Amanda Craig

was born in 1959 and educated in Rome and England. She won an Exhibition to read English at Cambridge before becoming a freelance journalist. She was voted young Journalist of the Year in 1985 and a *Cosmopolitan* Woman of Tomorrow in 1986, and she won the Catherine Pakenham Award for journalism in 1987. She currently reviews for the *Independent*, the *Spectator* and the *Literary Review* among others. She is author of two novels, *Foreign Bodies* - which was shortlisted for the *Yorkshire Post* Best First Book Award - and *A Private Place*.

AMANDA CRAIG

A Private Place

Flamingo
An Imprint of HarperCollins*Publishers*

Flamingo
An Imprint of HarperCollins*Publishers*
77–85 Fulham Palace Road,
Hammersmith, London W6 8JB

Published by Flamingo 1992
9 8 7 6 5 4 3 2 1

First published in Great Britain by
Hutchinson 1991

Author photograph by Jerry Bauer

The Author asserts the moral right to
be identified as the author of this work

ISBN 0 586 21692 8

Set in Sabon

Printed in Great Britain by
HarperCollinsManufacturing Glasgow

For Rob

Acknowledgements

I would like to thank Alexis Bowater, Anna Tanvir, Sophy Fisher, Ilona Dixon and Rod Williams for many invaluable details of school life.

Michael Lewis checked out my junior player of liar's poker, and Charlotte Lennox-Boyd took me into the mines at Morwellham. Su and Euan Bowater first showed me Dartmoor, which deserves better things than Knotshead and its imaginary inhabitants.

The encouragement of my agent, Imogen Parker, my editor, Robyn Sisman, and my publisher, Gail Rebuck, has been surpassed only by that of my husband, Rob Cohen. To all the above, my love and thanks.

'They base the importance which they assign to hypothetics upon the fact of their being a preparation for the extraordinary, while their study of Unreason rests upon its developing those faculties which are required for the daily conduct of affairs. Hence their professorships of Inconsistency and Evasion, in both of which studies the youths are examined ... The more earnest and conscientious students attain to a proficiency in these subjects which is quite surprising: there is hardly any inconsistency so glaring but they soon learn to defend it, or injunction so clear that they cannot find some pretext for disregarding it.'

Samuel Butler, *Erewhon*

'In the lower primates and the mammalia in general, each individual is born completely equipped with both primary and secondary sexual direction. They know without the need of any experience or teaching the natural method of satisfying the sexual sense ... and the behaviour is always identical in all individuals. Man has to be taught all this, and the teaching varies as widely as the races of mankind do. Most savage races have initiation ceremonies during which both primary and secondary sexual behaviour is taught to both sexes as they reach maturity, and I do not think that there are any two tribes in which the teaching is identical.'

Eugene Marais, *The Soul of the Ape*

PART ONE

1

The sudden acquisition of power does not go to the head, but to the groin. In some, it promotes lust; in others, supplants it. Those on whom its effect is purely cerebral may indeed be counted as fortunate.

Simon Hart was not a vain man, but he flattered himself that he had a talent for publicity. It was for this, he knew, that he had been appointed over the heads of so many distinguished rivals. Lank-haired, bespectacled, and with the choleric complexion of a slice of gammon, he was not on first appearances a likely maestro at presenting the silver lining to every cloud. Yet so he had proved, and would prove again. Sitting at the breakfast table on the first day of the autumn term, he opened a package from an Exeter printing firm with pleasurable anticipation.

'Dearest, we've got it!'

His wife, Poppy, paused in her attempt to push a spoonful of goo into the mouth of one of their twin daughters.

'Got what?'

'Ugh!' said the little girl, spattering her parents with glistening green slime.

'It.' Hart dabbed absently at his Next check shirt.

'AIDS? The *Reader's Digest* Lucky Dip? A recantation of my mother's will?'

Hart said, proudly, 'The proofs of our new corporate literature.'

'Ah. That.'

'We have to market ourselves as never before. Target our

niche. Position our strategic response to the environmental threat and opportunity profile. This is our shop window, a vital tool in the life cycle of our product. A new image for the New Age. Remember, we have gone from baby boom to baby bust. We are', said Hart, 'in a recession which is hitting even the chattering classes.'

'Yah!' said the other twin – Lily, or possibly Daisy. He still found it hard to tell the difference.

'Oh. The school brochures.'

'I must say, dearest, it's a great improvement on the old literature. Do look.'

Poppy said, 'You appear to have changed it from an upper-class borstal to Club 18-30.'

'Don't be facetious, dearest. Listen:

'"A FEW WORDS FROM THE HEADMASTER

'"The Knotshead tradition has always been to be free of tradition: the individual should mould the School, not the School the individual."'

'Did you really write that?' asked Poppy with feigned admiration. Hart held up a finger for silence.

'"Central to our approach is the belief that every male and female is capable of excellence in some sphere. We are confident that the unique atmosphere of the school ensures that each pupil discovers and develops his or her own individuality."'

'I've noticed,' Poppy interrupted, unable to bear his droning voice for long, 'that whenever institutions claim to be confident of anything, it means the precise opposite.'

Hart gave her a tolerant smile.

'Twenty years in education have taught me that prospective parents read a school prospectus as though it were a holiday brochure, not a court summons.

'"The atmosphere of the school is immediately apparent. By encouraging the process of self-education, self-discipline and self-motivation" – you can never go wrong emphasising the self – "individuals and relationships flourish."'

'Flourish? Surely that sounds a little . . . rampant,' said Poppy.

'Well, perhaps. I could substitute "grow". Thank you, dearest, for that suggestion.'

Hart made a small pencil mark in the margin.

'"THE HAPPIEST DAYS OF THEIR LIVES

'"In this, they are encouraged by the informal rapport between staff and pupil. Staff are addressed by their first names, uniforms are not worn. Males and females sleep in the main house and the Dower House –"' Hart made another mark. '"Males sleep in the main house and females in the Dower House, but every effort is made to break down the artificial distinction between the sexes, as it is between different academic years, or 'blocks'."'

'Coo,' said Lily.

'Yes,' said Poppy.

'"The two Houses, with their inevitable differences of tone, interest and cooperation, are happy units within the larger community."'

'Are you sure that is wise, after the scandal?'

'Yes,' said Hart, firmly. 'What's happened is in the past. This is a new, classless era. A new decade. We must look forward, not back. You, of all people, should know the importance of a fresh start.'

Poppy looked at him without expression. Hart continued reading aloud.

'"A UNIQUE APPROACH TO EDUCATION

'"With its progressive timetable and system of coeducation, Knotshead provides a marvellous opportunity for boys and girls of varying levels of ability and from different cultural backgrounds."'

'Why don't you just say, "We don't care if your kids are thick as long as they're rich"?'

'Because it wouldn't be true,' Hart said, annoyed. 'They aren't all rich or unacademic – look at your own sister.'

'Alice is different.'

'You know perfectly well that without my stipendiary benefits she'd never be able to come here. In any case, intelligence isn't only about passing examinations.'

'Oh, isn't it?'

'No. Developing a child's personality is equally important.'

'Developing its personality!' Poppy's voice began to vibrate with rolling Scottish "r"s. 'And do you also take credit for the fact they are all taller at eighteen than they were at thirteen?'

'"There are fifty pupils to each 'block', and great efforts are made to balance the sexes, although competition is stiffer where entry of the girls is concerned."'

Poppy snickered.

'You have a coarse mind, dearest,' Hart told her, coldly.

'Yes.'

'"NONCOMPETITIVE EXCELLENCE

'"Knotshead's reputation as a centre for excellence in music and craft makes it particularly attractive to the less academically oriented, although our GCSE and 'A'-level results compare well with most other public schools."'

Here Hart paused.

'"A-level results are now 80 per cent ABs."'

'Yes: you've imported a lot of high-flyers in the last two years.'

'That's only fourteen out of fifty in each block,' Hart pointed out. 'Most of those results are from Knotes born and bred.'

'From children brought up in traditional middle-class homes. Nurture over nature. And we all know how much easier examinations have become over the past ten years.'

'Would you prefer it if I were the head of an inner-city comprehensive?'

Poppy sighed. 'I just think you should be more honest about what parents can reasonably expect.'

'Parents today have far more conventional aspirations for their children than they have any right to, considering they were young in the 1960s,' Hart said, with some heat. He himself had spent the first decade of his own maturity drudging, as he had told Poppy many times, like some early Christian martyr in the bear pit of one comprehensive after another. He had seen the disintegration of grammar schools such as his own alma mater with satisfaction. When all but state education had been razed to the ground, the youth of Britain could start afresh. So he and many others had believed. But paradise had been, alas, postponed. Frustrated, impoverished and ambitious, he had espoused radical Thatcherism and joined the market economy. Promotion had followed fast: he became a housemaster at a boys' public school, then head of Knotshead. The state-school experience had counted for much with the board of governors. 'Of course, we think Knotshead is just another comprehensive,' one said at his interview. Hart had smiled deferentially, and kept quiet about his resolution never, ever, to have anything to do with the state system again.

Poppy, like so many of the parents he had to deal with, had

no idea about the real world outside, thought Hart. Her own career in education had been limited, to say the least. A belated attempt to put her life in order had led to a position as house-mother at a local girls' boarding school: the sort which always had distressed alcoholic gentlewomen to fill the post, and was not in a position to be too choosy as long as the applicant came from the right background. Beautiful, charming, vaguely aristocratic Poppy had been adored by all the girls. But then, everybody who met her fell under her spell. He wondered whether, even with the Knotshead offer, he would have had the confidence to overcome the memory of his previous disastrous encounters with the opposite sex if she had not told him, that extraordinary summer of his courtship, about certain matters. For Poppy, too, had been a rebel.

'"THE INDIVIDUAL HAS MANY SIDES",' Hart resumed.

'Like a diamond? Or like a lump of coal?' asked his wife.

'One is no less useful, dearest, than another,' Hart said. '"The emphasis on allowing pupils to work at their own pace rests on the conviction that pupils work better if the teacher is discouraged from doing too much of the talking and thinking. A competitive stance in class is gently but firmly discouraged as divisive. We have a policy of taking on pupils who have difficulty with more traditional public schools.

'It is inevitable that a close-knit community such as Knotshead should have its quota of personality problems, but normal children will always cooperate in the running and discipline of a school when their individuality is appreciated. With a little effort, round pegs can be made to fit into square holes, and vice versa.

'"THE EBONY TOWER."'

Poppy smiled. She was a great admirer of John Fowles, and kept an ancient copy of *The Aristos* by her bedside. Hart always teased her that this was a reversion to her roots when he saw her reading it. He never noticed her wincing.

'"Central to the Founder's beliefs was the importance of general experience and manual labour in the educative process. Young people tend to be excessively self-centred, and the inclusion of agricultural duties in the academic rota encourages them to develop a theory of life which stands them in good stead in the complex world for which they are destined. It is essential that healthy impulses should not be thwarted by meaningless tradition and culture: for this reason, we do not wish the atmosphere of the school to be disturbed by frequent exeats during termtime.

'"As the great number of Old Knotes, or OKs, returning to the school and sending their own children here indicates, our preparation for the modern world is a sound one."'

'Mrs Kelly tells me it's become impossible for local people to afford houses within a thirty-mile radius because of all the OKs who want to come back to live in Cornwall.'

Lily and Daisy began to wail.

'If you had had a taste of paradise, wouldn't you?'

'All paradises are there to be expelled from.'

'Aha! Ha!' Hart exuded two blasts of breath like old flower water. 'Very neat. I must remember to tell that to the Tore boy if he steps out of line again.

'"A BRIEF HISTORY OF THE SCHOOL".'

'Is there a lot more of this? The twins aren't even dressed.'

'Only a little. Besides, it's our USP.'

'Our what?'

'Our unique selling point. We're a very distinguished footnote to the history of liberal England.

'"Knotshead was founded in 1905 by the thinker and writer Ego Seymour and his wife Minnie, an American heiress. Members of the Edwardian 'Souls' and, later, the Bloomsbury Group, they decided to turn this remote rural corner of the West Country into a retreat for artists and thinkers.'

'Ah, Seymour,' murmured Poppy. 'Redolent of so many ironies, don't you think? Even without the extraordinary first name. He didn't have a brother called Id, I suppose?'

'No. Ivo, I believe. It was quite a common name for that stratum of society.'

Hart always talked of social strata: perhaps thinking he could bore his way through like a geologist.

'"Seymour's ideas on coeducation continue to influence independent schools to this day. He considered the educational programmes of other public schools, with their emphasis on the classics and muscular Christianity, too narrow. Believing in the equality of the sexes, he found it quite natural to introduce female pupils from the first day. A startling feature in the Edwardian era, coeducation eventually became one of Knotshead's most attractive and widely copied features. However, its setting remains unique.

'"Seymour bought the estate from the seventh viscount, 'Mad Ben' Anstey. With the advent of the Great Western Railway from London to Knotsmouth in 1880, the river Knot could no longer be maintained as a commercial waterway along the Devon and Cornwall border. Inland ports, which had provided considerable prosperity to the Anstey fortunes for 200 years, rapidly silted up, returning it to the wild West Country valley now enjoyed by so many pupils. In addition, Lord Anstey was forced to close the copper and arsenic mines beneath the estate after a disaster which killed three men in 1891. Finally, his hereditary passion for building follies completed the collapse of the Anstey family's fortunes at the turn of the century. Seymour bought the estate after a sale lasting two weeks which stripped the house of all its contents."'

'Is all this really necessary?'

'The parents – our clients, that is,' Hart corrected himself, 'love that sort of thing. The Fall of the House of Anstey. Besides, it's a famous house as well as a school.'

'Isn't one of the new governors a descendant? The lady magistrate? Kenwood or Kenward. The one whose daughter ran away from home.'

'Possibly. The English are always enthusiasts for failure.'

'Sometimes.' Poppy was silent, thinking of her own family.

'"The Founder's was a remarkable and, to many, eccentric venture, for the estate had not been properly maintained for some fifty years. Famous not only for its great Palladian house, begun by Vanbrugh and completed by J.C. Loudon, Knotshead is exceptionally blessed by lovely surroundings. Its grounds provide an inspirational setting for a host of outdoor activities."'

Poppy yawned.

'"Situated at the head of the river Knot, the estate was where Charles Bridgeman, forerunner of 'Capability' Brown, produced one of his earliest examples of the new English style of landscape architecture. After the original house had been rebuilt by the first viscount, his son swept away the rigid formality of the parterre designed by Henry Wise with mounts, rises, grottos and above all the five temples of Venus, Diana, Minerva, Apollo and Bacchus at the end of each avenue: temples which made Knotshead one of the most famous estates in Cornwall.'

Here Hart paused again, chewing his bottom lip. Those abominable temples! They might be photogenic, but the dead hand of classical learning lay on every one: precisely the sort of outdated nonsense that had made him committed to the progressive school system. Alas, they were Grade One listed. Worse, he was constantly nagged by busybodies like the Georgian Group to do something about their crumbling condition. He sighed.

'"The earliest temples, those of Bacchus and Apollo, were clearly inspired by two paintings by Claude Lorrain, 'The Embarkation of Theseus' and 'The Abandonment of Ariadne', now in the Wallace Collection. Brought back from Italy at the end of his grand tour, they fired the second viscount with the fashionable neoclassical vision of nature. Woods were planted, the Knot diverted, and the estate laid out in the *patte-d'oie* pattern of five converging avenues which may be seen today.

'"Improving the great park of Knotshead became a family obsession which required a constant supply of heiresses. The fifth viscount improved the design still further by flooding Anstey village to make way for the lake below the house, and rebuilding Anstey outside the park gates. Bankrupted by this last piece of extravagance, both the family and the estate began to decline."'

Poppy yawned again. The twins jiggled about in their high chairs, whingeing to be let down.

'"FROM THE MONUMENTAL TO THE MODERN".'

'You really think they're going to read all that?'

'No,' said Hart, suddenly depressed. 'I think they'll just look at the pictures, get an impression.'

'In any case,' said his wife, 'you're really preaching to the converted, aren't you?'

'I don't know. Am I?'

Beside him, the sun came out. The words he had written faded to invisibility; and in the laminated depths of the brochure cover, he could see only the reflection of his own face.

2

Denis Daniel Viner, commonly known as Grub, lay cocooned in a malodorous maroon duck-down duvet, listening. Clefs of damp red hair stuck to his forehead as his fingers played on an invisible piano. He grimaced with pleasure. This expression changed abruptly to dismay when the Walkman fell silent. Holding its plug in her hand, his mother demanded:

'Breakfast?'

'Nggah!'

'Breakfast?'

'Oh, *Mum!*'

'Breakfast?'

'Why did you do that?' Grub demanded, sitting up. His mother tugged at the blinds, and a sharp autumnal light penetrated the top of 1 Belsize Park with reluctance. His windows were smeared with grime and cobwebs, but so were the rest below. Grub's parents had bought their home on marriage, when everyone with money had wanted to live in the suburbs.

Sam and Ruth had not. They installed an Aga in the kitchen basement, stripped all the floors and, with the sublime self-confidence of the unmortgaged middle classes, had taken no notice of anything else. Now the rest of the street was unrecognisable, the crumbling stucco smoothed into fondant baroque palaces and divided up into condominiums for professional couples. Only their house – vast, shabby, painted dark green beneath its rampant ivy – maintained the same appearance it had had twenty-five years before. Many things had changed in the Viner family: children had grown up, pets had died, Sam and Ruth had divorced. But inside and outside, it still reflected a consistency of chaos, with furniture scavenged from junk shops or inherited from parents, Chianti bottles turned into lamp bases, an escaped boa constrictor in the bathroom and a perennial whiff of cat pee in unexpected places from the two Siamese, Leo and Pard. Four times a year, a firm of cleaning ladies would descend to keep the worst at bay (although even they could not face the boa constrictor, whose affectionate embraces were increasingly hard to resist), but otherwise the house remained an unconscionable blot on gentrification. In and out of its wide stained-glass doors bounced Grub and his two brothers, buoyed up by an inner tube of affection, laughter and the syndication of their father's, 'Felix's', cult strip cartoon 'Dum and Mad'.

Grub wondered which disc of complaint would drop from the maternal Wurlitzer. At present, the Top Ten were:

1. Prep (lack of)
2. Cleanliness (lack of)
3. Tidiness (lack of)
4. Noise (superfluity)
5. Pocket Money (superfluity)
6. Practical Jokes (superfluity)
7. Fat (superfluity)
8. Music (superfluity)
9. Energy (lack of)
10. Shaving (lack of)

'After shouting up the stairs for the last hour, I thought I might have a brain-damaged son.'

So it was 9, Energy, moving up the charts to number 3. He pushed his wire-rimmed spectacles up on his nose and said, 'Yes.'

'Oh, my God.'

'Yes to the breakfast ... please.' She wasn't bad, as far as mothers went; in fact, he secretly wished she would pay more attention to him and less to his aggravating older brothers, but she could be rather scratchy at times. At present, her glorious Manhattan squawk was in the clarinet rather than the recorder range, so he judged he was safe.

'What are you listening to?'

'Liszt's Piano Sonata,' said Grub, in a lofty and defensive

tone. 'The Richter recording. Some idiot keeps coughing and coughing. He should have been shot. Just think, a single bullet to the brain; a moment's hesitation, and then the divine fingers move on. Nobody would have given a toss.'

Ruth snorted. She was a psychotherapist, compact, pragmatic, with a nose that turned up at the end, like a skijump for the jokes which poured out of her. It was Ruth's unwavering belief that people were made to be happy, and that romanticism was responsible for most of the miseries she saw in her professional life. Her son had inherited her nose, her colouring and her relish for jokes, but not her intellectual tastes.

'This dreadful nonsense pouring into your head, day and night, all feelings and no thought. Such Technicolor egoists! If you're going to listen to trash, why not Chopin? But that awful Stendhalian creep banging on about his tortured soul – really, Grub!'

'You don't listen to him properly. It isn't about being in control.'

'Ha! Musical masturbation.'

'More like enjoying being raped,' said Grub, with a leer.

'You! And what do you know about such matters?'

'Ho, ho, ho.'

His mother eyed him speculatively. 'Oh, yes?'

Grub hunched over, like Lon Chaney in *The Hunchback of Notre Dame*. 'I lie in wait, and jump out of bushes on to innocent little girls.' A mortifying recollection surfaced in his mind, and he blushed immediately.

Ruth laughed. 'Ho, ho, ho, indeed! When you start dating girls instead of music, this house will become even more like a hotel. How your brothers ever manage to do any studying at Oxford I do not know. Now, then. As I expected, complete indolence on your last day. You'll never get packed in time for the school train. Why aren't you dressed, at least?'

'No socks.'

'It is my belief that your socks get up and crawl out of the house like caterpillars, in desperation to get away from those dirty feet.'

'We have a mutant teenage ninja washing machine. Is Dad going to take me to the station?'

'I don't know. We haven't talked today. I'll drive you if he can't get away from the office, don't worry. Unless the Deux

Chevaux packs up again. I took it to the garage, and they told me I've been floating around on a flake of rust, and the surface tension could go at any moment. But then, they always say that when they see an old car.'

Grub began to feel the familiar tension swarming all over his skin, and swallowed. 'Did you tell Dad it was my last day?'

'Yes,' his mother said briskly. 'But he's in the middle of a deadline, so I wouldn't expect much.'

'He's probably with that bimbo Bambi,' said Grub, under his breath.

It was well known in the Viner household that he had a mistress called Fiona Bamber in Lamb's Conduit Street who was a journalist on a tabloid newspaper. She was known to all the Viners as Bambi, although Ruth did not seem to bear her any ill will for breaking up her marriage. Grub had taken a photograph of her and used it as a dartboard.

'Do you really need all this stuff? What's this, here?'

Ruth dived beneath a putrefying mound of dirty clothes, ash, empty crisp packets, old chocolate wrappers, crusted mugs of coffee with cigarette stubs floating in them, used Kleenex and unused Durex. Uneasily, Grub wondered whether he had remembered to hide his copy of *Playboy*. However unshockable his mother might be, he still felt there was something shameful about his susceptibility to pornography. But Ruth pounced on a pair of moulded plastic handles attached to each other by a short piece of coiled wire.

'My bullworker. When you can stretch it all the way out, it means you've become like Arnold Schwartzenegger.'

His mother stretched it, experimentally, all the way out.

'Um, well, the spring goes after a few times, so you think you're getting stronger. But pretty soon, I'll be able to tear the telephone directory in half.'

'I can do that any day,' said Ruth. 'Want to bet?'

Two pairs of green eyes regarded each other with calculation. 'How much?'

'You have to tidy your room if I succeed.'

'OK,' said Grub. His mother picked up a telephone directory from the floor, and tore it down the spine.

'That's cheating!'

'No, it's brain over brawn. Now, you must keep your word. I'll keep the frying pan out for another twenty minutes, and then you'll have to fend for yourself. You could do with losing some weight anyway.'

Grub looked at her with love and fury, and she laughed as she went down the stairs. Then he poked a stubby finger vigorously in and out of his left ear, inspecting the orange crumb that emerged with deep interest: enough wax to make candles, he thought, yawning. Life at present seemed a continual series of movements to escape – sleeping from waking, waking from dreaming. He felt tired almost all the time, both before and after sleep. Something to do with getting taller, his mother said; she should know, having been a doctor before turning to psychotherapy. He could remember when he had been compact and energetic, before the tub of blubber that now encased him barrelled out, but it seemed like eons ago. The only time he ever felt really awake, or even alive, was when he was inside a piece of music, or performing in some way.

People accused him of saying things for effect, and it was true, he liked to make them laugh. It was good to play the fool; people liked fools, and Grub liked to be liked. What was wrong with that? Sometimes at Knotshead he spoke for another kind of effect, as a bat whistles in order to make out the contours of the objects around it by means of the returning echo. Yet this, too, evoked only laughter.

It was often observed that the Harts' house, with its low, humped roofs and curving beige walls, resembled a giant concrete fungus. How it had got planning permission so near a Grade One building was a mystery: it wasn't even designed, like the James Stirling Tower of Babel Language Centre, by a famous architect. But there it squatted, just across the river by the school walls. Often, when the streams poured off Dartmoor, the Knot would rise, and a fungal damp penetrated every coat of creosote. The first joke every junior pupil learnt when he or she came to Knotshead was:

Q: What is the definition of a mushroom?

A: A place where you keep the headmaster.

To Alice its smell of mildew was synonymous with unhappiness, as that of the Edinburgh house – bleach, fresh paint, her mother's Arpège – had been that of rational serenity. At times, she wondered whether Poppy had moved there deliberately, so vehement was her dislike for their mother, even after death.

'Neat' was to Poppy a term of contempt. It was unfortunate, thought Alice, that she herself could at best be summed up by this adjective.

They had the same short, high-bridged nose, but there any similarity ended. Sisters define each other by opposites, if not by opposition. Poppy was small, blonde, kittenish in bright Benetton clothes and flashing crystal jewellery: 'the thinking man's Julie Christie', as one bedazzled parent (male) had dubbed her. She had made the transition from beautiful little girl into beautiful young woman with no apparent effort, and was generally thought able to charm the birds out of trees provided she put her mind to it. Alice was tall and thin, with perfectly straight dark hair cut in a precise but amateurish bob, and the sallow Celtic skin which looks almost jaundiced in winter. She dressed only in black: a black made dusty by fastidious washing and ironing. Her manners veered between awkwardness and aggression, and when she laughed, it was not at the things other people found amusing. She was much addicted to speaking the truth and had no gift for anything but examinations. At Knotshead, these were not admirable attributes.

She looked now at the vertiginous hills above. Three tors, the last brown billows of Dartmoor, emptied their streams into the Knot as it rose in the mines behind her. Their steep sides, with the diverted stream that, below the lake, became a river meandering across the valley, effectively cut the Knotshead valley off from the rest of the West Country on a peninsula of land. Across the water, to the south, was Minedale, puffed by the railway to the size of a small town. Three miles down was Knotsmouth, and the nacreous slab of the Sound.

A dense confusion of boulder and bog, bracken and branch lay beneath, between the river and where Alice sat. The woods were pathless apart from a maze of deer tracks. Everything was tumbled about, great oaks and beech trees snaking out of the red earth, or crashed down in lizardly lengths, whole forests of new saplings sprouting from the old trunks. Dissolution sent waves of fungus rippling out from dead stumps, strangled by claws of ivy and the netted clouds of clematis. The ground crackled with unseen twigs, as if charged with static electricity. Intermittently, the prints of Alice's Wellington boots would fill with transparent, putrescent water, where she had followed the stream trickling beneath the decades of clotted, rotting leaves to the narrow shelf of turf before the ruin of the old copper mine.

Even on orienteering games, Knotes did not like going near the abandoned mine. Much of the hillside across the ha-ha was supposed to be out of bounds, riddled with shafts and pocked with adits which could collapse under an unwary foot. All along the river bank, as far as Minedale, there were milestones and other traces of the industry that had been discontinued a hundred years before, but nobody except Alice cared to get closer. At night, its crumbling lime kilns echoed with the hollow laughter of owls, and by day its entrance looked too much like a black mouth.

In any case, the stream was the only reliable way up. It had once been the original path of the Knot, until the construction of the main house and its lake below had caused Vanbrugh to fear floods. The stream was blocked and diverted to the east; then, with the development of the copper mines, straightened and used as an ore shoot. Now that the mines had been abandoned for nearly a century, this, too, had been abandoned. Often impassable after rain, the ore shoot was a sunken track, prodigiously overgrown, but navigable following the summer drought. After some forty feet, it became a small waterfall like a broken stair slippery with black slime; then a tiny stream, running straight and noiseless across turf out of the mine entrance, which now resembled a cave.

Alice went there to cry. She did this violently, silently, and with a sensation of shame, for all displays of emotion were wrong, and she considered self-pity more ludicrous than masturbation. Once begun, however, her tears were as uncontrollable as vomiting. She would cry until her face was tight and swollen and there did not seem to be a drop of water left in her body; after which, greatly to her relief, neurasthenia would pass into anaesthesia and her depression reduced to tolerable levels.

Often, she longed to ask Poppy, 'Why him? Why Simon? You had dozens of others, why choose this little toad of a man? How can you bear to listen to his pomposity, his venality, to have his flabby hands paddling your flesh?' But she was too polite, too painfully aware of all she owed Poppy even to think of saying this. Besides, her brother-in-law was a very small part of the problem.

Her mother had said, 'Don't you believe that balderdash about love being free. It's the most expensive thing there is, as your sister has discovered to her cost.'

If Mrs Godwin had been confounded by her daughter's marriage to the future headmaster of Knotshead, she was given no time to comment. The day of Poppy's wedding in the Exeter register office she had been run over by a drunk driver on Prince's Street, a particularly unfortunate ending since Mrs Godwin had been a trenchant teetotaller. She had left a will insisting that in the event of her death, Poppy's share of the estate came on condition that she take care of her sibling until Alice was eighteen.

Alice had shown no emotion. To thoughtful natures, events are like depth charges: the surface is calm, but the shock spreads further. Her stiff, adult manner repelled sympathy. For two weeks, while solicitors tried to trace her sister, she had chosen to live alone, refusing the leave the Royal Circus flat. Ringed by order, by gleaming black lampposts, by burnished brass kickplates and stony proportion, she had waited for Poppy to take her away. Then, to the cruel, bosomy south she had come.

The Godwin girls knew very little of each other. Twenty years, differing temperaments and several hundred miles separated them. Poppy had been born at the beginning of her mother's marriage; Alice at the end. Poppy, for all her ebullience, was unable to give affection, and Alice, for all her self-possession, was unable to ask for it.

Their parents had been much the same. They had met each other at two or three houseparties in the Highlands; it was thought a fine thing for a Lockhart and a Godwin to marry, so marry they did. The fact that they had hardly a single taste in common was not discovered until too late.

Each had misunderstood the other from the start. Mr Godwin had been a landowner with a farm in Ayrshire, a flat in the Royal Circus and one in Kensington. He spent most of his time at the last, regarding Scotland as a tedious source of income. Mrs Godwin had grown up in Edinburgh, the youngest daughter of an advocate, and a proud descendant of the Lockhart who had vilified Keats in *Blackwood's*. She despised the English almost as much as she came to despise men. Neither parent had been prepared to accommodate the other's tastes.

'Scots divide into two kinds: those who go to Fettes, then spend the rest of their lives counting sheep; and those who believe the only good thing about Scotland is, to paraphrase Dr

Johnson, the express train to London. My wife and I encompass the gamut,' Mr Godwin would say, with a charming laugh. As he became more hedonistic, Mrs Godwin became increasingly puritanical. She ran the farm, which her husband visited only during the grouse season, and refused to come to London on the grounds that the water was undrinkable. Eventually the marriage, though never formally dissolved, broke down completely, and the couple were separated.

Poppy was her father's daughter. At the end of the 1960s, she had run off to the bright lights as a dizzy sixteen-year-old. By the time Alice, a starchy, solitary little girl knew herself fatherless, Poppy had been in Chelsea for five years. Embittered, the widow had leased the farm, sold the Kensington flat and taken good care to ensure that Alice's upbringing was of a very different nature. A prodigy would replace the prodigal. Alice would be a true product of the Athens of the north, inspired by the noble names of Hume, Fleming and Lockhart.

Her material was ductile, almost docile. Alice and Mrs Godwin seemed more like two elderly companions than mother and child. Their social life was minimal.

'The only thing that really matters for women is education and career,' Mrs Godwin had told her daughter, over and over. 'If I had had the opportunities presented to your generation, I would never have accepted marriage. Men make women first into fools and then into slaves. Emancipate yourself from the craven need for love, and you will set yourself free.'

If only, thought Alice, it were really so simple.

She went back down the hill, feeling swollen and tired. At the bottom was the upper bridge which crossed the Knot at its narrowest point. A track led from this along the river to the Librarian's cottage. He had been away in Tuscany all summer, but was now presumably back, since a battered blue Volkswagen was parked in front of the cottage door.

Alice cast it a nervous, hopeful glance. He was to teach her Latin for the next two years. The last classics teacher had taken the few Catullus poems on the Cambridge course as an invitation to descant on how many times he could bring his wife to orgasm. This was thought to be really cool by all the other Knotes, most of whom were boys who had learnt Latin at more traditional prep schools. The thirteen-year-old Alice's silent distaste had led him to accuse her of being frigid and intellectually narcissistic about Edinburgh. Had he not been sacked by Simon, she doubted whether her freakish passion for the subject would have sustained her to A level.

Letting herself in through the sliding picture window by the kitchen, Alice hoped she had missed Simon, and lunch. Although the house was open-plan, it was easy to avoid her sister and brother-in-law at breakfast because they always took such a long time to get up. In her eagerness to get away, she had packed her trunk the night before. She looked cautiously into the living room.

Poppy was lying on the brown corduroy sofa, reading. The twins were absorbed in drawing felt-tip doodles on the walls. In the kitchen, dirty crockery was piled high; Poppy hated handling greasy plates, but considered wearing rubber gloves the stigma of the housewife. She had a vague idea that if everything was rinsed in cold water, it would somehow sort itself out.

Alice went to her room. She had made no attempt to stamp her personality on it. The trunk was just inside the door. It was ribbed, like the lung of a giant, and creaked as she pulled it through the living room by its leather strap. Poppy started, and looked up.

'Can you manage?'

'Yes,' said Alice.

'I was only asking,' said Poppy. They always went through this pantomime, but nevertheless Alice said, 'I thought you wouldn't want to be bothered – '

'How do you know what I do or don't want?'

'You tell people.'

'You remind me of all the reasons why I left Edinburgh,' said Poppy. 'All right, piss off, then. You only use this place like a hotel anyway.'

'How else am I to use it?'

'As your home.'

Alice said nothing.

Poppy sighed. 'I don't know why I bother.'

'You are too kind,' said Alice, without inflection. Neither met the other's glance. 'Can I borrow the luggage trolley from the garage?'

'If you want. Say bye-bye, twins.'

Lily and Daisy waddled over and hugged Alice round the knees. She knelt down and stroked their perfect peony cheeks.

She longed to put her arms round them, but was too stiff and shy to know how to do this.

'Are you coming back?'

'Not until Christmas.'

'Why not?' asked Lily.

'It's the rules.'

The twins proffered cold, soft kisses like frozen petals, and she returned them. She did not kiss Poppy, and Poppy made no attempt to help her. This was as it always was. She tied the trunk to the trolley and walked down the drive without a backward glance. The new year had begun.

The car he sat in was of burnished chrome, and burnt down the highway. Winthrop T. Sheen had wasted the last 450SL convertible Daddy had given him ('Fifty-five and stay alive! You're so full of shit!') but he had no difficulty in persuading the chauffeur to go over the speed limit.

'Man, I'll be roasted alive by the big white chief if I arrive late for the new semester,' he had said.

The goon obviously knew even less about British public schools than Winthrop because he increased the speed of the stretch so much that at this rate, they'd soon be in the Channel.

Winthrop dropped his copy of *Hello!* magazine and peered through his Ray-Bans in deep disgust. It was a small-screen culture, this; everything kept changing all the time. It really chilled him out. Just when he thought the scenery had settled down, and there was nothing but cows and stuff, it began humping around like a quarterback and two cheerleaders in a sleeping bag. No wonder Mummy had chosen not to accompany him. At least this new place was in the south, and had girls. Mummy had been very insistent on this.

'Poor Winkie, he's just too full of testosterone,' she had murmured to Bunny, her second husband. 'In another era, he would have been off drilling oil wells or something. Darling, I do think Knotshead would be preferable to Switzerland. He'd only turn into a ski bum and impregnate half our friend's daughters. The English are so much more . . . civilised.'

Winthrop had pleaded on bended knees (metaphorically, of course) to be allowed one last chance, even at a military academy, but in the end, his stepfather had provided the clincher.

'We could send him to Buxton or the New Lincoln, and he'd be leaving with the same chances – maybe Ivy League, maybe a Montana car-repair joint. After two expulsions, no traditional school is going to believe that all he needs is a little discipline. But if he blossoms in the less repressive atmosphere at Knotshead, you can always buy some Oxford college a new professor,' Bunny had pointed out. 'Those places are real hard up, but they still have class. If Win has a British education, he'll get a broader perspective on life.'

'His perspective has been nothing but broads,' said Winthrop's mother bitterly, but she had taken his point. Besides, Bunny had known someone who knew one of the governors, so this meant it was acceptable. Underneath the flaky exterior and the show-biz parents, Bunny's informant had told him, it was really a happy compromise between the Walden and Putney, with an element of *Brideshead* thrown in.

The big black car slid between a pair of granite gateposts.

'Hell,' Winthrop muttered, 'I'm going to be like a fucking prisoner of war here.'

Over his head, an iron shield announced: *Et In Arcadia Ego.*

3

Noise, noise, noise. The banging of trunks up stairs, the slipping and pounding of heavy feet along polished wooden floors, the yowling of radios and record players, the grunting of burdened males licensed to glimpse forbidden territories in return for carrying trunks, the high-pitched squealing of friends separated or reunited, the revving of cars departing or arriving.

Alice had found her year's lodgings on the lists pinned up in the hall, dragged her trunk up two flights of stairs unassisted, and was sitting on her bed. This, like every other bed in the Dower House, was covered with a pink candlewick material, which impressed a wavy mark on a sitter's buttocks. Sometimes she thought that the mark of the bedspread had franked her flesh as though it were an envelope, for all time: Knotshead, Cornwall, 1990s.

She felt overpowered already by confusion, loneliness, the necessity to remain constantly on guard. It was a relief to find herself the first to arrive.

The new dormitory was at the top of the Dower House, in what must once have been a servant's room, facing southeast towards the tennis courts and the Sound. It turned its back to the main house, including the converted stables and the 1960s prefabs (known as Flottage) curving along the Knot, and for this Alice was grateful. The classrooms were not on the whole an attractive sight; every year, the replacement of the prefabs was mooted, and every year, it was decided that although they leaked and looked phenomenally ugly, it was too expensive to replace them.

Across the river, the Temple of Minerva was still horrid with scaffolding, though no work appeared to have been done on its crumbling ochre stone since anyone could remember. Every time attempts were made to rebuild it, some objection was raised: the new stone was wrongly cut with modern instruments; the original designs had been misinterpreted by the builders; an inadequate number of experts had been consulted, and so on. So there it stood, year after year, crumbling away in the salt sea winds. Some people were standing on the bridge, taking photographs of the goats grazing. New parents, no doubt. For an instant, she saw Knotshead as they must see it: the embodiment of harmony between man and nature for ever suspended in the still, chill air.

The dormitories varied in size. Many rooms in the Dower House had once been beautiful, with elaborate cornicing that, because of the infrequency with which it was repainted, had kept its delicacy. Nearly a century as an educational establishment had overlaid proportions, fireplaces and functions but garlands of fruit, flowers and dancing cherubs still rioted overhead on the first and second floors, fossils of dead delights veiled, decade after decade, by distemper.

The girls countered institutional living according to ingenuity, income and inclination. It was remarkable how quickly each dormitory assumed a distinct character every year: the same room could, within a matter of hours, become a place of frilly femininity, slick chic or exotic ethnicity purely as a result of a few judiciously arranged props. Lockertops and windowsills acquired a floating assortment of potted plants, family photographs, rejects from craft classes and other knick-knacks. Stereos revolved ceaselessly with the records that each particular dorm became obsessed by for a term; this was believed to lend atmosphere, as in a boutique or restaurant. Posters and even Indian bedspreads were Blu-Tacked side by side to conceal the garish vinyl wallpaper, which rampaged in such violent violet efflorescence that it gave sensitive girls headaches if left uncovered.

The wallpaper was the choice of the housekeeper, nicknamed Shit Horder after her manner of signing her illegible first name on ferociously petty announcements. Shit Horder thought her wallpaper charming (though she did not dare to impose it on the males) and would inspect every dormitory in the Dower House to ensure that the blobs of Blu-Tack used to cover it up were not too big; if they were, she would rip every poster off with vicious satisfaction. Equally, if she thought a lockertop was too crowded with private effects, she would sweep the whole lot off to the floor, saying that the maids couldn't clean it.

The lockers were a plywood chest of six drawers, veneered to resemble a light mahogany, which had one small drawer on the left for valuables which could be padlocked. Pupils were told to provide their own padlocks, and to carry the key with them at all times. It was when Alice had understood that this drawer, measuring twelve square inches, was to be the sole repository of privacy for the next five years that the surface of her world had cracked, and she had fallen into a place of despair.

'You're the new headmaster's daughter, aren't you?'

'Sister-in-law.'

'Who's your father, then?'

Silence. The eyes probed her like needles.

'Is your mother divorced?'

'No,' said Alice, and the voice died in her throat. My mother is dead, she thought, and I can't say it. I will not milk these harpies for false sympathy, in any case.

'Oh. Well, most people's parents are divorced, here,' said one of her tormentors. 'Where do you live?'

'In the Royal Circus,' she replied, unthinking; for now it would be here, at Knotshead, all the time.

'In a zoo?'

'You grew up in a royal zoo?'

'Were you a lion tamer?'

'Alice Godwin is a liar. There's no such thing as a royal zoo,' said Olivia Paddington. Nobody who cut a bread roll or who called a lavatory a toilet in Olivia's presence ever forgot the mortification. She claimed to have lost her virginity at twelve to a member of the royal family, and since she was one of Princess Margaret's godchildren, this was altogether possible. From the beginning, she had been the leader of the females in her block, as Tore was of the males.

Alice recognised a natural enemy, and said boldly, 'It isn't a zoo. Royal Circus is a square in Edinburgh. Anybody knows that.'

'Anybody knows that,' Olivia repeated, imitating Alice's

prim Scottish accent. 'Och, aye, she thinks the whole wurrld knows that!'

Olivia and her friends burst into sniggers.

Alice was to be head of this dormitory, by virtue of being in 6i; there were a couple of girls from Block 4 and 5 whom she dimly knew, and a new girl, Fay Baron. It was strange to think of herself as having any kind of power or responsibility, even if this was only to ensure that lights were switched out before Veronica or Miranda, the housemistresses, came round. When she had first arrived, the dormitories had been mixed-age all the way up, but Hart had introduced separate study bedrooms for the final year in an attempt to improve the examination results.

The door was flung open, and a bald, middle-aged man wearing a velvet smoking jacket backed into the room in a simian crouch, followed by a trunk and a small, fluffy-haired girl of about fourteen. She was kicking the other end. Behind them teetered the girl's mother wearing a powder-blue suit with gold frogging and a head of hair which looked as if it had been sculpted out of Wondermash. She peered short-sightedly at the letter on the door.

'I think this is the one, dear.'

'I told you it was the one. Why don't you listen to me?'

'How could you tell, walking backwards?'

'It was obvious.'

'What do you mean, obvious? It wasn't obvious to me.'

'Look, every room has a letter of the alphabet, so P follows Q, see?'

'I know the letters of the alphabet, Saul, as well as you do if not better. You're embarrassing us all in front of one of Fay's schoolmates. Isn't he, dear?'

The girl Fay, who had been following this exchange with an expression of mutinous boredom, threw a look like a stone at Alice.

'Er, hallo. I'm Alice.'

'This is our daughter Fay. You'll look after her, won't you?'

Alice nodded politely. It was not for her to explain the consequences that would follow if she did so. 'What block are you in?'

'6i.'

'Oh. So am I.'

'But she's only fourteen,' said Fay's father, anxiously.

'A prodigy.'

'She has ten GCSEs.'

'Grade A, all of them.'

'Oh,' said Alice.

'Well, that's everything. We must get back to St John's Wood before the rush hour. Here's your music, dear. You won't forget to practise, will you?'

'No, Mum.'

'I'm sure you'll have a wonderful time. Just remember, we're only a phone call away if you get homesick.'

'Don't worry,' said Fay irritably. 'I'll be fine.'

'You'd better be, the fees they charge. Here are some biscuits in case you feel peckish.'

Alice buried her head in *Germinal* while they made their farewells. When they left, Fay unwrapped the box of biscuits and began eating them. Alice watched, curious, then, feeling that she must make an effort, asked, 'Is it your first time at boarding school?'

Fay nodded. 'Yeah. I was at a day school before, but my parents decided it was too limiting, socially.'

'Didn't you like it?'

Fay shrugged. 'It was OK. No boys, though.' Then she asked, through a mouthful of shortbread, 'How many GCSEs did you get?'

'Ten.'

'What marks?'

'Don't you think that's my business?' asked Alice, more gently than she would usually have done.

'They must have been bad, then. If they were good, you'd want to say.'

'Not necessarily. The new ones aren't very hard, after all, though they pretend they are. Quite a few people expected to be chucked out, and weren't this year.'

Fay was nonplussed, but rallied. 'But you're much older than I am.'

'Sixteen,' Alice agreed. She wondered when she would stop feeling surprised at people's inability to hear the crassness of what they said.

'My parents wanted to send me to a school for gifted children, but my cousin Izzy went here and said it was really great, everyone's much more balanced.'

'It's a high-wire act between anarchy and tyranny,' said Alice; but Fay, who was crunching into another biscuit, did not hear her.

'Do you have a boyfriend?'

Alice shook her head.

'I do. This is his photo. We went to Prague together this summer.'

She handed Alice a snapshot of the boyfriend, who looked at least six years older than she was, and began sticking posters of Madonna and Arthur Rackham fairies up on the walls. She was still doing this when the other two girls came in. They ignored Alice pointedly. Fay they eyed with some calculation. The next two minutes would seal her fate.

'Oh, yum, biscuits! Can I have one?' said the elder.

'Well,' said Fay, reluctantly.

'Go on, don't be Jewish.'

Fay stared at her in surprise. 'But I am Jewish,' she said.

Oh, God, thought Alice. It's going to be worse than ever, then.

4

Why did he feel terror whenever he was confronted with those over whom he was supposed to have power? Hart wondered.

The first Jaw, or assembly, of the year was never a particularly easy one to keep under control, he thought, surveying the fizzing confusion beneath him. Groups of friends clotted together and made little rushes for free spaces on the long wooden pews. Males lolled in the back rows, flicking through comics and furtively carving their initials on the panels beside them whenever they thought the staff weren't looking; in front of their gaze, the girls wriggled and giggled in a frenzy of self-consciousness.

At the very back of the Assembly Room sat the staff, their faces shadowed by the huge beams vaulting up and up. Their eyes gleamed at him out of the dark, like wild animals. His gaze flickered across their faces, searching for the one he most feared and disliked. There was Maggie Brink, scratching herself, so her psoriasis was no better for a trip to her beloved Communist China. Toby Hindesmith, with a vaguely punkish haircut and a disgusting hand-painted silk tie. Hart fingered his own knitted maroon job for comfort, as another man might have put his hands in his trousers to comfort his shrinking testicles. Sally Rupple and Norman Sproggs. He must remember to announce their marriage, perhaps with a little joke about the need for sport and physics to be linked. Norman was the sort of man who would shave his legs in order to increase his aerodynamic efficiency on a bicycle. Still, *mens sana in corpore sano* . . . Martin Mortmain, the English teacher almost drooling over that new German teacher, what was her name? Helge something. Miranda Jupp in yet another Laura Ashley dress, tossing her mousy curls pointedly and pretending to be in animated conversation with Kit Ricks. Daphne and Nicholas Crump, their handsome, iron-grey heads held perfectly upright. Philip Slythe, the bursar, his steel-rimmed spectacles so complex they looked as if he'd need an engineering degree, as well as an accountant's, to keep them on. Veronica Slythe, senior housemistress at the Dower House. A hundred feet away, Hart still felt the force of his deputy's basilisk glare.

This was his enemy. Never openly rude or contradictory, she made no secret of her contempt for his betrayal of the Founder's principles, either. A pupil herself during what was generally regarded as Knotshead's golden age, it was said she had inspired terror in staff even as a head girl. Certainly, as housemistress of the Dower House she inspired a greater degree of discipline than Captain 'Pug' Wash did in the Males' Flats. Whether she inspired any trust or affection in her charges was a different matter. Of all the school staff, she was the most fanatical about realising the Founder's vision, and the superciliousness of her manner was softened only towards the children of other OKs.

For months, now, he had sensed the staff wavering between their two camps. He had pushed through study-bedrooms for the Upper Sixth in the interests of improving examination marks, but both Slythes had succeeded in blocking plans for a new sports complex. 'Competition is antisocial and non-Knote,' they told him, with a faint sneer. 'We have no truck with Thatcherism here.' He had remembered something he had once read, that the last battle would be not between socialists and non-socialists, but between believers and ex-believers. In the case of himself and Veronica, it was all too true.

Together, the Slythes were a formidable pair. Philip Slythe was known to read *Spare Rib* and embroider Kaffe Fassett cushions in his free time. Veronica chose instead to patrol the grounds at night with a powerful torch in the hope of finding miscreants to punish with massive doses of outdoor work. Her wishes were frequently fulfilled. Hart sent her a toothy smile over the heads of his audience, remembering that the origin of the smile was the snarl.

Alice was in the first row. Only misfits sat in the front, or at the very back, under the eyes of authority. Hart glanced at her, briefly. A plain and sullen girl, he thought, so unlike Poppy and the twins. He had not anticipated taking on such a responsibility. A predictable penalty for late marriage, he supposed. He still could not believe the unfairness of Mrs Godwin's will; but his wife only shrugged and said it was what she had always expected.

At least Alice would be off his hands at eighteen. Had she been a daughter from a previous marriage, Hart might have thought twice before taking on Poppy. He had tried with Alice, goodness knew, but all she had ever done was gaze at him with those grey eyes, that made him think of shattered ice.

Stiffly upright in the William Morris chair, Hart was already sweating. The antagonism he encountered in three hundred pairs of eyes fuelled his anxiety and sense of failure and made him want to lie down and howl like a dog. He knew – how bitterly he knew – that he was not a leader of men. He was confident only in presentation, not in confrontation.

In the beginning, Hart had blundered by addressing them as 'girls and boys'. He had made references to their being 'the cream of British children' – a not unreasonable appellation, considering their school fees were among the highest in the country, but one that had given deep offence. He had even referred to Christianity, which was something only the lower middle classes now believed in. He surveyed the vaulted roof of the Assembly Hall curving over him like the ribs of Jonah's whale, and wondered whether he had not made a great mistake in accepting this post. He rose to speak.

'Welcome, welcome, everybody, to the first day of the winter term. I hope everybody had a good, hard-working holiday' (snickers) 'and has returned to Knotshead full of enthusiasm for the year that lies ahead. Whether you are old Knotes or new ones, I trust that you will remember that Knotes alone mean nothing: Knotes in harmony make music.' (Groans. Hart was disappointed; he had laboured long over that one, and was proud of it.) 'And notes in disharmony make pop music, aha-aha-ha.'

Hart found he was looking straight at Johnny Tore. Dead silence now, and a shuffling of feet. The boy raised his fashionably cropped head and stared back at the headmaster with his insolent, slitty gaze. Hart's nostrils twitched. He could smell the stench of cigarette smoke on him from here. Something would have to be done, famous father or not. He had wanted to expel him two terms ago, but even Poppy had interceded on his behalf. Hart finished his speech, unaware of the way his flat, droning voice set the collective teeth of his audience on edge, but in some way conscious of the fact that the brief moment of truce which had greeted his first sentences was now over. Sweating into the mushy grey wads of his anorak, he sat down and contemplated his Hush Puppies.

Hew Morgan thumped out a few bars of music with aggressive disdain. Hart rose with the school and droned;

> 'Once to every man and nation
> Comes the moment to decide,
> Tum, tum-titty-tum,
> Arumph, arumph, arumph,
> For the good or evil side.'

He had reintroduced hymns on Sunday, arguing with some success that his predecessor's taste for African bongo drums and slide shows about leprosy and schizophrenia did not accord with the religious requirements of British educational establishments. Morgan had then taken a barbed pleasure in choosing the gloomiest in the canon, although even 'Nearer, My God, to Thee' could not quite dampen Knotes' enthusiasm for singing.

> 'And that choice goes on for ever
> 'Twixt the darkness and the light.'

Unlikely, really. Evil, if it existed, would be some creeping process, not a single decision. The blotchy faces before him were erupting in violent pustules of crimson and mauve, diseased by hormones as by smallpox. Life was first a coarsening, then a disintegration, Hart thought. When he looked at the twins, at their perfect grainless complexions and blazing innocence, and considered this, his heart seemed to weep blood.

At the end of his speech, the staff lined themselves up on one side of the aisle to shake the pupils by the hand. This wearisome custom, nicknamed the factory line, had been instituted by the founder as a further method of breaking down the artificial distinctions between teacher and pupil. It was tolerated because it made it easier to spot pupils skiving off. Daily attendance was compulsory, as the only means of checking that every Knote was present unless specifically excused: now that London was only three hours from Knotsmouth by Intercity, there was a perennial fear that some would sneak off.

How they all revealed themselves by touch, those teachers, thought Alice. Unlike the pupils, they favoured the bunchy outlines, the beads, smocks and sandalled socks of liberal ideology. Here was Hew with his prehensile pianist's grasp, and Simon inserting his hand like a frozen haddock in a pop-up toaster. Then Poppy, holding herself like a poker player. The Slythes, with their faint, disdainful clasps. A Teutonic *Heil* from Nicholas Crump, German master; a turpentine palming from Hindesmith; a sweatily enthusiastic pumping by the deputy housemaster, 'Pedigree' Chumley. Then Mortmain, bending like a melting snowman towards a pretty new teacher. Sally Rupple, apparently practising press-ups. Dai Delus wrapped in the sickly sweet smell of tobacco and fresh wood shavings. Norman Sproggs proved that heat passed from the hotter to the cooler. Miranda Jupp gave a coquettish touch redolent of Diorissima. Ben Kenward inspected a page of an indifferent book. Hartley Leigh Hunt thought he was a combine harvester. 'Pug' Wash would have preferred to strangle every member of the opposite sex but crushed their hands instead.

'Three.'

'Two.'

'Five.'

'Zero.'

'Less than zero,' said Johnny Tore, and a guffaw went up. As it was the beginning of term, not even Nicholas Crump turned round to tell them to keep quiet.

'Why were the boys whispering numbers?' Fay asked Alice, as she emerged behind her. Alice was thinking of Prometheus having his liver torn out every evening. Fay repeated her question.

'Do you really want to know?'

'Of course.'

'That was the males rating the females as they passed up the assembly line. We get marks out of ten for looks.'

'Well,' said Fay. 'How dare they only give me five?'

*

The smell of school is polish and piss, Grub thought. At the beginning, it was more polish than piss; at the end, more piss than polish. At some point past Exeter St David's, when the earth turned red and Dartmoor heaved itself up out of the rippling plains, he always began to change into his school persona: wriggling out of home with every shake and brake on the track. But the process was never completed until the Brasso and floor wax rose up like a rubber skin to enclose him.

The Males' Flats were a different affair from the arrangements at the Dower House. Not even the James Stirling Tower of Babel was in such a bad state of repair as the Males' Flats (though Flottage came a close second). Scabby with marks made by sticking up and ripping off *Playboy* centrefolds and posters, they were thought by those who lived in them to be health hazards. However, they were made far more desirable than the Dower House or even the new study bedrooms by the fact that they enclosed and overlooked the inner quadrangle of the main house.

This was where the majority of Knotshurst social life took place. It was known as the Quad. Some fifty feet square and seventy feet high, it had a filthy parquet floor on which two badminton courts and a ping-pong table were easily accommodated. Mostly, however, Knotes of both sexes just spent their time hanging around there, as if it were a public square in a Mediterranean country. This suggestion was increased by the presence of a brick loggia supporting the corridors of the Males' Flats above. Boys would sit, legs dangling through the bars, and throw apple cores or rude remarks on to the heads of disliked passers-by, after Jaw or during the afternoon Free.

On the ground floor, staff, dining and common rooms were appointed along three walls of the Quad; the fourth, opposite the swing doors, had a row of tall fanlighted windows looking south to the lake and Temple of Venus. Half a mile beyond that, the winding estuarial waters of the Knot gave off a damp salt wind. Many noises were brought by this wind besides the continual high-pitched whistle which drove everyone mad for the first few days before they became deaf to it: the exhalation of waves in the Sound, the crack of trees in cold winters, the weird keening of seagulls, and sometimes strange, almost harsh groans, which led the superstitious to claim that the estate was haunted.

'If you go out to the temples at night, man, you see the ghosts

of miners that drowned in the flood, coughing and coughing,'
Naimh told Winthrop. 'And if they see you, it means you'll die
within a year.'

'More likely to be night wanderers having a fag,' Grub said.

'It's true,' Naimh persisted, adding, 'That's why that kid
topped himself. Everyone knows it.'

'Oh, bog off,' said Grub. 'You weren't even here at the time.'

Bang! The door was thrown open against the wall, making
everyone jump. A hand snaked round the opening and switched
the light off.

'Shit, man, who's that?' asked Naimh, in a shaken voice.

'Fucking Arabs! God, you make a stink in here!' said Tore,
cackling as he switched the light on again and slouched into the
dorm. 'Open the fucking windows. I think I'm going to suffocate in this maze of spastics. Hi, Grubster.'

'Torosaurus! Good to see you,' said Grub, bounding up from
his bed. They punched each other playfully in the stomach. The
last of his home persona vanished like smoke.

Tore drew attention wherever he went. Thin, dark, sallow, he
had the same androgynous Gypsy looks that his famous father
possessed. But there was something else, too: a wildness, a
barely suppressed nervous energy which could fly off in any
direction. He spoke in a hoarse smoker's croak, but when he
laughed, it sounded almost like screaming. When he lost his
temper with anyone, he could paralyse them with fear.

Tore was, to the whole of Knotshead, the epitome of cool. He
had discovered Jim Thompson, Fritz the Cat and Marilyn Mon-
roe years before everyone else; taken drugs even the *New
Musical Express* hadn't heard of; lost his virginity, and flown
on Concorde before he arrived in Block 3. He was beyond style
– or beyond good and evil, which at Knotshead amounted to
the same thing. Nobody else would dare to dress in biker's
leathers for fear of looking a pleb, but Tore did. Nobody else
would have burnt his own wrists with a lighted cigarette end for
a dare, but Tore did. Nobody else would have thought of putting Pug's telephone number in a gay encounter magazine, but
Tore did. Even the staff were frightened of him, Grub thought.
He was not, as far as Grub could tell, particularly good-looking,
yet he could have any girl he wanted with a snap of his nico-
tined fingers.

'Ah, leave us alone,' said Hussein, languid in his red and

cream silk dressing gown. Winthrop, clutching his knees beneath the sheets, looked at him in appalled fascination, for Hussein was clearly wearing nothing underneath except a gold ingot on a chain. Jesus, his dick hung out like a fucking salami! Vague horror stories about British public schools welled up in his memory. If this was how Mummy intended to punish him for having the normal instincts of an American male, she must be nuts. He put his retainers in his mouth and hoped they made him look as mean as Jaws in the Bond movies.

'You'll need the window open the whole time with these tossers,' said Tore. His black leathers creaked as he struggled with the swollen wooden frame. 'What's all this hag pong on your locker? Pheromones? Aw, fuck me, it's fucking aftershave!'

'I need it,' said Hussein. 'My beard grows twice a day since I was twelve.'

'Mine too,' said Naimh. 'Besides, the women, they like perfume. My father's mistress, she told me the first time we have sex.'

Winthrop sagged with relief.

'You shag your old man's tart?'

'Yeah,' said Naimh, yawning. 'My father, he tell me, when you are twelve, I get her to tell you how to make a woman come. Keep it all in the family. That way we don't get no diseases.'

Hussein sniggered.

'Yeah, well, my old man didn't need to set me up with some cunt like that,' said Tore. 'They queue up to do it for free.'

The others sighed enviously. Even the children of *Guardian* readers had heard of the floating gin palace on the Aegean, the château in Provence, the concerts to packed audiences at Wembley Stadium. Journalists occasionally made sneering references to Gore Tore as an ageing rock star, but he was still the most famous of them all, with a harem of models and groupies all clawing each other's eyes out to become the second Mrs Tore.

'Ah, man, at least they don't wish I were my father when I – ' Hussein's voice died in his throat as he caught Tore's eye. There was an electric silence.

Grub thought of a joke. 'Hey, what's the difference between a penis and a bonus?' he asked.

Immediately distracted, Tore grinned. 'I dunno.'

'Your wife will blow your bonus but not your penis.'

Everyone laughed. Only Winthrop had the vaguest notion what a bonus was.

'What's this?' said Grub, relieved, picking up something on Hussein's locker. 'A vibrator?'

'A portable phone, man.'

'So you can call up your Chinkos without even moving?'

'Nah, more likely so he can keep ringing his stockbroker,' Tore said, but without aggression. 'Fucking Arabs. Always tossing off.'

'So I like to make a little money, so what?' said Hussein in his glottal American, perusing his *Financial Times*. All the Arabs read the *FT*, particularly the 'How to Spend It' page on Saturday. It was, as far as they were concerned, the most educational thing about being in England.

Many so-called Arabs were not in fact Arabs at all. Knotshurst had a policy of allowing a couple of what the headmaster called 'our Third World cousins' in every year: these were not impoverished Africans but the sons and very occasionally the daughters of exceptionally rich exiles from the trouble spots of the world. Like an arms dealer, Simon Hart always knew when things were hotting up in some country or other a year before revolution broke out, because he would suddenly be deluged with calls from senior government officials related to the current prime minister, asking him to let their child in without taking the entrance tests.

Naimh and Hussein were from Lebanon and Iran; they and the other exiles had become allies, a separate faction in the school bound by their flagrant wealth. They had their own vogues, which were as urban as those of the rest of Knotshead were rustic, carrying their prep around (when they bothered to do any) in briefcases lined with ostrich-skin suede. Every month, they would order an enormous Indian or Chinese takeaway to be delivered by taxi from Knotsmouth, three miles away. This, when it arrived, gave them instant power over all the non-Arabs, who, in the hope of being allowed a share, willingly closed off a whole corridor and stood guard over them after lights out as the Arabs lolled around like Roman nobles, feasting in a mound of aluminium cartons. Most of these hopes were false. The Arabs ordered and dispensed their food with considerable acumen, taking care to time these banquets so that just enough food was ordered to bribe Tore and one or two of his Lads.

In the balance of power at Knotshead, the Arabs were a neutral element, interested only in self-preservation and profit. Their cunning was both loathed and respected: Hussein, within a week of arrival, stole all the plugs out of the basins and baths, and sold them back at 50p a time. Knotes despised them for making money in this mean way: the Arabs despised Knotes for not thinking of it first.

Tore left them alone unless very bored. Occasionally they bought dope off him, and could be extorted to give him money. He took another toke out of his jacket pocket and lit up as the fire alarm gave two deafening blasts outside the door. Lights Out. Everyone groaned.

'I got this for my birthday.' Grub took out a tiny black object, the size of a little finger, attached to his keyring. It was a torch. Torches were strictly forbidden, as it was believed (correctly) that they encouraged Knotes to go out night wandering. 'It's a spy torch, developed by the CIA, with an adjustable pencil beam and a spare bulb and battery in the screw. Isn't it ace?'

They all agreed, rather enviously, that it was.

Tore took something from his leather jacket and began to play with it, idly.

'What's that?' Grub asked curiously.

'I got a new toy, too.'

'What?' asked Naimh, his eyes lighting up.

'Flick knife. Look.' He pressed a button, and six inches of thin, shiny steel sprang out with a tiny click, making everyone, including Winthrop, start.

'Shit, man,' said Naimh, uneasily.

'Isn't it illegal?'

Tore shrugged. 'So?' He put it back in his jacket. 'Nobody here saw it, did they?'

'Pug will be coming round in a few minutes,' said Grub. Captain Wash was the senior housemaster of the Males' Flats. Resembling a depilated Pekinese, he kept the males, including his sidekick, Peter Chumley (a.k.a. Pedigree), in some degree of terror when he could be bothered to go on the rampage.

Tore shrugged. 'Such a fucking bore, treating us as if we were kids. He's been a real pain ever since he found out about Pedigree making me morning tea for a quid a throw.' Nevertheless, he yawned.

'Good summer, Jono?' Grub asked, casually, as his friend made preparations to leave.

'Yeah. We went island-hopping in the Aegean, all the way from Bathos to Pathos.'

Winthrop wondered if this was an example of British irony. His patrician nostrils dilated.

Tore, who had ignored him, caught sight of this. He narrowed his viperous eyes and said in a soft drawl, 'Hey, you, what are you staring at?'

Grub looked from Tore to Winthrop: one thin, cool, dark; the other an arrogant, neo-Nazi android. Something about the contrast made him shiver, as if he had a premonition of evil. He opened his mouth to make a joke, then found he could not speak.

Winthrop T. Sheen gave Johnny Tore his iciest blue glare.

'Chill out,' he said in a bored voice.

'Right,' said Tore softly. 'You're on.'

5

Familiarity breeds sentiment before contempt. For the first week there was a truce between every faction as it took stock of depletions, considered possible new recruits and changed from children into Knotes. Those whose metamorphoses were too slow, insufficiently backed up by new clothes, contact lenses or compact-disc players would be cast into the outer limits of social life at the first school disco. This took place on the first and last Saturdays of each term.

Alice watched the girls in her dorm preparing for the dance. The whole Dower House was in a ferment of excitement. Every mirror was steamed up by heavy-breathing pimple-poppers; in communal bathrooms, where six or more baths were ranged around the whitewashed walls, taps thundered hot water and bathers basked in the swampy heat, masked by concoctions of yoghurt, egg yolk or mud. Clothes were piled high on beds and changed half a dozen times. Even so, mistakes were made, particularly by newcomers. By the end of the evening, they would discover that eyeshadow, high heels and sequins spelt social death; but for the moment hope and excitement reigned.

'Aren't you coming?' Fay asked, smearing blue cream on her eyelids.

Alice was sitting in her usual pool of black, reading. 'No.'

'Why not?'

'I'd rather read.'

'Bor-ing!' said Olivia, like a suburban door bell. She was sitting on Nicola's bed with two other girls in 6i, riffling through

Jackie while her friend tried on different pairs of earrings. Nicola, the Block 5 girl in Alice's dorm, was a junior member of the Jet Set. Her father was an ambassador. She thought school was absolutely super, and hung on Olivia's every word even if she could barely be bothered to speak to anyone else. This behaviour was generally excused as shyness.

'Dancing is the only compulsory subject here besides agriculture and sex,' said Alice. 'You may find it entertaining to strut around like a headless chicken. I do not.'

'She's just frightened none of the males will ask her to dance,' said Olivia spitefully. 'Aren't you, Louse?'

Alice ignored her.

'A-louse
Is a Scouse
Like a mouse
Without a blouse.'

Olivia went out, giggling, to go to the Quad with Nicola.

'Is it true that dancing is compulsory?' asked Fay.

Alice's voice was strained. 'Not officially. But you get into trouble with Veronica if you don't go.'

After the first term, she had pretended to have a headache or too much prep every time, and had been lambasted in reports for being 'antisocial', the worst thing a Knote could be accused of.

'Can girls ask males to dance?'

'In theory. But,' said Alice, 'this is a place where they believe in the vaginal orgasm.'

'When I told an Etonian I was coming here, he said it sounded like paradise.'

'Oh, it is, if you're a boy. As long as you don't have glasses, braces, fat, the wrong clothes or are nervous of the opposite sex.'

'And if you're a girl?'

'There are worse defects than that, I'm afraid.'

'Oh. Shortness?'

Alice sighed. 'No. It won't do any good if I tell you, anyway.'

'I think you should come. You're always reading.'

'I like reading better than anything. Sorry.'

'I think you're mean,' said Fay. 'You promised you'd look after me, and you won't even come to the disco. It's just cowardice, as Olivia said.'

There was a pause, in which her lips trembled. Alice remembered that Fay was, after all, only fourteen, even if a week of shepherding her to and from classrooms and meals had proved her as maddeningly self-centred as suspected. Her heart sank. It was quite true: she was frightened. It was painful to be reminded of her ugliness in so public a fashion. She loathed pop, and always came away from such events sunk in the deepest depression, despising herself, as her mother would have done, for going to such a cattle market in the first place. Yet she had promised to look after Fay. Nobody had looked after her in her own first term. Perhaps things would have turned out differently, if they had. Perhaps thing would turn out differently for Fay, if she did.

'It won't do any good, but if you really want me to, I'll come.'

Fay, typically, did not thank her. 'Aren't you going to change?'

'No.'

'Do I look OK?'

'Well ... I think, perhaps, the eyeshadow ... '

'But then, you don't wear make-up, do you?'

'No. There wouldn't be much point, would there?'

'No,' said Fay. 'I suppose not.'

The thump-thump-thump of rock music came very clearly through the Quad roof. A great glass cupola, it had been one of J.C. Loudon's earliest achievements: inspired, according to his 1805 'Hints for Laying out the Ground in Private Squares', by a reading of 'Kubla Khan'. Occasionally, fears were raised at staff meetings that the vibrations caused by school dances could dislodge panes on to those beneath, but these were pooh-poohed.

'You couldn't stop it even if you wanted to,' said Martin Mortmain. 'Mnyah, mnyah, "The association of man and woman / In daunsinge ... Two and two, necessary coniunction". Eliot puts it so well.'

Helge giggled as Mortmain leered at her pneumatic cleavage.

Pedigree Chumley rose to the opportunity with all the eagerness of a hard-won Cambridge 2.2. He was desperate to make the German teacher notice him.

'He encapsulates Life Itself.'

'Too ghastly. They are scarcely men and women,' murmured Toby Hindesmith, cleaning manicured, if paint-flecked, fingernails. He had taken his first art class of the term, and was still reeling from the horror of it all. Although there had been a rather fetching, faunlike creature in Block 3, who might make it rather more tolerable. Yes, distinctly so.

'"Earth feet, loam feet." It's a force of nature,' said Mortmain.

'Life Itself.'

'Simulated public copulation,' said Hew Morgan. 'How anyone can endure melody of such staggering banality is beyond me.'

'What would you prefer? A massed male-voice Welsh choir?' asked Hindesmith, with a delicate shudder. 'Now that really might bring the roof down.'

'I seem to remember that the whole thing is organised by one of your favourite pupils, in point of fact,' said Maggie Brink. The asperity of her tone was marked; she was secretly trying not to scratch herself. Her psoriasis had been so much better in China, but this morning she had woken up to find the map of the USSR on her stomach was gradually disintegrating around Poland. She scratched, surreptitiously, and wondered whether to try wrapping her torso in clingfilm, as suggested by a recent article in the *Independent on Sunday*. 'Grub Viner.'

Hew rolled his eyes.

'Is there really a chance it might be unsafe?' Hart asked. He could never repress his unease about these events.

'The glass panes are quite secure,' said Veronica, her cold, precise voice falling on them like a shower in a public swimming bath. 'I personally inspect them at the start of every term.'

'Darling, if you told us you went down the school sewers with a torch and a pair of Rottweilers it wouldn't surprise us a bit,' said Toby Hindesmith. 'The indefatigable Slythes! What would we do without you?'

There was a slight pause. Veronica clicked the Biro attached to her clipboard with deliberation, in-out-in-out. Like a scorpion deciding whether to sting or not, thought Hart. It was well known that Hindesmith and the Slythes entertained a strong and mutual detestation. All arts and the sciences staff lived in a state of some antagonism, but Veronica disliked homosexuals. Had Toby not been such a cult figure, the headmaster would have been very tempted to get rid of him, just to keep the peace with Veronica. The alternative was tempting, but impossible.

'What indeed?' said Hart, with a sigh. 'In any case, we can't cancel such a popular event.'

'They're such nice kids,' said Delus, sucking on his pipe. A sweet, sightly sickening scent filled the staff room. 'These dances really seem to break the ice for newcomers. I've noticed it time and time again.'

The balding, bearded crafts teacher was, like the Crumps, a generation older than Hart, but his charity and sincerity always made him seem much younger. An old-fashioned socialist, he had come to Knotshead with his son after an attempt to produce some of his patented inventions had foundered during the last recession. Hopeless with money, Delus had signed a contract which effectively bound him to the school for the rest of his future in return for a loan from the trust. He found it a frustrating bargain, if only because it left him so little time to get on with his own work. However, his appointment had been such a success that even difficult pupils like the Tore boy could be contained by him. If he thought the dances were a good thing, then there was no question but that they would continue.

The popularity of Knotshead discos was manifested by the universal attendance at such events. Vigilant for signs of drinking or other misdemeanour, staff never noticed that at least half the school never danced, remaining shadowy spectators. Instead, they lined two walls of the Quad, jerking their Adam's apples in and out or else smiling fixedly in the shadows while the same fifty males danced with the same fifty girls.

This was the underclass of the school: those who were, except for purposes of persecution, completely invisible. Preponderantly female, and usually scientists, they were not, to the adult eye, strikingly unattractive. One or two might be volcanically pimpled or excessively fat, but by and large they were not notably freakish or frumpish. What they lacked was the particular Knote style, the mix of *haute* bohemianism and debonair poise. Knotes knew by instinct that it is easier to afflict the comfortable than to comfort the afflicted: the line of those whom it was fair game to persecute was always drawn at their own heels.

The existence of a rigid social hierarchy among pupils was something that Knotshead staff chose to ignore. While some of those approaching retirement were vaguely conscious of an

absence of sandals and socks, they blamed this on ten years of
Tory misrule. In any case, the healthy life of farming, craft and
music would show them the way. For it was a truth held to be
self-evident that children were naturally good unless perverted
by the outside world.

'Every Knote,' the Founder had written, 'is to be a *tabula rasa*
free of the artifice and shoddy industrialism which suffocate our
natural impulses and affections. Every schoolchild should be
able to know what it is to have lived in Arcadia.'

Teachers only had to look out of the window to be reassured
of this – the young in one another's arms, the inspiring landscape, the general air of grand simplicity. Dances encapsulated
all these happy themes. So the staff thought as they watched
those in the grip of the stroboscopic lights.

Occasionally, some well-meaning teacher such as Dai Delus
would register the fact that one particular girl had been part-
nerless for the entire duration, and instruct a male to dance with
her. Such chivalrous interventions invariably paralysed both
dancers with humiliation, and were tantamount to an instant
seal of Reject status. It was better not to dance at all than to be
forced to do so.

Those at the top had, of course, a very different time of it.
They whirled, they twirled, they jumped, they bumped; they
hopped and bopped and even knew a few steps of the ceroc. It
was here that Winthrop came to grief.

Winthrop had been taught to dance by his last girlfriend –
actually, a teacher at his last prep school, but that was another
story. She really knew how to tango, as if the two of them had
been joined at the hips and elbows by a piece of elastic. Winthrop thought it was almost as good as sex, and much longer-
lasting.

He had been watching Olivia as she wriggled and giggled on
the floor, and decided that here was one hot chick. He was
ready for some heavy dancing action, and judged that now was
the time to strut his stuff.

'Hi,' he said, walking up to her and grinning whitely. 'Let's
move.'

Olivia stared at him and snickered. Like all Knotes she automatically despised Americans, and found males with athletic
physiques repulsive. Winthrop's looks, which alternated be-

tween those of a film star and a killer rabbit, were the antithesis to the government heroin poster campaigns generally admired. Had it not been for the Knote rule never to turn down a male, she would have refused. As it was, she went out on the dance floor making faces to all her friends. Winthrop caught sight of this, and became uncharacteristically nervous.

'What do you like doing?' he asked, as the music started up.

Olivia could not even be bothered to look at him. She waggled her fingers at Tore, who watched with a faint sneer.

'I said, what can you do?'

'Actually, all sorts of things,' said Olivia, in a bored voice. 'But only with people I like.'

'Well,' said Winthrop, displaying his large white teeth, 'I was kinda hoping you'd like me. Hey, let's boogie.'

Olivia rolled her eyes.

Annoyed, Winthrop seized her hand and they began to dance.

She moved with such disdain that he became more and more nervous. It was like manhandling a corpse. Nothing he could do seemed to wipe off her expression of bored indifference. It went right through from her face to her entire body language. His hands started to sweat. His elbows made contact with other dancers. People made irritated noises as he hit them in the solar plexus.

Winthrop started to panic. This was terrible; he had never danced as badly as this in his life. He kept missing the beat but not, mysteriously, her toes. By now, Olivia was not only bored but angry. His hands were sweating so much they felt like pretzels. He had to keep moving at all costs. Perhaps something fancy would help him out.

There was a complicated two-step like a figure of eight which usually broke the ice. It involved reeling your partner in, twirling her about and then flinging her out to arm's length. He tried it. It worked like a dream: but when he flung her out, she kept right on moving, spinning out of his grasp and across the parquet. She crashed straight into Alice and Fay, who fell over. Everyone stopped dancing and began to laugh.

'Hell, I'm awfully sorry,' said Winthrop.

'Bog off,' Olivia hissed. 'Just bog off.'

'Are you hurt?'

He ignored the other two girls picking themselves up off the floor. Alice, who was quite badly bruised, was trying to comfort

Fay, who was not.

Tore came over. 'You heard what she said.' He looked at the American boy.

Tore could inspire terror in anyone when he looked like that. Everyone melted away.

Normally, Winthrop would have been able to turn the whole situation to his own advantage, but the embarrassment of what had just occurred was underlined by the sudden, appalling realisation that he was in a completely foreign country. In America, he could smash someone's car, reputation or career and know he'd escape because the victim, or the judge, would have turned out to have, say, been a member of Skull and Bones like Sheen Senior. But here, he was in a whole new ball game.

Win with ease, lose with grace, he told himself.

'Hell, I'm really sorry about that,' he said to Tore, putting out his hand.

Tore looked at it. 'Bog off, wanker,' he said, jerking his thumb towards the stair to the Males' Flats above.

Winthrop thought it wisest to bog.

At the end of the dance, all agreed that it was 'a really good bop'. No other conclusion was possible.

6

Winthrop had expected things to be bad, but not as bad as this. It was one thing to reject a new school, and quite another to have it reject you. That really jacked him out.

'Son,' his daddy had told him once when he was a little boy, 'look at those fuzzy things up there, and tell me what you see.'

'They're geese, Daddy, aren't they?' said Winthrop.

'Right,' said Sheen Senior, taking a pull on one of his miniature bottles of Jack Daniels. 'And you know why they always fly in a V?'

'No.'

'Because one goose, son, yes, one alone is *born to lead*. Remember, leaders are born, not made. And you come from a long line of leaders, Win, which you can be very proudful of. It's the law of the jungle thing out there,' said Winthrop's father, swallowing emotionally. 'We're all restrained kind of guys, but now and then we have to vent a spleen. I want to be upfront about this, without getting into semantics. A lot of people think people like us are doomed to failure. That is not so. Basically, son, you kill or be killed. Don't forget.'

'Yes, Daddy,' his son breathed. 'I won't.' And he had not.

A flock of wild geese were migrating overhead now, honking high above the onyx leaves of the valley. Across the reedy, steely lake, the twin domes of the Temple of Venus shone white and rounded through the grey gloom. The geese flew on, towards Knotsmouth and the Sound. Their calls sounded like raucous, mocking laughter. Winthrop wished he had a gun.

He trudged from one class to the next, from one meal to the next and from one sports field to the next in a state of growing resentment and bewilderment.

I have a problem, he kept thinking, I have a problem with all of this.

Instead of treating him with the respect due to two generations of East Coast trust funds and West Coast real estate, Knotshead made it clear it considered him a total nerd. He didn't look like a nerd, dress like a nerd or talk like a nerd, but the mere fact of being American was enough to make him an underdog. He couldn't believe it. All his life, he had been a success. Even as a rat, he had been a Big Man on Campus. 'Moby Dick', he had been called, and 'Poon Man Sheen, the American Dream'. Hell, he'd been tossed from two prep schools because he was so popular. Yet this spaced bunch of British kids thought he was a dork. They called him Superbrat, and laughed as soon as he came into a room. Outrageous, astounding – but fact. He had to face facts.

'Tomorrow there'll be another tidal wave, so keep your snorkel above the water level,' he muttered grimly to himself, remembering one of his daddy's adages. If only his trustees had not been so mad at him.

At first, he thought the key must be money. It usually was. The Sheens were one of the richest families on the East Coast. Maybe these guys needed a foghorn. He tried mentioning the fact that he had a trust fund a couple of times. But that was no good, either.

'Look,' Grub had muttered to him, 'you just don't talk about money, ever.'

Evidently, flower power was still key. Half the kids looked as if they'd stepped straight out of a 1960s time warp. He considered cutting the alligators off his T-shirts with the scissors from his manicure set, then decided it would be too awful. If they were anti-American, that was their problem not his. Fuck the lot of them. He would keep his Weejuns, and his pride.

The fat boy had given him a rapid tour of the main buildings, leaving a snail trail of chocolate wrappers which filled Winthrop with disgust.

Each looked on the other with profound dislike, mixed with resentment. Winthrop could not understand why a guy like Tore, an asshole but a cool asshole, would want to associate

with a clown who had red hair and glasses. Grub found it hard
to keep a straight face every time his dorm mate opened his
mouth. Those awful teeth, so large and perfect and white.
Thank God Mum isn't like this, he kept thinking. At the same
time, he found Winthrop's ignorance and political naivety made
him painfully aware of his own first term, the tightrope he had
walked as a fat, clever half-Jew, before Tore had decided to like
him. He did not want to remember that time.

'Why is it so bad to even mention money?'

Grub pushed his spectacles up his snub nose in embarrassment. 'You just don't.'

'You mean, I've got to pretend I'm ashamed of having a trust
fund?'

'Yes. No. I don't know,' was Grub's confused and confusing
answer.

'No wonder this is such a half-assed country,' said Winthrop
angrily. 'What do you think capitalism is – death or something?' Grub shrugged before disappearing into the building
Knotes called the Tower of Babel, from which a cacophony of
different instruments seeped out. Winthrop did not care to follow, mooching back through Flottage to the empty dorm.

He wished, yet again, that Mother had not had this weird
Anglophile fixation. From what he could see, they were just
Eurotrash: snotty, lazy and cliquey.

There was no sport to speak of. That was a big blow. He had
always relied on sport to win him friends, but here they hated it
so much they even had an anti-sports day. Anything competitive
was completely déclassé, although the younger Blocks played a
little soccer. In winter, there were only two compulsory sports
afternoons in which you could basically jog, bicycle or do yoga.
Rugby and crew were out, of course, and as for squash, they
seemed to think it was some kind of fruit drink.

His courses were English, humanities and French. At first,
when he had heard that he had to concentrate on only three
core subjects, he had thought he had touched goal. No math!
No more economics or physics, only the subjects he was best at!
But then, to his dismay, he had found that the level of work expected was not the kind he had been accustomed to – even if nobody seemed to notice when some students didn't turn up for
lessons. If you did, it was not good enough to have read *Plot
Outlines of 100 Famous Novels* and identify strongly with Hol-

den Caulfield and Huck Finn. In any case, the British idea of a famous novel did not include Fitzgerald or Hemingway or even William Burroughs. They had no idea that America had anything to offer apart from films and *Dallas*. The professors 'corrected' his spelling, and the others laughed at his pronunciation the one and only time he was asked to read aloud.

Maggie Brink, the humanities teacher, seemed to have taken a particular dislike to him. Her pilot light had been blown out long ago, but unlike his fellow students, she knew about his family – all socialists were terrific snobs, really – and seemed determined to carry on the class war in her lessons. It was said that when she had first come to Knotshead she had stuck posters of Marx, Che Guevara, Stalin, Fidel Castro and Chairman Mao all round her classroom. One by one, either as the Sellotape became too brittle or the ideals bombed, each had fallen from the walls, leaving only the head of Marx in place.

In his second class, Winthrop had yawned.

'I know it's all incredibly boring for you, but do try to show a little interest,' Maggie had snapped.

'I'm sorry, ma'am. My retainers keep me awake at night.'

'Your retainers!' The woman had completely lost her rag. 'I'm sure they do. Well, those of us without an army of servants could perhaps answer my question on the ethics of famine.'

Winthrop had been completely confused by this. It was only later that he realised that what he put into his mouth before sleeping, the English called braces. What he called suspenders, they also called braces, but what they called suspenders was what he called garters. Sometimes, he didn't think they were speaking the same language at all.

It was the accent that made him feel outclassed. Back home, he had never considered the way he had spoken, confident that it was neat. Here, he felt like an idiot as soon as he opened his mouth. He suddenly remembered how, at his last school, there had been two British guys: nothing special to look at, but all the girls would start talking in this stupid way when they were around – 'Eoh, your burger looks gorgeous' – just because they thought it such a classy accent. It had been, like, they knew Shakespeare personally.

Winthrop kicked a fallen apple along the path from the Library to the main classroom block in the Stables. He was only just beginning to get his bearings in this place; so far, the woods beyond the lake filled his head with a kind of fog. He hated the suffocating trees and the dense, acrid mass of rhododendrons underneath. He hated the maze of buildings, sprawling between the main house and the girls' house; the classrooms all with weird names like Flottage or the Tower of Babel, or even the Old Harness Room. Boarding schools were pretty much the same up to a point: intense, bad food and full of furtive smokers, but here there was nobody with whom he could share the experience. Nobody bothered to explain anything. He was lonely and hungry. The food was just unbelievable, even compared to the fruit salad Jell-O of yore. There was no fresh orange juice. How could anyone live without fresh orange juice? Winthrop kicked the apple again, viciously, and hit the ankle of a tall, thin girl walking ahead of him.

'Shit!'

'Ow.' She bent down and rubbed it. Her face was vaguely familiar: from class, he supposed.

'Sorry.'

'It's only my Achilles heel,' she said. She wondered why she bothered to make jokes when nobody else understood them.

'I feel the heel,' said Winthrop.

'Can one person feel the pain in another's foot?' asked Alice sarcastically.

'Only if our souls were touching,' said Winthrop.

Alice, amazed by this delightful pun, looked at him with more interest. Pleased, Winthrop returned her gaze. He was programmed to respect people who looked him straight in the eye: it was like a strong chin, it meant someone was OK. She had strange eyes and a short, arched nose, but was otherwise nothing special. He wished he could decode the way English girls walked. In America, he could tell exactly how rich a girl was because of the trust-fund walk, that loping stride that became easier and easier the more money Daddy had. Here, they were sort of all scrunched up inside themselves. This one was a classic example.

'So, what's with the total design concept? Did somebody die?' He gestured towards her clothes.

'I am in mourning for my life,' said Alice, with the irony which made her much disliked.

Winthrop had heard this sort of line before, perhaps in a Woody Allen film. It made him feel secure. He remembered that he had had chicks back home creaming in their jeans for him, and flashed his whitest smile at her. On second thoughts, Alice did not look like the sort of girl who would wear jeans. He removed his smile.

'Can I ask you something personal?'

'You can try,' said Alice. The good impression he had made was rapidly fading. She disliked the way he questioned without inflecting his voice upwards at the end, as if he assumed she would answer.

'I've been watching you,' he said, improvising (girls always believed this, for some reason), 'and I see somebody who doesn't look like she's, like, brain-dead, right?'

He paused. She said nothing, but he sensed he had pressed the right button.

'So, I was wondering, how does this place work? I mean, you must know.'

'You want the worm's eye view?'

'Any view is a help.'

She shrugged, and he saw her breasts rise and fall against the fabric of her long black sweater, like something almost surfacing out of deep water for an instant. He wondered, idly, what they would be like to touch.

'It won't do any good. Schools make up their mind about you the first week. There are the Lads, or Jet-Setters if you're a girl, at the top; then the Groovers, the Semi-Groovers, the Semi-Rejects and the Rejects. You and I are Rejects.'

It took a moment for this to sink in.

'That's absolutely outrageous!'

'It's going to rule your life here for the next two years.'

'And is it fixed, just like that? I mean, don't they change their minds?'

'Rarely.'

'How? What do they judge by?'

'Oh. Everything. Anything. Whether your parents are famous; but if you boast about it, you become a Reject. If you have a title. If your parents aren't divorced. Where you live. Whether you have an Aga.'

'The Aga Khan? But my mother's a great friend of his.'

'An Aga isn't a person,' said Alice patiently. 'It's an oven. Incredibly expensive to run because you can never switch it off, but if you're anyone in Knotshead, you've got to have one.'

'An oven? Why not a Rolls-Royce in the garage?'

'Oh no. Americans have cars; we have Agas. Like the Continentals have sex and we have hot-water bottles.'

'This is incredible. So, what else? Clothes?'

'Well,' said Alice, looking down. 'Not moccasins.'

'These are Bean's.'

'What?'

'You haven't heard of Bean's?'

'Of course. Flatulence of one sort or another is endemic to the Knote population.'

Winthrop could not decide whether she was being deliberately stupid. 'It's a store,' he said. 'A very famous American store. L. L. Bean's, in Maine? I can't believe you've never heard of it. It's symbolic.'

'Symbolic of what?'

Winthrop looked at her with irritation. 'Just symbolic. Like wearing pink and green. People like us – people like me – oh, hell.' He gave up. How could he describe what it all meant?

'Oh. That kind of symbolism.' Alice was disappointed; she had hoped for something more than mere snobbery. 'Of course, Knotes have colour codes, too. Green gumboots – you must have noticed them. Black ones mean you're a townee, so nobody wears them.'

'You do.'

'Well, yes. Cheaper. And unlike them, I spent my childhood on a farm. But green ones mean you're a country person.' She said, with repressed savagery, 'All Knotes love the countryside, even if half of them live in Fulham. Especially if they live in Fulham. Or Hampstead. They look down on real farmers – but everyone is a Friend of the Earth.'

Winthrop thought of the time he had gone walking at a summer school in Vermont and was stung by poison ivy, and gave a faint shudder. As far as he was concerned, large grassy spaces were acceptable to people of good breeding only if you were accompanied by a set of golf clubs. Nothing would get him to like the kind of thing that surrounded Knotshead. Hell, there could be anything out there.

He smoothed back his straight blond hair.

'Whether you're good at acting – no, not whether you're actually good at it, whether you're chosen to act in the school plays. A very different thing.'

'What about . . . ' Winthrop paused. 'Personality?'

Alice grimaced. 'If you're a girl, you're not supposed to have any. The great crime is to be antisocial: not in the sense of being unpleasant, but in not smiling at the staff, or – ' She stopped suddenly, and said, very fast, 'You probably think I'm just saying this out of disappointment. Well, I am. Not just because it's beastly to be spat on all the time, or because it's unfair, although it's both those things, but because – I'd like people to be better than that. I'd like them to be valued by what's inside them.'

She was like one of those trick drawings, where the same lines depicted Cinderella and her old godmother.

'You want them judged by moral worth?'

'Yes,' said Alice.

'How can you tell, though? I mean, it isn't something you can see, like clothes or a good body.'

'Oh, I know all right.'

'How?'

'People make sounds, like bells. You can hear if something isn't right about them.'

Winthrop laughed, for the first time since he had arrived at Knotshead. 'That's one of the weirdest things I've ever heard!'

At once, he could feel her withdrawing from him.

'Hey, I didn't mean – '

'I'm late for Latin,' she said abruptly. 'And things get worse for Rejects if they talk.'

'Oh. Catch you later.'

'Ha!' she said, and went up the Library steps.

At lunchtime, when he was hesitating in the Quad whether to join her in the queue, someone shouted, hoarsely, 'Hey, Superbrat!' and emptied a bucket of ice-cold water on to him from the Males' Flats. The whole lunch queue laughed at him, and when Winthrop raced, dripping, up the stairs to catch his assailant and beat him to a pulp, there was nothing there but the acrid tobacco stench of Johnny Tore.

7

By general consensus, the Library was the only new addition to the original estate that was a pleasure to use. A world away from the 1960s prefab scrum of Flottage, where most of the lessons were held, it dated from the school's inception, and had been the Founder's greatest gift to Knotshead.

Overlooking the lake at the eastern end and shadowed by the hills at the west, it was a long, two-storey edifice whose every detail, from the rose-red bricks and mullioned windows outside to the long oak tables and chairs inside, had been designed by Lutyens at the start of his career.

Inside, the Library had twenty-eight bays: seven on each side of the ground floor, and seven on each side of the galleried upper floor. Each bay was devoted to a subject, which could be anything from art history to astronomy, and each contained a thousand dusty books judged to be the best of their kind.

This was the domain of the Librarian, and of his parrot Horatio.

It was a rule of Knotshead life that every teacher, irrespective of age, sex and position, should be addressed by his or her Christian name. Yet it was also an unspoken rule that those whom pupils instinctively respected were invariably addressed by their surnames. The Librarian was Mr Kenward.

Nobody knew how old he was. A tall, spare man, tonsured by age but otherwise pickled by book dust, he lived in a large, dilapidated cottage by the upper bridge, below the abandoned copper mines. Some said he was a retired Eton master; others that he was the scion of an ancient local family, perhaps even the Ansteys themselves. He lived alone with Horatio, and taught Latin to the occasional pupil who, like Alice, wished to pursue it for A level. Impish, acerbic, formidably intelligent, Mr Kenward and his familiar terrified even the boldest of Knotes.

Unlike the other members of staff, he did not surround himself with a clique, but there was no way pupils could avoid encountering him several times a week. Up to the last year, when the Upper Sixth had the enviable privilege of study-bedrooms and minimal contact with the rest of the school, there was nowhere but the Library in which to do prep during Frees. Each Knote was assigned a table in a particular bay. Down the centre of the ground floor, there were long oak tables, where particularly disturbed pupils were placed. Up and down this centre well would pace the Librarian, parrot on shoulder, eyebrows bristling at the slightest whisper. A dressing-down from him was an experience greatly to be feared. Alice, tiptoeing in across the creaking floorboards, was given a beetle-browed glare and beckoned through the glass window into the inner sanctum of his office opposite the door.

'You are late,' said the Librarian.

'I'm sorry. A new boy in my block was lost,' she said. Knotes learnt to lie automatically to members of staff.

'Humph!' said the Librarian.

'Youth: possibility,' the parrot squawked. Alice jumped.

'Horatio,' said the Librarian sternly, 'back to your perch.' Sulking, the bird sidled off the Librarian's shoulder and on to the stout pole by the radiator overlooking the lake. There, he ruffled his feathers and sharpened his beak with ostentatious indifference. Alice and the Librarian exchanged smiles, but did not laugh.

'Please, may I stroke him?'

A month had passed, and after eight lessons she felt bold enough to ask.

'That's up to him. Remember, he can take your finger off it he wants. Horatio?'

The parrot considered with one wicked, cynical eye, bobbed twice on the perch, flapped crimson, green and indigo wings, and sailed on to Alice's shoulder.

'Accord: harmony,' he remarked with supreme condescension.

This time, the girl and the Librarian laughed.

'Oh, the angel!' said Alice.

The Librarian gave her a sharp glance. 'A delicate spirit, perhaps.'

'How polite he is, to bow.'

'Miss Godwin, you must avoid attributing human behaviour to animals, even those of such exceptional intelligence as parrots. That motion is not mandarin good manners but the remnants of his desperate attempts to escape from the cage where he was kept confined. Some experiences leave too deep an impression ever to be completely eradicated.'

'Please, how did you find him?' asked Alice.

The Librarian put out a hand, and Horatio stepped mincingly off Alice's shoulder.

'He found me, you might say. He was in a pet shop, the kind of establishment that should carry a sentence of imprisonment no less barbarous for the owner. I detest all creatures being kept in captivity, but this was evil even of its kind.'

The Librarian paused and scratched the parrot's head. 'He was by no means the handsome macaw you see before you. He had survived the most terrible voyage from South America, like many of his unhappy race, only to be put into a brass cage for the entertainment of cretins. He had plucked out most of his feathers, and would not speak. In revenge, the owner was starving him to death. Oh, you were a most wretched creature, were you not, sir?

'Well, I do not often lose my temper, or I would be foaming and biting the floor every other day, but the sight was unendurable. I took his cage and ripped it apart with my hands. He uttered the words, 'Impunity: wealth,' before taking a large chunk out of my jacket and clinging to my arm as if his life depended on it. It was, I may say, love at first bite.'

'O, the horror, the horror!' said Horatio.

'He seems something of a philosopher.'

'He is more of a plagiarist, I fear, but "*plus ave docta loqui*", as Ovid says. Now, where were we?'

'Catullus 64.'

Namque fluentisono prospectans litore Diae
Thesea cedentem celeri cum classe tuetur
Indomitos in corde gerens Ariadna furores,

Necdum etiam sese quae visit visere credit . . .

'Translate, please.'
'Here Ariadne, on the wave-booming shore of Naxos,
  looks out
At Theseus and his shipmates quickly escaping,
And, unable to believe that she sees what she sees,
Feels love tearing like an untamed beast in her heart . . . '
Alice's voice became strained.
'Tell me what you think,' said the Librarian.
Alice thought, It reminds me that my mother is dead, but
said, 'It's the only bit of the poem which is felt, isn't it?'
'Why do you say that?'
'The rest is very clever and beautiful – that conceit of the pine
trees rushing down to make themselves into a ship at the begin-
ning is brilliant – '
'Yes, Ovid copies it in the *Metamorphoses*.'
'But it doesn't vibrate, like the Lesbia poems. He knows
what it's like to be rejected, how close it can bring you to
madness.'
'Don't you think the description of Ariadne losing her clothes
as well as her mind is more lascivious than pathetic? After all,
he seems to be stripping her for the reader, rather.'
'I think it's lascivious *and* pathetic.' Alice's voice shook
slightly. 'The misery of her betrayal isn't lessened by the fact
that she's beautiful.'
'Note, the "*lactentis papillas*" are not just milk-white breasts.
Theseus has made her pregnant.'
'I think she's a fool ever to have trusted him.'
'She had led a very secluded life.'
'Yes, but to show a complete stranger how to kill your own
brother, even if he is the Minotaur and a monster, just because
Theseus had blond hair – it's so silly.'
'Sex is a powerful and mysterious thing,' said the Librarian.
'Much less common than people suppose.'
'I thought it happened all the time.'
'Oh no. Animal attraction is overrated, particularly in the
case of animals. Those deprived of reason lead extremely chaste
and well-ordered love lives.' The Librarian's voice was dry. 'But
only fools despise the real flame, which knows neither sense nor
moderation. It's much rarer than, say, intellectual compatibil-

ity. Obviously: even today, people have far more friends than
lovers. That does not mean passion like Ariadne's should be
welcomed or invited. But it is still a very remarkable thing.'

'But, to judge by the marriages of people's parents, passion
doesn't last. Why love, when there is no fidelity?'

'It is not the nature of living things to remain constant,' said
the Librarian. 'Change and decay; and out of decay, change.'

'But you can be true to yourself, can't you?'

Horatio made a rude noise. The Librarian looked at her.

'Can you?'

Grub spent most of his free periods on the Liszt Piano Sonata.
Music A level demanded Grade Eight on an instrument, as well
as competence in harmony, composition and notation. These,
he found he could do without thinking, having perfect pitch.
What drew him was the piano, and the B Minor.

It was way beyond what he was supposed to be doing for
Grade Eight – a hard piece even for Diploma, said Hew, who,
like Grub's mother, thought Liszt 'an old ham'. Grub was supposed to be doing the usual melange: a Bach fuge, a Mozart
sonata, and the only other piece which really taxed him, Ravel's
Sonatine. But it was the Liszt that he wanted.

Practice, practice, practice, practice. Let it slip for a single
day, and pianism deteriorated inexorably, not just in terms of
suppleness but in mental ability. It was odd: he was restless and
irritable if he didn't play, and yet every time he approached a
piano, the effort of will just to start playing made a part of him
want to scream, or faint, or be sick – anything, rather than start.
And then, when he started, it was dreadful. His fingers would
not make the exact sounds he heard in his head, the pianos were
all crappy Korean Young Changs or clapped-out Chappells and
Bluthners, he could hear half a dozen other musicians practising
because the walls of the Tower of Babel were so thin, he was
frightened of sounding foolish or inept. He hated anyone who
wasn't a musician hearing him, and yet he feared the judgement
of those who were. Hew nagged him to perform something for
Parents' Day, but the idea of it gave him goose pimples. Music
was a private misery, a vocation of unhappiness. Yet there was
the B Minor, waiting for him with all its abysses and mysteries.
He had to have it.

Over and over, he crept up on it: the opening bars, so deceptively short and simple, as if it were snoring. And then it spotted him, and the struggle would begin, the music slipping and sliding this way and that, twining round and round him like a fantastic protean snake, slithers of shimmering, iridescent semiquavers pouring through his fingers, trying to strangle him in its embrace. It would turn itself into anything: a monk, a nest of ants, a beautiful woman, a saint, then back into the snake and he had to hold on at all costs, stubbornly, as if his life depended on it. Sometimes he thought he had beaten it, and sometimes, trembling with nervous exhaustion, he had no doubt that it had beaten him.

He hated the B Minor, and loved it passionately. It was an obsession which not even Hew could fully sympathise with.

'Historically, I agree, it is an important piece in the development of Romantic music, but it has no shape. It's all bombast and self-indulgence. Where does its climax come? It keeps seeming to end and then coming back again. At the end, it merely dies away.'

'It has a shape,' said Grub. 'I know it does.'

'Well, you tell me when you find what it is.'

He had thirteen different recordings of it, and listened to them so often in the dorm it drove everyone mad. Grub, who hated pop with a passion, would come close to quarrelling with Tore about music.

'It's all just music for toffs,' Tore said. 'Toffs or religious maniacs.'

Grub tried to explain in language his friend would understand.

'It's a great horror film, Tore. Listen. First you get the gates of Hell opening, dah-dah-dah-da-da, and this great devil's claw coming out. That's the devil's mode, which the Catholics banned because it sounds so evil. Then there's this bloke who's in love, which is all the soppy bits. The devil attacks him, and is crawling all over his body like a disease. The man is screaming and writhing and tearing at himself to try and keep the germs of evil at bay. Then Liszt thinks of God, and beats the devil. Then the devil comes back at him. Then Liszt wrestles with him again, and thinks he can concentrate on love. So the devil creeps back up. But finally, Liszt becomes a priest and beats him back into Hell, although the devil is always waiting for him.'

'Sounds like he just wanted a good wank, and didn't dare,'

said Tore.

Grub snorted with laughter. 'I wonder what Hew would say if I told him that?'

'Ah, you can't embarrass a Taff who wears Day-Glo clothes. How many times did you manage to get "orgasm" into your English essay for Pedigree this week?'

'Twice. It's not so easy this term.'

'Yeah. That turd burglar, he was dead easy.'

'D. H. Lawrence.'

'Yeah, him. Not so much bonking now, is there? That tosser with the nightingale, he's a dead loss.'

Grub imitated Chumley on Keats. 'For beauty *is* truth, and truth is Life Itself.'

'He thinks everything he reads is Life Itself, stupid git.' Tore loathed and despised all teachers, on principle. He made no secret of the fact that he was only staying on at school because his father insisted. Attempts to keep him under control had been hopeless ever since the apocryphal time in Block 4 when Beatrice Bassett had attempted to fine him £10 for smoking. Tore had pulled out a wadge of £50 notes, peeled one off, and held it out to her. Beatrice, naturally, had not been able to give him any change.

'You can keep it, Busy Bea,' said Tore, sneering. 'But I want the change by lunchtime.'

Only Dai, the crafts teacher, had any influence over him, and this was not great. Tore liked cutting and sawing and hammering, but had no patience with finishing things properly. Throughout his time at Knotshead, he had half completed three projects: an inlaid cigar box for his father, a magazine stand for the Hut, and a crossbow. Dai insisted on perfection before he allowed something to leave the workshop.

'Attention to detail is everything,' he told his pupils. 'If a thing's worth doing, it's worth doing well.'

Dai had a peculiar compassion for Jono, and would limp over to watch him, sucking on his smelly pipe, and try to infuse him with his ideals.

'A piece of wood is like a person,' he said. 'If you work with the grain, it will have the strength of the whole tree. If you go against it, it will snap, or take your hand off. Find people whose strengths dovetail into your weaknesses.'

Tore listened to this with an odd, half-comprehending look

on his thin face, then mooched off with Delus's son to mock the crafts teacher. Sparks, though a whizz at electrics, was bored by craft and embarrassed by his father's flights of homespun ideology. His own interests were confined to taking massive amounts of acid, which he would sell to other Lads.

'We're only stuck in this cruddy place because he was such a dickhead about money,' he said. 'One of these days, I'm going to hotwire a teacher's car and fly away.'

When he could no longer practise, Grub would spend most of his time with Tore, Sparks and the Westler brothers, instead of doing runs or outdoor work. The Lads' numbers were always sadly depleted after GCSE, and vanished altogether before A levels, but those in 6i still felt it incumbent upon them to continue the traditions of night wandering, smoking, drinking and generally skiving with younger Lads, like Mongol, Knife and G-Force. (Only at the top and the bottom of Knotshead were pupils graced by nicknames.) They had several venues for this: the bike sheds, the changing rooms, and the Stagehands' Hut.

Officially the temple of Bacchus, the Hut was decorated with delicate swags of grapes and carvings of dancing figures. Unlike the other follies, it was a tiny house, complete with door and windows, and had been accorded a grudging acceptability as being the place for storing all the lighting equipment for plays and discos. A tattered piece of carpet matted the floor. At some point, electricity had been run up to it. From the ceiling hung a single red light bulb, and a coal-look fire kept it warm.

The chief attraction of this reechy den was as a place to have sex. Staff such as the Crumps and the Slythes, suspecting this, made regular raids which succeeded only in making the Lads hate them. Names and dates of those who had copulated on the Hut's torn chesterfield (upholstered, appropriately enough, with a fabric resembling gigantic black sperm thrashing across a green background) were entered in a book. This, it was said, even contained the name of a junior member of staff who had drunkenly succumbed to a Lad many years ago. The precise location of this book was kept a deadly secret, and passed from head Lad to head Lad in 6ii. It was Tore's great ambition to obtain this. The walls were papered with centrefolds and posters: the usual mix of soft-core porn and soft-pore corn.

'Rule One: all girls are tarts,' Tore would say. 'If you don't get your end away here, then, quite frankly, mate, you never will. That's why our parents sent us here, so we don't turn into a bunch of fucking lesbos or turd burglars.'

It really was wonderful to be surrounded by so many incredibly pretty, charming girls. Grub fell in love at least once a fortnight, and sometimes twice. If only he could work up the confidence to make a pass at one of them, he knew he would not be rebuffed. After all, it was not a girl's place to say no. All the others had done it, right down to the Semi-Rejects – or said they had. Once, in Block 4, he had admitted he was a virgin to that cretin Hussein, and all the Arabs had called him 'Cherry' until he came back the next term and lied that he'd lost it.

Grub was reminded of a cartoon his father had once drawn, one of the 'Dum and Mad' strips. Mad finds Dum with a skin mag and asks him, 'Why do you read that stuff? Does it make you feel happy?' 'Well,' Dum answers, 'yes and no.' 'How d'you mean, yes and no?' Mad shrieks. 'Well,' says Dum, 'it makes me feel that everyone in the whole world is having terrific orgies. Except me.'

He could never imagine himself having the cool to jump on a girl and do all those things to her. How on earth did you keep a straight face? How did she? What if she laughed at you? What if you had got the whole thing utterly, ludicrously wrong? He still couldn't quite work out where the noses went when you kissed, so what about all the other bits?

Tore thought sex was dead boring. He and Olivia had been going together ever since the first disco in Block 3, but they still went with lots of other people, in and out of school. Both the Westler brothers claimed to have had it off with Olivia at one time or another, and Tore had done it with two girls at once, right there in the Stagehands' Hut, the week after GCSE. But he still thought it was overrated.

'Give me a good wank over a *Playboy* centrefold to a tart with a whiplash tongue any day,' Tore told him. 'Tarts are always such a shag. It must have been great before the poison of women's lib came along. I mean, my old man, he could just stuff it up them and they'd thank their lucky stars. Now, you've got to hang around for hours waiting for them to come, just like you do when they're having a piss, because they're all into multiple orgasms and the crap they read in *Cosmopolitan*. Quite frankly, tarts should be chained to the kitchen sink with a mattress on their backs. The rot set in when we were born,

Grub, and all we can do is try and keep it outside the school gates.'

'Yeah,' said Grub, trying to make his snub face look tough and knowing. 'Absolutely.'

Tore's cynicism, his nicotine croak of defiance against received ideas, was endlessly illuminating. Lessons went past in a dream; Grub learnt things, but they hardly ever touched the quick of his imagination. (Music was, of course, a private matter.) With Tore, you were like a piece of uranium bombarded with radiation; you mutated, you became someone to be reckoned with. When Grub's parents had divorced, Tore told him:

'Most parents are better apart than together. Look at how fucking miserable everyone is whose parents have stayed married: they gang up against you the moment your balls drop. This way, they have to really work at being nice to you, and you can play one off against the other or else they just won't see you any more.'

'But that's so calculating.'

'Calculating! Listen, you got to get reality behind those gogs of yours. Family is all politics. Everyone hates each other's guts, if they're honest, not like they say in those barf-making Sunday mags, all lovey-dovey and how clever little Trevor was aged three. That's a load of crap. Most brothers and sisters try to top each other given the chance; you always gets the worst wars in countries with big families. I hate my steps, and so does my old man. If it wasn't for the paternity cases, he'd never send them a penny.'

'Why do grown-ups bother to have children at all, then?'

'Because they don't think it through, Grub,' said Tore impatiently. 'People have kids because they go soft in the head, tarts especially. They forget what it's like to be a kid themselves and want to remember through their own. They don't want us, not real, brand-new people who puke and criticise and tell them to bog off: they want their own frigging innocence back. They want to have their own lives over again, with the bad bits taken out. Quite frankly, they'd be better off with a dog. Parents are a bunch of losers from the word go. Take, and don't thank them. After all, they got you into this shit heap, didn't they?'

Grub could never think of any argument with which to counter his friend's philosophy. He felt, dimly, that it was flawed, but couldn't think how. He knew Ruth and Sam both loved him, but it somehow didn't have any reality for him when he was away from them. Only Tore and the Lads existed here, just as only his family and their friends existed in London. He imagined his brothers had felt the same way, because they had never discussed their real experiences at Knotshead, either. They continually told stories about the times they had had at school, even though they had left years ago. It was as if nothing had ever been quite as real, after.

8

The Lads were not the only people to find Veronica a thorn in their flesh. Had he known quite how much Simon Hart loathed his deputy headmistress, Tore would have been agreeably surprised.

'That bloody woman,' Hart said to Poppy. 'She makes me realise why every Englishman is right to hate the opposite sex.'

'What's she done now?' Poppy asked.

'She got a vote passed cutting out doughnuts at elevenses.'

Poppy began to laugh. She found pettiness quite inexplicable. Then she saw Simon was on the verge of one of his cold rages, and became solemn. It was difficult being married to a man who had no sense of humour; but humour, though highly rated by the young as an antidote to their own embarrassment, was a luxury she had, with experience, found it possible to live without.

'Slythe worked out that it cost an additional £15,000 a year to provide them, and they both say kids can make do on hot cocoa alone. The pupils will blame me, and she'll get the credit with the governors for saving the school money.'

'Aren't you exaggerating, Simon?'

'You know that she was one of the people who was considered for my job, three years ago?'

'Yes, but all the same, I thought she has always been very friendly towards us,' said Poppy, with an almost frightened look. 'When there was all the scandal, she was awfully kind.'

'Dearest, you have the political sense of a gnat.'

'But you liked her, too. You were always going on about how efficient she was, and how you wished more of the staff took their responsibilities so seriously.'

'Not seriously enough as far as the outside world is concerned. I had a call from the chief constable at Knotsmouth today about suspected drug-dealing in the school. He says that unless something is done, the police will be coming round with sniffer dogs. Veronica says that we have to continue to sort problems out in the traditional democratic way, and most of the staff are behind her. They seem to be treating me as some sort of mole to the authorities ... I admit I was fooled by her at first, dearest. I thought she was on the side of law and order. But now I think she was just biding her time. She's very ambitious, you know. She plays chess. The mathematical mind.'

'So unlike life, the queens having all the power and the kings needing protection.'

'She'd beat me any day.'

'Are you talking about chess or work?'

'I don't know,' said Hart, unhappily. 'I don't know.'

Everyone looked forward to mealtimes with Pavlovian enthusiasm, although the meals were always the same: Monday, macaroni cheese; Tuesday, toad in the hole; Wednesday, shepherd's pie; Thursday, faggots; Friday, cod au gratin; Saturday, bacon and cauliflower cheese; Sunday, roast beef and Yorkshire pudding. At least, the names changed, if the tastes did not. Mostly, pupils lived on toast made in the common rooms by smuggling sliced bread and butter out of the dining hall. Such vast quantities of this would disappear every mealtime that Veronica would make a habit of standing by the exit to catch people stuffing it from their trays to their pockets. There was an ongoing battle by the members of 6ii to be permitted kettles in their study-bedrooms, persistently turned down by the house staff as an electrical hazard.

The dining hall, once the library of the old house, was always a scene of noise and confusion during meals. Cliques would attempt to bag a whole table for themselves; anyone thought socially inferior would be frozen out. This included unpopular members of staff, such as Hart, who would sit down and cast everyone into silence or fits of sniggering giggles with questions such as, 'And what does everyone here think about the

unification of Germany?' or, 'The British Constitution needs re-
form, wouldn't you agree?'

Then the school would wonder why on earth the governors
had ever appointed him. It never occurred to anyone that, just
as pupils regarded the staff as Them, so the staff themselves regarded the governors as an authority to be distrusted and confounded, yet blamed when they did not absorb problems by
osmosis.

The most painful incidents, however, always surrounded Fay.
Some bores are the equivalent to stodge in a meal, necessary in
order to throw taste into relief. Others unite the rest in irritable
malice against them. Fay was of the latter type. She droned on
interminably about the superior central heating in her parents'
house in St John's Wood, and could not let a bright autumn day
go by without quoting 'Season of mist and mellow fruitfulness'.
At the sight of her slight figure marching towards them, whole
tables would bolt, screeching with laughter. The dismay on her
face every time this occurred was thought pricelessly funny, particularly by other Rejects. She became a mascot of awfulness.

It was noticed that the tip of her nose had a broad and bony
point, which went white under strain; after this, a game called
Snout would be played around her. The purpose of this was to
get her to say 'nose', or become so upset that the white tip
would show.

'Hey, Fay, what's this on your face?'

'Is that a Jewish penis, Fay?'

'Fay, Fay knows sweet FA. If she wasn't such an ugly Jew
she'd be an easy lay.'

'Oink-oink! What's the difference between a boar and a pig?
Fay will beat one and not eat the other.'

And on and on, until she got up and ran away.

Day by day, she became harder and uglier. Unlike Alice, she
cried openly when Tore and Olivia baited her, though nothing
seemed to dent her tiresome demand for attention. Alice knew
or guessed what she was suffering, and pitied her, although she,
too, felt distaste: distaste as much for her craven relief at having
the burning focus of malice partially diffused on to another. Fay
was, after all, only fourteen, and until her arrival Alice had been
both the youngest and the most unpopular member of her
block. There was nothing she could do to help except to try to
curb her impatience at Fay's defects and not let her feel as

utterly isolated as she herself had been since coming to Knots-head.

To defend Fay would only redouble the attacks on both of them, and to advise her would only be seen as patronising. Fay had the most tedious and common kind of sensibility: that of being acutely sensitive to her own feelings, and completely blind to others'. Like most egoists, she was clever but not intelligent. Yet even dead meat may be tenderised by repeated blows, and poor Fay was very much alive.

She – or the Baron parents – had taken too much to heart the adage that genius is nine-tenths perspiration and one-tenth in-spiration. She would spend hours over every essay, and asked people doing the same subjects what marks they had had for theirs – crowing triumphantly if they deigned to make any answer. Every book was something to be read for the sake of being able to say she had 'done' it, as though the mere action of running the eyes over paper and grasping the most obvious points were sufficient. Knotshead, which believed in a minimum of perspiration and a maximum of inspiration – preferably schi-zoid or drug-induced – found her approach as objectionable as Alice's puritanical classicism.

Nor was her competitiveness confined to academia. During languid games of volleyball in the Quad, intended to show off the legs of the girls who played, she almost scratched eyes out in her desperation to hit the ball.

'I must, I must increase my bust. The bigger the better, the tighter the sweater,' she would mutter in the dorm, jerking her elbows back and forth across her chest like stunted wings. Oli-via and Nicola would shriek with malicious laughter, and mimic her afterwards to the Lads. Even Alice, who looked upon these antics with more compassion, found it hard not to smile.

Worst of all was her attitude to music, which, like Grub, she was taking for A level. Everyone was informed Fay had passed Grade Seven on the piano; Grub, who had heard her in the music rooms, declared that she must have used a pianola.

Normally quixotic in his pranks, he loathed her as he had never loathed any other pupil. Alice he thought of as humour-less and hysterical, but Fay was pure filboid studge. Her piac-ular pianism made him grind his teeth with such force he invari-ably had a splitting headache after ten minutes practising beside her in the Tower of Babel. To hear her do Chopin – there was no other verb for it – made his whole day go grey. He hated her as only a good musician can hate a bad one, without pity or comprehension. Her Jewishness made her a nightmare carica-ture of his mother, for, like Fay, Ruth had a gritty irrepressibil-ity. Yet around Ruth, the charm of femininity had formed pearls. Fay was just indigestion.

'I'm so alone. I feel like Captain Oates, going out into the Antarctic,' Fay told Alice. It was remarkable, Alice thought: even in a depressed state, Fay expected other people to be in-terested in her.

'Nonsense,' said Alice. 'You aren't sacrificing yourself for anyone else. Don't inflate yourself with false comparisons. You shouldn't have corrected the spelling in Grub's essay when you saw it in the Library.'

'I only did it as a joke,' Fay said sulkily.

'No, you didn't. You did it because you thought you were better at music than he is.'

'I am better. That's why they all hate me.'

'If you honestly think that's the reason,' Alice said, 'then you have entered a self-perpetuating system of delusional beliefs which can't be penetrated by reason. Persecution is bad, I know, but a persecution mania is worse.'

'It's not persecution mania. To be clever and female, here, is worse than being a criminal.'

'Oh, quite,' said Alice. 'But then, it always has been. We should both count ourselves lucky not to be burnt at the stake for passing examinations.'

'How can you make a joke of it?'

'What else is there to do? Apart from just keeping going?'

'It's all very well for *you*,' said Fay. 'Everything just rolls off you. You always go on answering back, even when they call you Louse. I don't have your self-confidence.'

Alice scowled, then said, 'The only way to be free of them is not to care what they think.'

'Everyone cares what other people think about them. I bet you do, really.'

'Oh?'

'If you don't care what anybody else thinks, then you've also got a system of delusional beliefs. Everyone else is out of step but you.'

'Now, that I don't believe. How easy it would be if I did! I

could look out at the world with such a marvellous sneer of egotistical self-satisfaction!' said Alice, half laughing. 'I could live
quite happily in a hermit's cave, writing love letters to myself,
enjoying the sound of my own voice, with only a mirror for
company. I wish it were possible to be so insulated against spite
and stupidity. But there are, thank God, people who are not
either of those things. Malice is the loser's hallmark. If I were
you, I'd value the opinions of people you respect. Even if you
only find them in books.'

'Oh yes. A system of delusional beliefs based on another
system of delusional beliefs,' said Fay, with magnificent disdain.
'God, you are such a prig, Alice!'

'Yes,' said Alice. 'But at least I don't make the coward's mistake.'

'What's that?'

'To be charming,' said Alice.

Alice lived for her Latin lessons: a taste, others thought, as
eccentric as longing for prunes, but nevertheless genuine. Partly,
this was due to the Librarian himself. She had had no friend or
mentor since her mother, and loneliness had become a state of
identity. The Librarian was too reserved to be a friend, but his
mixture of tact and asperity prised her away from the worst of
her introversion.

She hoped that her enthusiasm did not make her seem more
callow than the reality. The pleasure of being able to discuss
books and ideas without fear was literally heady, for she came
out of his lessons feeling light as a balloon. She was almost
frightened at the speed with which she had decided to trust him.
His face made her secretly think of him as a kind of eighteenth-
century God, without a beard and reduced to a single angel in
the shape of Horatio, but still almost supernaturally wise.

She told him a little about how uneasy she was living with her
sister and Hart.

'What else are relatives for?' asked the Librarian. 'Whether
you are an orphan or not.'

'What do you mean?'

'Well, they are the only people in your life whom you never
choose. All the rest – whom you fall in love with, or marry, or
work with, or befriend – are in some sense chosen by you. But
relations never are. That's why it's one of the cruellest things

people can do, to judge others by their parents, or siblings, or whoever.'

Alice thought of Fay. 'Can't you judge parents by their children, though?'

'An interesting question. To some extent, perhaps, but not much. The most atrocious people can turn out quite enchanting sons or daughters, and vice versa. Of course, in a school, one very often only has to clap eyes on the child's parents to see where it's all coming from. But in the end, the fashionable idea that the parents deserve all the blame, or indeed the praise, is to my mind quite false. You yourself make choices as to who you are and what you are going to be, all along, irrespective of nurture. Every one of us has to learn through the same elementary mistakes, every time.'

'That seems such a harsh idea.'

'It does not accord with the Founder's philosophy,' said the Librarian, with a touch of acid. 'But then, one of the things you have to decide is whether you are a classicist or a romantic; or, as that ass Nietzsche put it, an Apollonian or a Dionysian.'

'Is it always one or the other?'

'Well,' said the Librarian, 'that, too, is for you to find out.'

9

Winthrop spent his afternoons jogging. Every Knote had to do three hours a week of either noncompetitive sport or outdoor work with Hartley Leigh Hunt. Initially, since he could drive, he elected to do the last. However, after he crashed the school tractor into a group of newly-planted saplings in front of everyone, the latter was not a viable option.

'Oh, dear,' Leigh-Hunt would whinny in his snotty voice, 'it's Agent Orange coming this way again'; and all the other kids would laugh. This was a reference to Winthrop's favourite sweater, which was in fact red and a three-ply Ralph Lauren cashmere.

'Don't you have anything practical to wear?' said Leigh-Hunt. 'We're on a farm, not *Vogue*.'

'No, sir,' said Winthrop.

'Didn't your mother read the list of what to bring?'

'No, sir,' said Winthrop politely. He thought the information that his clothes were packed by Filipino maids would be an incendiary subject.

Winthrop rapidly discovered he didn't give a flying fuck about farming. Nature sucked. The only way he could stand all the green was by moving through it at high speed listening to his Walkman. The woods scared the shit out of him, but any time spent with his nostrils up the ass of a nanny-goat was worse. Not only did their stink make him feel nauseous, they had slitty yellow eyes with rectangular pupils, like in *The Exorcist*. He had seen them grazing in flocks from across the lake, and thought they were some kind of mutant sheep until Leigh-Hunt mentioned that the school made goats'-milk cheese for sale.

'All the food here is made from organically grown vegetables,' he barked, bald head shining like a beacon of ecological fanaticism.

'No wonder it looks like shit,' Winthrop muttered.

Jogging was OK. Jogging was prep. Jogging was American. It was a biological leadership trait. Screw them all. After a couple of days, the tracks became familiar, and he even quite enjoyed the Lone Ranger sensation. Eventually, he guessed his ego would burst through the box, but for the time being it helped. Once over the lake, he had his back to the school and the moors for most of the run, and could pretend he was in Deerfield, Massachusetts. He never thought he'd miss that place so much.

Half-term would bring no prospect of relief. Winthrop had tried dialling his trustees in Boston and Mummy in the Hamptons, to find out what was happening. Standing in the ammoniac reek of the one telephone in the Quad, rereading a tattered notice warning Knotes not to speak to members of the press, he had come up with zip. The trustees said they could do nothing without authorisation. The dumb Filipinos had no idea where either of his parents was. Daddy was drying out in some clinic, and his stepmother hated him. He was too embarrassed by the recent past to contact any of his friends.

It burnt him up when he went to withdraw money from Pug. Nobody was allowed a chequing account, so every Wednesday and Saturday the males queued up for cash. This had to be spent quickly, or it was stolen within twenty-four hours. The Arabs, who had credit cards and talked plastic all the time, got sums of £50 or £100, while he himself was stuck on embarrassingly low sums. Tore never queued, but then, he never had to.

Pug would sit in his housemaster's study reeking of stale BO and getting increasingly irritable by the minute.

'Why do you need so much?' he asked Naimh, gobbling aggressively.

'I, uh, need to check out a new stereo,' said Naimh in his grating pseudo-American.

Winthrop knew perfectly well he and Hussein were going to spend the weekend with a couple of whores they would pick up at Tramps, for the whole plan had been discussed in the dorm, and Tore had agreed to cover up in exchange for a large bribe.

'I've never heard of anything so ridiculous in my entire life. What's wrong with the one you have now?'

'It's been stolen,' said Naimh.

'What? What? Why didn't you tell me?'

'Please, I am telling you, now. I only just found out.'

'Are you sure? Was it valuable?'

Naimh shrugged.

'About £2,000,' he said. The Arabs usually made a tremendous fuss over money, but couldn't care less if something was insured.

Pug glared at him. 'I'll have to report this to Simon,' he said heavily. 'Permission?'

'Uh, yeah. Today.'

'You know you are not allowed an exeat to London without a week's notice and written permission.'

Naimh's face assumed an expression of ludicrous woe.

'Why can't you wait?'

'Please, I also have to see my oral hygienist,' said Naimh. 'He has already made an appointment. He's a very busy man. Also, my uncle is over from the Lebanon, and expecting me.'

Pug sighed, defeated.

'Very well, then. But you must be back by Jaw tomorrow.'

'Of course,' said Naimh, in a tone of injured innocence.

Hussein also withdrew a large amount of cash, but did not ask for an exeat. Two of them going up to London, and even Pug would have smelt a rat.

What a pair of assholes, thought Winthrop, signing for his own modest demand for £10. He himself was going into Minedale for a reality check, if nothing else. Most necessities of life, from vitamins to soft toilet paper, could be bought from Shit Horder's stores. Minedale had nothing much apart from the railway station. That is, it had a supermarket with one rotting avocado and a few shrivelled apples, a Tea Shoppe patronised by various senior citizens whose dogs wound their leashes round and round the spindly chairlegs in paroxysms of boredom. Also a health-food shop called Full 0' Beans where the same old cows attempted to prolong their crap lives by means of pap and mineral water, a gift shop which sold balls of knitting wool, and a hardware store. Finally, there was the Anstey Arms pub, where no Knote was allowed. Alcohol was strictly prohibited in case it encouraged pupils to fuck. The fact that this did not deter anyone seemed to have bypassed the staff.

Winthrop crossed the lower bridge and walked along the valley to Minedale. It was an easy three-mile walk, because the river soon became a clogged canal with a wide bank leading all the way to town. There, he cruised up and down the main street, despondent. He thought of the typical British village which adorned the postcards sent back by his parents' friends on vacation: whitewashed places with thatched roofs and historic associations with Shakespeare. No way was Minedale picturesque. Its buildings were covered in a kind of thin grey stone, like scales, as if the roof had gotten some sort of disease, or else painted a dirty white. The flat grey light and the turd-coloured moors filled him with something approaching despair. As he turned round to go back to the school, he saw Hussein follow Naimh into the little railway station and board the Intercity to London. The only thing that stopped him from following, even without a ticket, was the sight of a woman he dimly recognised as a teacher, hurrying to the station door. Hussein, he thought, was going to catch it. Well, it was no affair of his.

His loneliness and frustration teetered on the verge of fear. What if they forgot about him altogether? Daddy had a new family, after all. He might be the only son, but he was no longer the only heir.

He had never been one for writing letters home, but now he wrote, and longed for the sight of a US envelope in his pigeonhole.

Day after day, he would see those smug white or blue corners cocking their tails out of every slot but his own. He didn't even get junk mail, now that his credit cards had been taken away. Winthrop Senior had really been mad at him after the second expulsion. Mummy sent a postcard from the Nile, saying that they were staying in the suite where Princess Michael had been, but then Bitsy was a royalty fetishist and had probably sent the identical piece of news to everyone in the Social Register, and maybe her maid. He took his frustration out on jogging for longer and longer periods.

'I can't get no satisfaction', Winthrop sang tunelessly, feet pounding the wood-chip paths back to the estate as though he would pulp them to felt. Everywhere he looked, he could see the decadence of the British: the crumbling temples, the cruddy food, the complete lack of ambition. Only the other day, he had heard Maggie Brink tell a guy that if he didn't work harder, he'd fail his Humanities examination.

'So what?' the boy had replied. 'I don't need it. I'm going to run my father's estate.'

Winthrop's jaw had dropped open. If your dad was rich, you had to be richer, that was an axiom of male existence. Only girls didn't have to prove themselves in the marketplace. Jesus, didn't these guys have any balls?

There was another mystery. He couldn't understand why none of the girls seemed to find him attractive. They weren't dykes; that cute blonde, Lady Olivia, was definitely going all the way; but they seemed to go for guys who were practically ano-rexic, or couch potatoes like Grub. On any campus back home, someone like Tore would be thought a mush-head, but here he was, like, Mr Ultimate Cool. It was no coincidence, thought Winthrop as he jogged again the following day, that 'anguish' sounded so much like 'English'.

Two Block 4s had gotten hold of a bottle of vodka, and the changing-room floors were spattered with vomit. Wrinkling his nose, Winthrop went in by the back entrance to shower and change upstairs. A stench of boiled cabbage and carbolic soap assaulted his olfactory system. How much more could he take?

Coming into his dorm, he pulled off the sweater round his waist and threw it on the bed. Then he saw Tore and the other Lads laughing at the other end of the room. Sparks and Mongol were holding something out of the window. Not a thing: a kid. He was being held upside down, forty feet off the ground, by the waist of his pants. Pants which were, with infinite slowness, giving way with a rending of seams. Jasper and Sebastian West-ler restrained his kicks. Outside the window a tiny voice shrilled:

'Please! Please!'

Winthrop's trainers squeaked. At the sound of his approach, Tore yanked the kid back inside. It was the albino, a new boy who crept about like a white rat in a way which annoyed every-one. He huddled on the floor at Tore's feet. Across the boy's body, their eyes met. Winthrop's heart pumped hatred, systole and diastole.

'It's only Superbrat,' Tore said.

'Fuck you.'

'Bog off, Yank.'

Tore jerked up the kid's head by his hair. The albino looked completely stupid with terror, his eyes glowing red as if the blood behind them had burst. He was chalk white, apart from the pustulant mounds of pimples splotching his face and neck. There was a sudden stench. A pool of yellow urine dripped on to the floorboards between the kid's knees. Winthrop felt a violent disgust.

'Give him a break.'

'But he's enjoying this, aren't you, Ratlet?'

'Yes,' gasped the albino.

'See?' said Tore to Winthrop.

'Let's do a coat-hook crucifixion and see how long he takes to pass out,' said Jasper Westler. 'He stinks too much to hold, now.'

Out of the fog of his loathing, Winthrop spoke. 'Let him go.'

Tore made no move, but stood there, grinning. He fingered something in his pocket. Sparks, Mongol and the Westler brothers shifted around uneasily. Winthrop bent his knees slightly, feeling his centre of gravity. It was unlikely, he thought, that any of these slobs had ever done karate. If he took even one of them out, it would be Tore.

'Let him go, asshole.'

'Why don't you pick him up, then?' said Mongol.

'Let's dump them both in a cold bath,' suggested Sparks. 'Superbrat is dripping with sweat.'

It was well known that Sparks was gay; only Tore's grudging respect for the crafts teacher kept him in the Lads' group, for popular teachers, like famous parents, surrounded their children with a kind of invisible wall. Small and spiteful, Sparks was always trying to get younger boys to suck him off. Those who refused would often find Tore sicked on them on some pretext or other. He put his long, damp hand on Winthrop's arm, and pinched a bicep. The homophobic loathing which rose in Winthrop's throat almost choked him. He never realised how much he hated faggots until they made passes.

'*Fuck off!*' Winthrop's voice rose in such a yell that all four of his opponents fell back against the window. Out of arm's reach, they began to shout back.

Flump, flump, flump. This time, the sound of the housemaster's overburdened feet along the corridor was unmistakable. Pug's voice echoed as he bellowed, 'What? What?'

Instantly, silence fell. Pug in a rage could still command some awe.

Tore looked at Winthrop with his viperous dark eyes. The menace which surrounded him intensified. 'You say anything, you're history, Superbrat.'

The albino turned even paler, and fainted.

'What? What? What?' Pug gobbled, seeing the prostrate figure. The boys crowded round with expressions of concern.

'We were just wondering whether we should try mouth-to-mouth resuscitation,' said Sparks, leering.

'What? I've never heard of anything so ridiculous in my entire life. Here, you, Wesley or whatever your name is, don't hang around like a sick camel. Help us pick him up and take him to the matron.'

'Sure, sir,' said Winthrop.

Pug looked around the dorm with a lowering eye. 'Where's Hussein?'

Everyone assumed an expression of innocence.

'Mrs Crump says she saw him getting on the London train.'

Silence.

'Yet I see that last night, he was ticked off by Johnny on the dorm check list,' said Pug.

Silence.

'We shall get to the bottom of this. Follow me, quick march!'

'Yes, sir!'

Winthrop swung the sodden boy up on his shoulder in a fireman's lift, treading heavily on Tore's foot as he did so. Tore yelped. Winthrop turned smartly. The unconscious kid's feet hit both Westler brothers on the nose. They yelped.

'Come on, come on,' said Pug, not bothering to turn round – as for a big ship, this required a series of complicated manoeuvres.

Tore lost his cool and hissed, 'You evil fucking bastard!'

Winthrop looked down his perfect, patrician nose at him. 'The root of all evil is fear, Tore. And what can I tell you? You're a very frightened guy,' he said.

But, when he returned, he found both Tore and the red cashmere sweater he had left on his bed were gone.

Simon Hart had a headache. He swallowed two aspirin, tried breathing deeply, and rolled his head through 360 degrees. He tried snatching a few minutes' sleep. He tried splashing his face with cold water. Nothing helped. Sunday was supposed to be his day off, but, as he had discovered, there was no such thing in a boarding school.

So many parents clearly used the school as a dumping ground for problem children and the casualties of their own adulteries, it was not surprising that there were difficulties. According to Philip Slythe, they could not afford to turn them down, particularly if they were boys, because of the pressing need for fees. Yet the rot seemed to be going deeper than a few borderline psychiatric cases.

He reviewed the disasters of the current term in his mind.

A famous film director had discovered his daughter was pregnant by another pupil, and had removed her from the school threatening dire retribution. Hart had persuaded him that this would not be advisable. George Wash reported the theft of yet more valuables from the Males' Flats, including a cashmere sweater and a stereo worth £2,000. The Librarian reported that an edition of Pope's translation of the *Iliad* and the *Odyssey* printed by the Nonesuch Press had also vanished. Following some discreet telephone calls, a Knotsmouth book dealer had come forward with the stolen library books. Two pupils in 6ii had sold them to him for £100.

'I thought it was strange they had them,' the bookseller remarked, disdainfully, identifying them. 'They were wearing rags I wouldn't wash my car with.'

When confronted with their crime, the two males – one the son of a Cambridge philosopher – had argued that, as their parents paid for the school, its possessions were their property. They were sent home for a fortnight. In an open meeting, both school and staff criticised Hart for a lack of diplomacy and sensitivity in his handling of the matter. Afterwards, crossing the Quad, he had been followed by boos and catcalls from the Males' Flats above.

Furious, he had called the police in to investigate the other thefts. While searching for stolen possessions, they had come across a lump of marijuana in a Block 5's gym locker sufficiently large to get a pupil arrested. Hart was immediately blamed for 'shopping him to the pigs', and spent many wearisome hours on the telephone talking to the boy's parents denying this.

Then Mrs Crump claimed she had seen Hussein boarding the London train without permission for an exeat. When Hussein had reappeared, just before Jaw, he denied the whole thing completely.

'Mrs Crump, she sees Naimh, not me. Naimh had permission. She thinks all Arabs look alike,' he had said earnestly to the housemaster. Confronted with Daphne Crump herself, he had stuck to his story.

'Mrs Crump,' he said, staring at her with huge, sorrowful eyes. 'I really don't like to say it, but I think you making a racist mistake. It was Naimh you see, not me.'

'I'm afraid not,' said Mrs Crump, shaking her handsome grey head.

'Honest to God, Simon. Would I lie to you?'

'Ah, well,' said Hart, uncomfortably.

'You think I'd fucking lie to you? You think I'm a liar? You think like Mrs Crump because I'm a wog I must be bad?'

Hussein knew, like all the pupils, that staff could always be boxed into a corner if confronted with their own desire for fair play.

'No, no, of course not! Ah, let's discuss this peaceably, shall we?' said Hart.

Naimh had supported his story. The register for Saturday night showed Hussein as having been ticked off by Johnny Tore. Tore had also sworn he had seen Hussein in bed. Hart hesitated. Why believe Mrs Crump, after all? Both Crumps were due for retirement and very much on the edge of the power struggle between himself and Veronica. Nick Crump had a small following among German lieder enthusiasts, but was in no way comparable to the big bruisers in Delus's or Mortmain's camp. Both the Arab boys brought in large sums of money which, though erratic, was desperately needed.

He put off making a decision for a week, and now the staff room was divided into pro- and anti-Crump factions.

At least the governors' termly meeting had gone well. Hart had been able to get the proofs of the new school brochure passed. Half the staff, including Veronica, had been out chasing a boy who periodically cut his arms and legs with any available blade. While looking for him all over the estate, they came across eight Block 4s dead drunk with a bottle of vodka in the Temple of Venus. Two, discovered in flagrante, had been instantly expelled. The remaining six had been sent home for a week. The day after, Hart was rung up by the Earl of Paddington.

'Is that Mr Hart?'

'Speaking.'

'Ah, Hart, Paddington here. I just wanted to thank you for sending back one of my little gels in time for my birthday. We're all going to get ten times more pissed than she would have at school. I only wish young Olivia had been caught, too.'

'If so,' said Hart stiffly, 'I'm afraid she would have had to be expelled, as a third-time offender, Lord Paddington.'

Olivia's father had roared with laughter. 'I'll tell her that next time I take her out to the pub. Your very good health, sir!'

How Hart hated and feared the upper classes. Try as he would, he could not rid himself of an inner servility, an astonishment that he was actually speaking to a member of the aristocracy. It would have been easier, he thought, if he had been able to share his troubles with Poppy.

When Poppy had seduced him – and there was really no other word for it – that long, hot summer, he had been too astonished, too grateful to stop and wonder why. Now bitter phrases like 'a meal ticket for life' floated through his mind. She had hated being a housemistress in the school she called St Crumpet's, but, on the wrong side of thirty, had lacked the energy to get out. The dullness of her professional life had been compensated for by a rich and varied number of erotic encounters during the holidays; but even these were losing their charm, perhaps as her flowerlike beauty faded a little. Hart, never easy in the company of women, had fallen hopelessly in love, grovelling before her nakedness like a shelled prawn. Her impatience, her coldness towards him since the birth of the twins, he secretly regarded as no more than his due. He knew he was not physically attractive; he was unimaginative, anxious and probably boring. But he did love Poppy and the twins; and he had wanted to make Knotshead work.

Looking around his oak-panelled study, he felt oppressed, as so often, by the weight of the Founder's aspirations. Shelf after shelf was lined with books: Plato's *Republic*, Bacon's *New Atlantis*, Morris's *News From Nowhere*, Campanella's *City of the Sun*, Lord Lytton's *The Coming Race*. Later heads had added *The Time Machine*, *Brave New World*, *Nineteen Eighty-*

Four. Hart, who preferred to read books on competitive strategy, had struggled at first with this accretion of utopias and dystopias. Now he stared at them as a man in the dock pleads silently with the jurors.

What had once been minority views, held by a select band of actors, editors, writers and film directors, were now held to be conventional. What was there left to do but push at the limits? So his disgraced predecessor, Quirk, had thought. That ten-year regime left a shelf full of books on ecological disasters and failed experiments. *The Decline and Fall of Liberal England*, said one title. *Silent Spring*, said another.

How was Hart to market pessimism? Those who had once been aggressively confident in their vision of education were now on the defensive, even in the state system. The governors had been very specific about what they did not want for Knotshead.

'We don't want to go the way of other failed progressive schools and become liberal orthodox,' said one. 'We want to make our children part of the real world, not part of a ghetto. This school is a reaction against the depersonalisation of industrial society. We have a unique opportunity to show the world that the Founder's ideas really work.'

Naively, as he saw now, Hart had seen Knotshead as an overgrown garden, much like the estate itself, in need of assertive management and new directions. The pioneering educational enthusiasms of his youth had come back, tempered by pragmatism. If revolution was no longer possible, perhaps evolution would do. Then the suicide had come during his first term, and in the confusion that followed, he had let things drift for nearly three years, concentrating on improving the farm and setting up study-bedrooms for better examination results. The spiritual malaise had been left to go or stay. It was important not to let the children have their faith in the future destroyed by apocalyptic visions of the society within its walls, when society outside them was so riddled with pessimism.

Yet something would have to be done. He switched on his office tape recorder, and began to dictate.

10

At half-term, Hart sent every pupil home with a letter. 'Dear Parent,' he wrote:

> For some time it has been evident that theft has reached unacceptable levels in Knotshead. Not only money, but valuable items including jewellery, cameras, a £2,000 stereo system and a cashmere sweater have recently been stolen from lockers and dormitories. Over thirty items have disappeared, and the police have been called in to investigate.
>
> While we request pupils to deposit articles of significant value with the appropriate housemaster or housemistress, I feel it is necessary to warn you that you should keep an eye open for any signs of inexplicable affluence among your own children. We cannot combat this breakdown of law and order without your assistance.
>
> In addition to the above, there is an unacceptably high level of vandalism to school and staff property. Two pupils have had to be expelled for indulging in sexual intercourse in the school grounds.
>
> If this school is to progress, we cannot remain stuck in the 1960s, with under-age sex, wanton vandalism and drug and alcohol abuse becoming endemic. The ideals on which the school was founded are turning into a cynical shell of materialistic self-interest. I ask you all to support me in eradicating this blight from our school.

The idea that any of their offspring could possibly be accused of involvement in criminal activities caused deep offence, even to those who believed that property was theft. Knotes who had sent their own children to Knotshead were especially incensed: either something was wrong with the new generation, or the founder's vision was being gravely misinterpreted.

'This man sounds hysterical,' Grub's mother remarked.

'I told you so, Mum. We all hate him.'

'He seemed fine on Parents' Day.'

'What do you expect? Green slime shooting out of his mouth? He's always on his best behaviour when parents are around. You're his clients, aren't you. But we're his raw materials.'

'You make school sound like a factory.'

'So it is, in a weird sort of way. He's just a marketing man, packaging us up as some sort of concept. Not – ' Grub hesitated, and thought of Tore – 'not a leader.'

'Do schools need to be led?'

'I don't know. Maybe. We don't just hate him, we despise him. He called us 'the cream of British children', can you imagine? He's even worse than the one before.'

'Those governors are a hopeless bunch. You only had to meet Quirk for five seconds to realise he was a schmuck.'

'But it took them seven years to get round to sacking him. Masses of people's parents have written to complain about Hart, honestly, but they don't want another scandal.'

'I might mention it to your father for the paper,' said Ruth Viner.

'Too late, Mum. Look.'

Grub, a devoted reader of tabloids, spread out a copy of the *Sun*.

SIR BLASTS TOFFS AT SEX SCHOOL

A Headmaster last night spoke about the amazing goings-on at his exclusive £8,000 p.a. public school. He admitted that

GIRLS were indulging in secret under-age sex

DRUGS were circulating in the school

POLICE had been called in to investigate over 30 thefts

VANDALISM was rife. But Mr Simon Hart insisted, 'Knotshead is not a den of vice.'

He added, 'I believe in honesty and openness and that is

why I wrote to our parents. Most of our pupils are very nice children, but parents should know the truth. There are no more problems here than at conventional public schools.'

One parent who is not bothered by it is the Earl of Paddington.

'Two of my kids are there, and I'm an OK myself,' he says. 'Don't let's get too suburban about this, quite frankly.'

'Oh, Lord, he didn't really say that, did he?' Ruth murmured.

'Have you never seen Olivia's dad, Mum? He's the one who turns up to Parents' Days in flares and tunics,' said Grub.

'Are you really happy there, Grub?' Ruth asked, after a pause. 'I know Josh and Tom loved it, but that doesn't mean – '

'Oh no, Mum,' said Grub. 'I can't wait to go back. It's just Hart the Fart making a fuss about a few people, that's all.'

Winthrop found the semi-deserted school as eerie as a ghost town. As far as he could tell, he was completely alone; even kids whose parents were diplomats had someone to go to. Being alone was just awful. The scurfy plaster walls seemed to be closing in on him. Floorboards creaked, faucets dripped. He cursed his parents and his trustees, over and over.

On Saturday, the sun came out. Light hardened on autumnal beeches, the leaves swirling from bronze to violet like metal at melting point. He crossed the Quad, frightening a few depressed-looking sparrows, and went into the deserted dining hall, where Formica trays displayed the usual congealing bacon and eggs. There was a soft clink of china. He picked up a bowl of cornflakes, and saw Alice eating toast by a french window, gazing out at the lake. Hesitantly, he went over to her table.

'Hi,' he said. 'You over at your sister's?'

She turned, her hair shining like a helmet.

'No.'

'Why not?'

'We don't get on.'

'Why not?'

'Why do you want to know?'

'I'm just curious. Besides, what else is there to do?'

'Prep,' Alice said.

'You want to work, even on a day like this? You must have some blood in you that's not English.'

'I am Scotch, in fact.'

'Are people in Scotland very ambitious?'

'Ambitious?' She seemed to taste the word like wine, then spit it out. 'Not necessarily. Better educated. We had universal education a hundred years before any other country. Perhaps we believe in reason more. It isn't like this place, where everyone is half-asleep all the time. I have – I don't know how to explain it – a restless desire to know . . . '

'Know what?'

'Everything. I am a compulsive reader.' She fell silent, ashamed, as always, of sounding a prig. 'It's not something to be proud of, more a kind of neurosis. I even read the labels on bottles of detergent. I like to find things out.'

'But you don't find out about things by reading,' said Winthrop. 'You find out by living.'

Alice's lip curled.

'Do you call this, where we are now, life?'

'You don't?'

'They always claim it is. That it prepares us for the real world outside.'

'Oh no. Really, no. This is worse than a summer camp for web-feet. Do you mean you never get out of this place?'

'I go to Knotsmouth sometimes, for special things like dentist's appointments, and Minedale occasionally. To London, once, after my mother died. To France, a couple of times for a couple of weeks, with my sister's family. Otherwise, no.'

Winthrop stared at her. 'How can you stand it?'

'All's well that ends,' said Alice.

'If I had to be here for five years, I guess I'd commit suicide.'

'Yes. Someone did, a couple of years ago. It's a decision one makes every day. You know, get up, get dressed, brush your teeth, decide not to cut your throat.' She smiled, to take the misery out of her own words.

'So this is, like, the advance mourning? The black.'

'Why does it worry you so much? It used to be very fashionable.'

'Not since the Beat Generation.'

'Well. Self-projection is self-protection, here. But the real reason is, I don't have any money. It's cheaper to get one colour.'

Winthrop stirred his coffee. 'Who pays your fees, then?' he asked, curious.

'They're free, because of Simon. He and Poppy are my guardians. There's a little when I'm eighteen, but nothing else. I work in Minedale during the holidays.' She said this with defiance, for Knotes considered it plebby to work, unless as a model or an actress. To Winthrop, however, there was nothing extraordinary about student employment, so he made no reaction. She noted this, and thought better of him.

'Everyone pretends not to be interested in material possessions, but at the same time every single thing you have here is like a counter in an invisible set of scales. If you wear trainers, you're one sort of person; if you wear Timberland, you're another. If you've got both, you are superior, though not as superior as someone who walks through the mud in Manolo Blahnik. So it isn't surprising that some people end up stealing.'

'Why doesn't everyone just find the best image and buy it?'

Alice thought this a very American solution. 'Firstly, the majority of Knotes do not have analytical minds. Or hadn't you noticed? They're descended from well-meaning wafflers and taught by ideologues, and by the time they arrive here, they've become adept at believing in mutually contradictory creeds, such as the wicked lack of council houses, and their own right to buy second homes in depressed rural areas. Secondly, by the time parents have set aside thousands of pounds to educate them privately, there isn't money left over for clothes. Unless they're very rich, or have had a very messy divorce. So then it becomes even more important.'

'Some of that isn't so different from the States.'

'Yes, but . . .' Alice was not used to talking so much. 'At the same time, the grander you are, the smarter it is to wear Oxfam and Indian jewellery. Only Arabs wear awful designer labels, you know, Gucci and Yves St Laurent.'

'Weird. Like being stuck in a time warp.'

'Well – Marie Antoinette playing at shepherdesses.'

'Does that bother you?'

'If there were a uniform, we would have no choice. It would be dreary, but this way, people devise their own, which is far more rigid. Everyone's in fancy dress, all the time. When I first arrived, I was doomed before I'd even opened my mouth. You see, Poppy believed the prospectus when it said you only needed things that were practical. We went off and bought everything from Marks & Spencer. We didn't know that the only thing you can *ever* have from them is underwear. It's the first question Knotes ask each other, you know: not 'How are you?' but 'Where did you get that?' If you haven't cut the wrong label out, you're dead. Isn't it like that where you come from?'

'The dress code is different.'

'Why do you wear your watch on a grosgrain strap?'

'I couldn't hack the bad karma of one more dead lizard,' said Winthrop.

Alice gave one of her rare, snorty little laughs, then covered her mouth as the sound echoed round the dining hall. Winthrop grinned at her. She looked better when she had some animation, he thought; less long and yellow, like a sick Spic. It occurred to him that she must be very depressed most of the time to look like she did. He found it odd to think of someone being more jacked off with the place than he was.

A dinner lady from the village shuffled over, pushing a trolley.

'Lunch is off, dearie, just cheese sandwiches. You'd better collect them from Mrs Horder.'

'Blast,' Alice muttered. She envisaged having to take meals with Poppy and Simon.

'Could we, uh, possibly have some leftovers, please, ma'am?'

'I'm sure you can, dear, as you ask so politely,' said the dinner lady.

People who had no manners were so off-base, Winthrop thought; they just made life difficult for themselves.

'Thanks.'

'What are you going to do?'

'Have a barbecue,' said Winthrop.

Cooking was not part of the Knotshead syllabus. Pupils emerged at eighteen competent to weave a blanket or make an inlaid coffee table but not boil an egg. At the beginning, Block 3 had a lesson on how to make nettle soup over an open fire as part of an orienteering course. Invariably, the soup was quite inedible, but every Knote felt after it that he or she had come to grips with both nature and nurture, and that it had been a vaguely disagreeable and embarrassing experience, although, of course, a very spiritual one. After that, cooking was left strictly to proles.

Winthrop had learnt to barbecue during his time at summer camp. It was acceptable for a man to cook if it was over an open fire – even if, as at the Hamptons, the fire was run off the gas mains indoors. The dinner lady donated some boiled jacket potatoes and foil, and these they baked with cheese and sausages. It took two hours and many matches to get the fire hot enough in the lee of the Temple of Venus, but after much coughing and blowing they succeeded. A tint of pink crept into Alice's skin.

'This,' said Winthrop, 'is the first edible meal I've had since I came to this place.'

'I'm afraid it's part of Knotshead philosophy that food always tastes better in the open air,' said Alice.

'Screw the open air,' said Winthrop. 'All I mean is it tastes of something, even if it's just woodsmoke.'

Alice looked at him, and smiled.

They were on the farthest point of the peninsula, and the Knot glittered sluggishly through the rhododendron bushes some seventy feet below. The brackish smell of mud, salt and mould was almost overpowering as the tide sucked out. White gulls bounced up and down, as if on invisible strings; Alice could see the bones through their wings when they were against the light, so fine and long she would never have guessed them to be strong. It was impossible for a head as well formed as his to contain any real brains. His next question confirmed her fears.

'So, why did this Antsy guy build so many Wendy houses all over the place?' He regarded the stone tracery of doves and scallop shells, blurred by salt and wind, as if it were a series of syphilitic lumps.

'They aren't Wendy houses, they're temples. Or follies. They were just to give focus to the landscape, remind the owner of classical virtues. Also to punctuate each avenue.' She hesitated, then said carefully, 'I think the temples are beautiful, even if most people find them sinister. I like the way they shine out so against the long dark avenues.'

She was looking, almost absently, at his hair.

'Like light at the end of a tunnel?'

'Yes. Yes! That – and everything they represent. Order and culture and proportion and truth.'

'Do you think buildings can be truthful?'

'I didn't mean buildings, I meant landscape. All this. To control and contain disorder, the natural chaos, without spoiling it.

She took a bite of sausage.

'The temples are supposed to be haunted, you know, from when it was all mined. Nobody knows how deep the tunnels go.'

'What did they mine?'

'Copper. This used to be the biggest source of it in Europe, before they discovered it in Australia and America. It's been mined for centuries. When the copper gave out, they mined arsenic instead, for the cotton plantations. Maggie taught us about it for Humanities. It was the most horrible job in the world, although it made this area, and the Ansteys, very rich. The men all died from rock falls in their twenties, and the drills they used were called widowmakers. But the Ansteys were determined to go on building temples. Now – well, the Lads have got one. This is used for Venus parties.'

'What are those?'

Alice kicked a log. Sparks whirled up with an astringent noise.

'Oh, you know. People come out at night, and drink and smoke dope. Like the four who got caught. You may have noticed a number of condoms in the bushes.'

'Have you been to one?'

She turned, blushing. 'No, of course not!'

'Why of course?' The longer he looked at her, the more interesting her face became.

'I'm not that sort of person. Either to go. Or to be asked. If you're in a dorm with Tore, you must know that.'

'Uh-huh.'

Alice said, 'When so many things are permitted, even tacitly, the only way you can be your own person is not to do things.'

'What did Tore want you to do?'

'Oh, the usual thing, I imagine,' she said, her voice flat.

'What is the usual thing?' asked Winthrop, though he could guess.

For a long time, she made no answer. He thought she had dried up on him completely, when she began to speak.

'My first term, he – I was walking back in the dark after Jaw, and he and Grub and Sparks came after me. They wouldn't let me pass. As if it was some sort of game. Except that it wasn't. Tore said he wanted to go with me. I didn't know what he meant – I hardly even knew the facts of life. I'd never thought of myself in that way. I still don't,' she said in a rush, not looking at him. 'I don't like – So, I thought he meant walking, you know, walking me back to the Dower House. But I didn't like him, so I said no, that I walked alone – He said that walking wasn't what he meant.

'Then I was dreadfully frightened. Anyway, he sort of lunged, and they ripped my blouse off.'

'Hell!' said Winthrop, startled.

'They said I was asking for it, not wearing a – I had just begun to –' Alice blushed, painfully. 'That was almost the worst thing. So then I boxed Tore into a holly bush.'

'You did *what?*'

Her skin was almost translucent, alive with blood.

'I punched him on the nose, and he fell into a holly bush.'

'Oh, boy.' Winthrop looked at her with admiration. 'He must have been red as a tamale.'

'Well, his nose bled. So after, he hated me.'

'You surprise me. Did you report it?'

'No.'

'Why not? In an American school it would have made an absolute scandal.'

'What could I do? If I made trouble for them, it would only have rebounded on me – or Poppy and Simon. And then where would I have gone? If I couldn't last out here, how could I in a state school?'

'So he persecutes you instead.'

'I suppose it was worse, punching him in front of the others. He's not used to being on the receiving end.'

'The guy's practically a psycho.'

He told her about the boy he had seen being held upside down out of the window after his run. Alice shivered.

'Are you cold?' he asked, moving closer.

'No.' At once, she shrank back, then considered. 'You have a lot of guts to stand up to him like that.'

'It wasn't a matter of intestinal fortitude,' said Winthrop, quoting his father.

'He does that sort of thing all the time. It's not just him. Anyone who has power, or who wants it. They take new boys and strap them into the dirty laundry baskets, and throw them down the stairs. Or blindfold them on the parapets, and turn them round and round, then shove them off, so they don't know whether they're going over the edge.'

'Not me,' said Winthrop. He liked the way she made him feel confident. 'What do girls do?'

'Oh, they're nasty in subtler ways. Not talking. Some of it's just silly, like apple-pie beds. Or being made to hold a raw egg in the dark, and being told it's spunk.'

'Spunk?'

'Sperm,' said Alice seriously.

Startled, Winthrop grinned. The girls he had known in America talked like this; if you were Episcopalian nothing shocked, that was the creed. His other, quite surprising, re-action could remain invisible as long as he was seated. Frustra-tion, he supposed. Nobody could call her pretty.

'No wonder the British have so many hang-ups.'

'I thought you were the nation where everyone had to have two jobs to pay for psychoanalysis.'

'Well, it's true my parents' generation are incredibly uptight. I mean, at a certain age, your father takes you aside and says, 'Well, son, I guess you know all about that stuff, don't you?' And even if you don't, you say, 'Sure.' So you learn it on the streets, which is just about the last place they want you to be. Or with one of the maids, because you figure, if Dad is fucking her, then why not you?'

Alice looked at him in alarm and distaste, and he grinned. So many teeth, she thought; as soon as he smiles, he becomes iden-tical to all those people on television.

'Not my style, actually, but there are plenty of kids who do it. It's a given.'

'What about the maid?'

'Oh, she's probably Mexican or Filipino. She doesn't get much choice.'

'That's awful.'

'Maybe. But to have sex at prep school, unless you live in California and can go to the beach, you have to be very creative.'

Alice smiled, despite herself, at this novel use of the word. 'You get expelled here, if you get caught, so I suppose it's not so different.'

'It's crazy, isn't it? They take us at a time when we're all programmed to feel hornier than at any time in our lives, lock us up
together and tell us to concentrate on getting the right grades.
What do they think is going to happen?'

'If you see someone with spots over the marmalade pot every
day, you have no romantic illusions about them. That's what
Simon says at headmasters' conferences.'

'Yeah, and people who work together in offices never screw
around, either.'

'You sound bitter.'

'Well, I got caught. In two different prep schools.'

He grinned at her again. Alice, increasingly uneasy, jumped
up and started kicking the fire out.

'I must go back,' she said.

'Why, what's the hurry?'

'I forgot something.' She was a hopeless liar.

'Oh.' Winthrop could see something had gone wrong. He
thought of offering to walk back with her, then decided against
it in case it looked too eager. 'Well, catch you later.'

'I don't think,' she said.

He watched her quick, straight-backed walk until she disappeared into the shadows of the trees.

11

The weeks before half-term had gone slowly, like pushing a stone up to the top of a hill. After half-term, they moved faster, rolling down towards Christmas.

Winter arrived quite suddenly, blowing all remaining leaves off the balding trees, dulling the air with mist, and fog from the sea. November days were strung together by threads of rain like numbers on a calendar.

'The English have more words for rain than any other nation,' said Mortmain, bouncing in and out of classrooms with a swirl of his duffel coat. Pallid and swarthy, he resembled, as Grub had once remarked, a vampire who had shrunk in the wash. His pupils sat on the radiators like shivering birds on a wire. English classes were held in the Tower of Babel, so everyone either froze in winter or broiled in summer because of all the glass.

> 'Western wind, when will thou blow
> The small rain down can rain?
> Christ, if my love were in my arms
> And I in my bed again!'

The 6i English class snickered. Mortmain's amours were well known. They had included Maggie Brink some twenty years ago, before her psoriasis had struck; Holly Broom, the Sanatorium nurse, on whom Mortmain had foisted an illegitimate daughter; and, more recently, Miranda Jupp, Veronica's deputy at the Dower House. The French mistress had been discarded: it was, as Toby Hindesmith observed, too much of a cliché even for him.

Bets were already being made as to whether Mortmain or Pedigree Chumley would succeed in bedding Helge, the trainee German-language teacher. Both English masters were openly pursuing her, and what Mortmain lacked in youth or beauty was more than compensated for by his rival's extreme timidity and conventionality with the opposite sex.

What Mrs Mortmain thought of this was not known; a stony-faced invigilator and a shadowy housewife, she elicited little sympathy. Mortmain, while distrusted, had a powerful clique of Groovers and even the odd Lad behind him. A graduate of Sussex University, he had enjoyed a rise sufficiently meteoric to be addressed by his surname, though without the polite prefix accorded the Librarian. Draping himself in Eng. Lit., Mortmain convinced the more impressionable in his audience that he, like Wordsworth, thrilled to the dawn of revolution, raged with John Osborne or suffered quadruple agonies of T. S. Eliot's conversion. His real interest was the theatre, but his forte was the A-level course on the Romantics.

Grub listened to the English class with half an ear, itching to get back to the piano. He found reading a slow and painful process, demanding all his powers of concentration. Words were so flat and dull, compared to music. How could you have art in the same medium as that in which teachers wrote their end-of-term reports? He began to work out the fingering for Ravel's G Major Concerto on the desk, humming under his breath as the music coursed through his head. He could hardly remember a line of poetry, but a piece of music, once heard, would be fixed in his memory for ever. Hew had played a record of the G Major and the Concerto for Left Hand for the music class the day before. The latter had been written for Wittgenstein's brother, a brilliant pianist who had lost his right hand. Grub had shuddered, looking at his own long, ugly, muscular fingers with their bitten nails. They were not ideal for pianism; even if he could stretch over an octave easily, the palm was too big. At some point in the summer, his future was going to lie in those hands. It made him feel astonished, this thought: the possibility of having art, truth, his own spirit and the composer's commingled on the keyboard.

Mortmain droned on. Up and up went the Ravel allegro like a brilliant child ascending flights of stairs acid with yellow sunlight and blue shadows, shooting off a toy pistol, sliding down the banisters, jumping on his mother's bed. It burst into a nursery full of Gershwin toy soldiers. The soldiers pranced about in wilder and wilder formations, until everyone flopped down. Then the adagio told him off for making such a mess, with such tenderness that Grub-Ravel's heart swelled with love. How could his father ever have left her? The piano burned with rage. Grub-Ravel waved his hand and the Gershwin toy soldiers suddenly grew to glittering cohorts, charged, and stuck the hated Fiona full of swords until she –

'"Bliss was it in that dawn to be alive!"' Mortmain cried, making Grub start out of his reverie. 'The egotistical sublime was loosed upon the world! After centuries of stultifying classicism, poets discovered pantheism. Can anybody tell me what that means?'

Mortmain darted this question out at his class. They shifted uneasily, like cattle in a tight corner. It was well known that English was an easy option because if you took down every word Mortmain said and regurgitated some of it in examinations you would get a pass, but the downside was that, unlike most of the staff, he occasionally asked awkward questions.

'Anybody?'

A deepening silence. Olivia and Jasper giggled nervously. Mortmain's head swivelled round. His expression of enthusiasm shrivelled away into weariness.

'Does anybody know what pantheism means? Can't you work it out? Pan-theism?'

Silence. Pitying him, Alice put her hand up.

'Mnyah. Yes?'

'The doctrine that everything is God.' Alice paused. 'As opposed to the doctrine that God is everything.'

'A somewhat pedantic definition, but it will do. It meant that the Romantics saw God in nature: a discovery which was not only aesthetic but political. Consider Rousseau, the greatest thinker of all. Who knows about Rousseau?'

Silence again. Mortmain was evidently in one of his stickier moods today.

'Come on, come on, don't just sit there like a batch of puddings! Winthrop?'

'Uh, Princess Caroline of Monaco's first husband?' Winthrop

drawled.

'Do try to pretend there's something other than muscle between your ears!'

The class fell about. Winthrop was mortified by the acute humiliation of having said something in irony and having it mistaken for genuine stupidity. Seething with rage, he snapped his pencil in half. Perceiving this, Alice again raised her hand. A low growl of hatred, led by Tore, went up from the males. Any girl who answered even one question in a class was asking for trouble. Alice wondered when individualism became a consolation prize and hoped the patches of fright under her arms had not begun to stink.

'Yes?'

'An eighteenth-century French philosopher of bad morals, filthy habits and mendacious confessions,' she said.

The growling turned to hisses.

'Fuck off, Louse,' said Tore, audibly.

'A philosopher. Thank you. Your puerile Scots morality is of no interest to us,' said Mortmain, winning the class back with a stroke. Tore and Grub burst into raucous laughter. Alice began to shake. 'On the eve of the Industrial Revolution, this great Frenchman saw that competition and the march of materialist culture was stifling the human spirit. Consider the conditions in which people worked the arsenic mines in this very valley a hundred years ago. Rousseau was the harbinger of social revolution, a revolution in sensibility celebrated and expressed by the poets of the Romantic era.'

'Christ, this is so fucking boring,' Tore muttered.

Grub whispered something back. Tore cracked with laughter.

'Grub,' said Mortmain sharply. 'I'm sure we would all like to share your joke. Repeat what you have just said.'

'My heart aches, And a drowsy numbness pains my sense,' said Grub, in Mortmain's squeaky voice.

The class erupted. Even Alice smiled.

Grub gazed back at Mortmain, his snub face the picture of innocence. 'You did ask,' he pointed out.

'Mnyah, mnyah. I'll see you later,' said Mortmain, angrily. He was very annoyed, although, like most of the staff, he had a soft spot for Grub. His mischief had a different quality to it from Tore's. In Knotshead terms, he was a particularly successful product because he lacked all competitive instincts, and seemed not to realise his unusual intelligence.

Grub, claiming a spontaneous overflow of powerful feeling, escaped as lightly as he expected, and rejoined the other Lads in the orchard. They were jostling Alice.

'Hey, Louse,' Tore was saying, grinning. 'How many times do you masturbate? Once a month? Once a week? Once a day?'

'Oh, for God's sake,' said Alice wearily.

Sparks and Jasper seized her bag and tossed it between them. 'Catch, Louse, catch!'

'Give it back. I've got a Latin lesson.'

Other Lads from lower blocks gathered to watch.

'Jump, Louse, jump!'

'How many times, Louse? I'll tell you: I think it's once a month. Yes, you're not much of a wanker, are you? But then you're so ugly, you must really hate it.'

'Ugly, ugly!' chanted Jasper.

This was what was shouted at her every day, when she crossed the Quad. It was hard to ignore it, or pretend it didn't matter.

'Jump for it, Louse!'

Grub watched, grinning. Alice was such a spastic. She began to jump, hopelessly, and the Lads all yelled with laughter. Backwards and forwards went the black cloth bag, impossibly high. And then, quite suddenly, there was a blur of motion as Winthrop leapt up and up and up into the air, caught the bag in a single fluid motion, and handed it back to its owner.

December. Grass lay in long frozen clumps. Crows criss-crossed the blue air, their metallic cries like the vibrations on a railway track as an express train approaches. From every class, Winthrop could see them blackening the frosted lawn, their heavy heads jabbing down at a worm as mechanically as digging machines. Nobody in the feathered world would fuck around with those guys, he thought enviously.

Everyone was full of plans for Christmas. The whole school practised carols; Hew conducted the choir in twice-weekly assaults on Milton's 'At a Solemn Music'. Strands of moulting tinsel had appeared in two of the common rooms, and Block 4 had whited out their windows with spray-on snow, although snow was a rare sight in the valley.

Winthrop had no idea whether he was even going to be able

to take the flight home. Without his credit cards, he was stuck as completely as any prisoner. He went into the Library and then into the Quad, restless and shivering. He did not know how it had come about, but he was looking for Alice.

His curiosity about her puzzled him. She had none of the attributes which he usually found attractive. But that was part of her appeal. With his former girlfriends, what you saw was what you got: cheerleader, Jewish princess, debutante, it was all so obvious, like choosing a make of car and having it customised for a few extras. Alice was too smart to be predictable.

She was the only person who had been at all sympathetic to him, and she was unhappy. Being unhappy himself made him notice. He sucked up little pieces of information about her like a Hoover; in a school as small as Knotshead, you heard about everyone, sooner or later. As she spent so much time in the Library, so did he, which indirectly improved his grades because he couldn't spend all the time listening to the clock tick and staring at her dark head. He found himself fantasising about her, not least because she had made it so clear she wasn't interested in men.

Tore absolutely hated her. Fay was a legitimate target, but Alice brought out the real sadist in him. He had been the one to call her Louse, saying that it was ungrammatical to have 'a lice'. The nickname had stuck, like all nicknames; there was one girl with bad acne called Crater Face who was even called this by some of the teachers.

Between Tore and Winthrop there existed a state of antagonism which deepened by the day. Winthrop was certain Tore had stolen his sweater; Tore and the Lads were furious after the bag incident. They taunted the American about fancying Alice, and laid booby traps of waste bins and even bottles over the door when he approached. Once, the Westler brothers had gone on the rampage, flicking everyone with wet towels, and had tried to hit him in the face, but his reflexes were too fast. The sensation of living under siege was worse than Manhattan, he thought. When would he be able to go home?

Every afternoon, a steady procession of Knotes would cross the ha-ha by the gates and, as there was no tuck shop, walk a mile down the drive to buy sweets from the village.

It was a pleasant walk, lined with leafless chestnuts and

pleached limes. Beyond, the park had already been churned to a swampy mass by the males in Block 3, whose naive enthusiasm for football was encouraged by the increasingly dispirited Bruce, jogging and jingling on the sidelines, yelling, 'Come on, fellas, go for it! Think of Gazza! Come on, fellas!' Then, quietly, 'Oh, Christ.'

The second viscount had built a model village for the miners forcibly displaced from the original Anstey, but his single row of Georgian cottages had been infilled with brick bungalows to accommodate the teaching and grounds staff. The latter were all that remained of the native villagers. Their children worked as cooks or cleaners at the school, and were referred to as plebs or proles. Whenever a Knote wanted to raise a laugh, he or she would attempt to imitate the accents in which these villagers spoke; for it was axiomatic that such an accent denoted extreme stupidity, comic rusticity and, worst of all, bad taste. Proof of this was found in the villagers' disinclination to take up the sub-sidised places offered, in accordance with the Founder's wishes, at Knotshead. Instead, their children went to the local compre-hensive in Knotsmouth: after which, they invariably became cleaners and dishwashers just like their parents.

Addicted to chocolate, Alice walked to Anstey at least once a day, and sometimes twice.

'You should meet my uncle, Sir James Zuckerman,' say Fay, running to keep up with her long stride. 'He owns Sucro, you know, and anyone who works there is allowed to eat as much chocolate as they like, so after a week, they hate it.'

'Really?' said Alice.

'Do you know, chocolate is supposed to have the same chemi-cal that you get when you're in love? Perhaps you're just sex-ually frustrated. I am.'

'Oh, for God's sake! You're only fourteen.'

'So? In Holland, they're going to make sex legal at twelve. And boys can be prosecuted for rape at that age, now.'

Alice shuddered. 'The parents who send their children here must either have complete amnesia about what their own ado-lescence was like, or else the libido of the giant panda.'

'But it's unnatural to separate the sexes.'

'Natural! That stupid, stupid word! Do you think the fact that we are clean and warm is natural? Or that we haven't each had three children since puberty? Or that premature babies live and we don't die of smallpox or a swollen appendix? You're like everyone else here, you think natural means wafting round the park in Laura Ashley dresses listening to Beethoven. Nature is the cruellest thing in the world.'

'But everyone at single-sex schools is so neurotic. I know, because I went to one, and it was awful,' said Fay, stubbornly.

'And you got your ten As. Look, why should we be happy at our age? We're supposed to be bored and miserable now so that we don't spend the rest of our lives drudging behind the check-out counter. Happiness is rot.'

Fay skipped a few paces to catch up again. 'You only say that because you're not,' she said, with childish spite.

'Oh yes; better to have the mark of Cain on your forehead than some brains behind it,' said Alice, wearily. Her craving for chocolate was becoming intolerable, the closer they came to the sweet shop. 'Don't you know human intellectual development is due to neoteny, or the prolongation of childhood? The lower down the evolutionary scale you are, the earlier you discover how to fuck your brains out. Literally.'

'Winthrop fancies you.'

'Ha! A likely tale!'

'You're blushing.'

'Oh, bog off, you little brat!'

The bell tinkled violently as Alice shoved the door of the sweet shop open.

Inside, Grub was poring over a fiesta of metallic wrappers beneath the button-backed eye of the shopkeeper. There were chocolate bars with names of stars; there were Rollos and Crunchies and Polos and Munchies. Alice's entry annoyed him, though not as much as the sight of Fay.

'Cadbury's Fruit and Nut, please, Mrs Blacker,' said Alice, ignoring them.

'Which bits are for the fruit, and which for the nut?' asked Grub. Fay tittered.

Alice did not find this kind of humour remotely amusing. She smiled at Mrs Blacker, and paid.

'How are you, dear?' Mrs Blacker asked. 'Still studying hard?'

'Yes. How's Carol?' Alice was almost trembling with impatience to start on her chocolate bar, but was painfully aware of the rudeness with which most Knotes treated the villagers.

Once, she had been standing in a queue and the Westler brothers had elbowed their way to the front, waving £20 notes and demanding instant service. The shame of being in any way associated with such behaviour had made a profound impression on her.

'She's got a job at Kwik Save,' said Mrs Blacker, beaming.

'Oh, that's good. I'll be working at the Post Office at Christmas again, I hope. Give her my best wishes.'

'I will, dear.'

The bell tinkled again, and Olivia came in with three friends. The tiny shop became crowded. Fay lingered, hoping for acceptance. Both Grub and Alice left immediately.

As soon as she was out, she unwrapped the gold foil with fumbling fingers and bit off a single square. O ecstasy! Sweetness flooded her mouth. Everything suddenly became bearable again.

Grub was wolfing down the second of his bars already. He reddened as, fastidious in her own greed, she broke off another square and ate it slowly.

'Don't blush,' she said acidly. 'It clashes so badly with your hair.'

Grub rubbed his snub nose, as if considering this. 'Do you always do everything the way you eat?'

'Yes.'

'Why?'

'Oh, bog off!'

'No, go on, tell me. Why?'

'It's more – sensible.'

'And you never, ever let yourself go?'

'Why should I?'

'Why shouldn't you?'

'Do you really want to know? Because it's so boring. The uniformity of nonconformity. You're all the same. You're all such craven cowards.'

'Do you know what everyone hates about you?' said Grub, as they walked down the long straight drive. 'You're so – so judgemental.'

'You cannot be judgemental, what a disgusting word, without having the ability to judge,' said Alice coldly. 'You can't discriminate because you don't believe in any rules – moral or social or intellectual. I can, because I do. Hate away. As far as

I'm concerned, it's a compliment to be hated by people like you and Tore.'

'Everyone wants to be liked,' said Grub. 'You're lying if you say you don't.'

'Then I'd sooner lie to you than with you,' said Alice, turning off along the path to the Dower House.

'I wasn't asking!' Grub shouted after her. 'Bitch,' he muttered to himself. 'What a conceited bloody cow.' But the sting of her replies remained under his skin, and itched.

12

The week before the Christmas dance it snowed up on Dart-moor, and in the rest of the country. The river became brown with rushing water, bursting its banks and flooding the Venus Vale, so that even the most half-hearted games of football and lacrosse became impossible. Pupils, irritable with inactivity, mooched round the Quad at all times of day, ripping up chairs in the common rooms.

There were the usual complaints about eighteen-year-olds not being allowed to go to the pub, and a vote forbidding the cater-ers to buy South African oranges. Fay was sent a mystery parcel, which she opened excitedly at elevenses before the rest of 6i to reveal a vibrator. Olivia and Nicola were chased by Nicholas Crump after having a quiet fag with Tore and Mongol during a Free. A line of huge yellow footprints was spray-painted on the Quad floor, leading from the dining room to the headmaster's office. Hart, excessively annoyed, cancelled the afternoon Free for the entire school because nobody owned up.

The fuss over his letter to the parents died down, though it had earned him a sharp reproof from the governors for drawing 'unwelcome attention to problem pupils'. In public, they claimed to support him, but in private one or two younger governors began to voice doubts about renewing his contract. Sensing this, Hart fired off letters to influential parents telling them how well their child was doing at Knotshead, which most believed implicitly. An earnest woman in tweeds and beads came down to give a Sunday Jaw on leprosy in Africa, and a famous actor lectured them on the plight of Romanian orphans. One Tory MP was heckled, and an elderly publisher who came down to talk about Trollope was completely ignored. Several pupils converted to Buddhism after a visit from the Dalai Lama, and everyone agreed that Gerald Kaufman was simply frightful.

It seemed a normal enough school term.

Alice trudged in the rain. The trees lining the hillsides looked like bar after bar of an endless cage, tall and thin after hundreds of years of charcoal-burning for the mines.

The ascent to her private place was inaccessible, with the rains. Instead, she made a circuit of the peninsula, a flock of sheep running complainingly before her, swaying like fat women in crinolines. It was all so drearily familiar, she knew the tracks would be grooved on her memory for the rest of her life.

The symmetries of the Knotshead estate simultaneously consoled and distressed. She feared chaos, yet felt oppressed at seeing views in which human intention was so evident. The careful siting of every coppice and knoll, the tyranny of a decrepit order exercised a compulsion on body and mind.

Alice preferred the austerity of winter, which reminded her of Scotland even in its soft, southern form: the way grass was suddenly foxed with frost, like mildewed velvet, the blunt catkins spurting from hazel coppices, dogwood like the weals of a whip. Fields quilted the hills towards Minedale, then petered out into a dark, cloudy mass of moorland nearer the school. Branches turned a startling, fluorescent green whenever the sun shone on them, some so heavily encrusted with lichen it looked as if they had been dipped in calcified foam.

Alice went as far as the bridge to Minedale, then turned back. Below, the Knot looped and scribbled to the sea, straightening out as it sliced through the miniature red cliffs of Cornish soil. After the shallow rapids where the lake emptied and joined the thin trickle of the original stream came a long, quiet pool. A solitary swan, nesting on an island, followed her, gathering light in its wake.

She had some slices of bread. Winthrop, higher up in the woods, watched her throwing it on the waters. His trainers were heavy with mud, but he no longer wore his Walkman, for it had been stolen immediately after half-term. He had fallen into the habit of jogging at the time when he knew she would be out, running in the opposite direction so that it would seem accidental if they met. Sometimes they exchanged cautious smiles in passing; mostly, she didn't even know he was there.

He felt kind of stupid spying on her, like the man in the ballet Bitsy had once taken him to see at the Met, about a girl who was really a swan – he couldn't remember what happened, but it had a sad ending like those arty things always did. Quietly, he walked down the hill, trying not to trip on bits of rusting railway track.

'Hi. Do you always feed it?'

'Him. Yes. Usually.' She tore up her pieces of bread with nervous irritability. 'Swans get very hungry in winter. They have a very inefficient diet of weed.' There was that rustling quality to her voice, again. How beautiful some people become when they speak, he thought; how ugly others. It was such a cliché, the American falling for the British accent, but then all clichés became so because they were true. Ultimately, Winthrop was a great believer in clichés.

'Inefficient?'

'Yes. That's why they mate for life. Weed takes ages to digest. They're faithful because they don't have the energy to be promiscuous, like grain-eaters.'

'Oh. I thought it was because they, you know – '

'Fell in love?'

'Yeah.'

'No,' said Alice. 'Animals don't fall in love. You anthropomorphise, like Walt Disney. But perhaps it's the same with people, too,' she said, feeling she was too harsh. After all, she had made a similar mistake about Horatio.

'You think it's all sex?'

'Don't you?'

'No,' said Winthrop. He met her eyes, and she glanced away.

'Why not?'

'Well, it's different. It's just different. I'm not very good at verbalising these things.' Alice winced.

The weight of what he wanted to say almost paralysed him. 'I mean, I'm not good at talking about feelings.'

'Why not?'

'Well.' Winthrop considered. 'I've always gotten along on sports, and family, and that kind of thing. Before I came here.'

'Oh. You mean, the experience of not being popular is alter-ing your perspectives.'

'You put it so well.'

The dryness of his tone startled her. Alice said, with surprise, 'You understand irony. I thought – '

'That I'm stupid? The trouble is – you don't learn here about the Great Vowel Shift, do you? We do. That's why preppy Americans try to sound English. Basically, every American sounds stupid to you because we flatten our vowels, like low-class people in this country.'

'I hardly think people are stupid because they talk dif-ferently.'

'Well, you personally may not, but it's my impression a lot of my fellow students do. Like, the cleaners being called "proles"?'

'The underbelly of the liberal intelligentsia is always their children.'

'Also, where I come from it's, you know, bad form to talk, much.'

'I suppose it is in England, too.'

'But you do.'

'Well,' she said, 'as I've told you, I'm Scotch, and a noncom-formist. Besides, I don't usually. Except to the Librarian.'

'But you answer in class, despite freewheeling psychos like Tore. That takes a lot of self-confidence.'

'Self-confidence!'

Her sarcasm made him wince. 'Doesn't it?'

'I have *no* self-confidence. What you see is a different reaction to fear.' She paused, then added, with difficulty, 'You can choose flight or fight – I choose fight.'

Winthrop felt admiration, and unease. This was the way he should square up to Tore. 'The other girls don't, though.'

'They're more craven. Or better survivors. Take your pick.'

'If you didn't answer back, I think you'd be – '

'Less difficult.'

'Less attractive.'

Startled, she looked at him. 'You can't make less of nothing.'

'I do not think,' said Winthrop, 'that anyone can be described as *nothing*. Least of all you.'

Alice shrugged. 'Girls are all holes of one sort or another, here.'

'But every zero has the power to multiply by ten.'

'Oh, don't be so bloody metaphysical.'

They walked in silence along the sodden banks, past miniature sandy bays and serpentine tree roots. Branches were crys-
talline with rain. The river rushed and muttered, interrupted by
occasional splashes, perhaps from fish, perhaps from timid,
shadowy moorhen. Like two sticks in the eddy beneath, their
thoughts kept ducking and surfacing to the same point.

'Are you going to the dance tomorrow?'

'No.'

'Not even for a few minutes?'

Her head ached in the vice of pressure and depression. 'No.'

'Oh. But you'll go to the Christmas dinner?'

'I have to eat.'

'It would be a pity to lose out.'

'There is a difference between choosing and losing.'

'But if you choose to lose, because you're afraid?'

She flushed.

'What are you thinking?'

'I keep forgetting you are intelligent,' she said, deliberately to
embarrass him. But Winthrop only grinned.

The swan glided towards them as they reapproached its
island. When it saw that no more bread was forthcoming, it
arched its neck down into the water, forming the outline of a
perfect white heart with its reflection. Down, down, down. The
great feathery body became seemingly headless. It floated on the
darkness for seconds, heartbeats. Then slowly, slowly, the neck
began to rise again, transformed. Green with slime, it coiled up
and up. Out of the water came a scaly head which opened its
beak and hissed like a snake.

'Shit!' said Winthrop, jumping back.

'Do you still think swans so romantic?'

'He seems kind of cranky.'

'He doesn't have a mate.'

'I thought you said he was diet-impaired.'

'That, too.'

'It's kind of bad if you don't luck out, isn't it?' said Winthrop.

For those to whom coeducation had made intercourse less
mysterious than aerobics, Knotes were curiously prurient. Both
the Slythes, for instance, would have been surprised at how
eagerly glasses were pressed against the floorboards of X dorm,

above their bedroom in the Dower House, to discover how many times they had intercourse (once a week, it was generally agreed). All staff copulation was discussed with graphic detail by both sexes, although their own encounters were naturally different. Girls would recount their experiences in whispered gasps after lights out:

' . . . So he said, do you want to go with me, and I was wearing my new jeans, and he put his arm round me – and it was, oh, oh . . . '

'Go on,' the girl's friends would say, panting with vicarious excitement.

'Well, we walked as far as the lake, and he gave me his jacket and then, and then . . . '

'Go on.'

'And then he kissed me.'

Ecstatic sighs all round.

'French?'

'Of course.'

'Good?'

'Fab.'

'Come on, did he get an erection?'

'I thought he had a torch in his pocket.'

'And then?'

'Well, you know.'

'Oh, go on. Length, breadth, timing and position.'

'Ectually, I had the menarche.'

'Oh, bad luck.'

'But it was all so wonderful. He told me I looked like a drowned water rat. Don't you think he's gorgeous?'

'Well, if you look between the spots . . . '

In the Males' Flats, the same event was described as: 'Gobjob, three minutes.'

Sitting smoking a joint with Tore in the Stagehands' Hut, Grub listened to the usual golden oldies and thought about his problem with girls. Each school dance demanded a rehash of favourites; even if he hated pop, he still liked the feeling of controlling some Bacchanalian orgy as the school's D.J.

For thirty years, Knotshead taste in pop music had barely varied: the Beatles, Bob Dylan, Elton John, Paul Simon, Joan Armatrading, the Rolling Stones, Gore Tore, Bowie. With a few additions (the Gypsy Kings, lambada) they danced to the same music their parents had moved to, hoping to enjoy being young. Occasionally, some Old Knote would turn up in beads and flared trousers, like a dinosaur perfectly preserved by the Ice Age, embarrassing everyone. Mostly, however, the nostalgia was all their own.

Grub pressed a button, and a cold pulse of electronic music filled the hut. A voice at once hoarse and pure, like that of a depraved angel, began singing. Grub stared at the ceiling, where, in 1987, a previous Head Lad's high velocity champagne cork had permanently dented a fat frescoed cherub agape, and thought about the burden of people's dreams. 'Some of them want to use you, some of them want to be used,' sang the voice.

Such cruel clarity. Which category did he fall into? User or used? Did it matter? For if the user had power over the used, so, too, did the used have power over the user. It was not a relationship of appetite, like that between predator and prey, but one which, like the roles of lover and beloved, had to be arrived at by a kind of mutual agreement. 'Some of them want to abuse you, some of them want to be abused.' Grub thought of the boy who had hanged himself in block three and shuddered violently.

'Fucking feminist,' said Tore, dragging on a joint before passing it to Grub. 'Not the Eurythmics.'

Tore was in a bad mood. Boredom and exhilaration virtually coexisted in him. He could change in a blink from being completely charming, entertaining them all with stories about how one of his old man's loopier tarts had taken the legs off the billiard table with a chainsaw when she thought Gore wasn't paying her enough attention, to extremes of violence. This afternoon he had got out some joke-shop handcuffs, locked a Semi-Groover to the bed, and kicked him all over. The boy had complained to Pedigree. Big mistake.

'Ah, Johnny, I've just been writing your end-of-term report,' was Chumley's response. 'I was thinking of saying, you have a good sense of humour but a rather cruel one.'

Tore had pushed his face up into the housemaster's.

'Don't you dare fucking write that,' he said. 'Don't you *dare*!'

'No, no, of course not,' Chumley said, backing down at once.

Grub riffled through some old LPs until he came to *Bulldancer*, an old Gore Tore record. This was always popular. It had famously boppable tracks and the glutinously surreal cover of many 1970s productions: Gore in a gold bull's mask shafting a blonde. Even now, the effect was more like a skin mag than a rock record. Banned as obscene, it made him a star. Tore had told Grub (he knew every twist and turn in his father's rise to success) that this had been the image which made him popular with the aristocracy.

'Toffs like to have my old man to stay, so they can say how civilised he really is and feel they're really hip at the same time. He likes them because they're the only people who aren't after him for his dosh. I think that's why he sent me here. He wants me to grow up like them.'

Grub gazed at the blonde. She was exquisitely beautiful, despite thick 1970s make-up. He could never look at the cover without going into a dream so lurid that he blushed even as he palpitated. She was really lovely, not just sexy, like a fairy-tale princess. In the silence between tracks, Grub glanced again at the girl on the familiar record cover. Bleached and airbrushed into anonymous perfection, her body was slick as a mechanic's wet dream, and yet ... how strange that he had never noticed that short, arched nose.

'Hey, Jono,' he said softly. 'Look at this.'

'So?' said Tore. 'I've seen it a million times.'

'No, look at the face. Add sixteen years, and who does she remind you of?'

Tore stared. 'Some tart. They're all after him. Probably sold her story to *News of the Screws* six times over.'

'No, *look*.'

Tore looked, then bared pointed, greenish teeth. Grub had seen that expression before. It always meant trouble.

'Well, well,' he said.

'Do you really think it's her?'

Tore began to laugh, his voice high and cracked with excitement.

'Can you doubt it, once you look? Poppy Hart. Jesus, Grub, you're a frigging genius. Right under everyone's nose for years, and we were all too busy staring at my old man's dick! I'm surprised he never mentioned it, he must have seen her the time he came for Parents' Day.'

'Perhaps he didn't recognise her with her clothes on,' said Grub.

Tore didn't hear him. 'God, what a laff! Just let Hart the Fart try and cause any trouble for me, now.'

Veronica paused outside the door of the temple. She had been peering through the little window, searching for signs of misdemeanour. Beatrice Bassett might be intimidated, but Veronica was not. Her eyes shone in her chalk-white face, and her long red nostrils dilated. Marijuana! This time, she was going to catch them in the act, however practised their ability to conceal a glowing end. She listened, waiting for the moment to pounce. Tore's voice reached her with unmistakable clarity. It took a second for its meaning, its importance to sink in. Then she felt giddy at the opportunity that suddenly presented itself to her. She peered again through the crack, trying to see which record they were looking at; and, when she saw, Veronica, too, began to smile.

13

Greatly to her surprise and embarrassment, Alice found Poppy perched on her bed when she returned to the Dower House. Her sister had never been known to set foot in any school buildings other than the Quad and the Assembly Hall; having left her job as housemistress she was open in her dislike of dormitories. Yet here she was, reading a copy of *Elle* and looking little older than Olivia. It was only when you looked into her face and saw the immobility, the slow glacier of disillusion, that you realised she was middle-aged.

'Hallo. What's your sign of the zodiac?'

'Our fates are in ourselves, not in our stars. I don't believe in all that.'

'Come on, what are you?'

'Don't you know?'

Poppy gave her a strange look. 'Perhaps I do. Perhaps I don't.'

'Virgo, then.'

'Oh. Yes, of course. You would be. Well, "the process of re-building your life reaches the end of its initial stage now. Problems in your relationships will come to a head on the 18th" – that's tomorrow – "when conflicts between work and love will endanger those high standards which are the Virgo hallmark. You will regain the initiative –"'

'What utter tosh!'

'I think they're frightfully funny.'

'I think they're frightfully stupid. They are written in a style which can always apply to anyone at any time. In any case, they don't apply to me. I have no – relationships, to use that detestable word.'

'What about your relationship with me?'

Alice said, dryly, 'I don't think that's quite the kind of thing they have in mind in a magazine like that.'

'You don't come home much,' said Poppy, tracing the pink candlewick waves with one perfect, tapering finger.

'You didn't ask to have me dumped on you by fate.'

'I thought you didn't believe in fate.' Poppy smiled, tightly.

Alice stood there. She had longed for her sister to visit her like this all through her first two years, but those times were over. Now she wished Poppy would go. Her stomach creased with nervous tension whenever she thought of the Christmas party, no matter how many times she considered the pointlessness of it all. She wanted to be alone, to have a bath while most of the bathrooms were empty, to lie in a coffin of white steam and think of nothing.

'Did you come for any particular reason?' she asked, politely.

Poppy looked at her, the faint, wintry smile still on her face. Then she shook her head. 'I came to give you a present.'

'Oh. That's kind of you.'

'Simon and I thought it was time you had something nicer to wear. Something that wasn't black. I was doing some Christmas shopping in Knotsmouth, and saw this. Look.'

She drew out a heap of fluid material. Alice looked at it with horror.

'But it's *red*.'

'Garnet. Jersey.'

'The skirt is miles too short.'

'You're tall and willowy, it would suit you. And this.' Poppy brought out a long silk shawl, heavily embroidered with red roses, with a fringe at either end. 'It was Mama's. Chinese, I think. You should have it, now you're growing up. Black makes you look like an old lady.'

'Why shouldn't I, if that's what I want to look like?'

'Because you aren't one,' said Poppy. 'Look, I know you don't want to talk about Mama, but you can't go on mourning her for ever. Life must go on. She was my mother, too, you know.'

'Yes,' Alice said.

'Yes,' Poppy's voice was equally ironic. 'But we had a difficult time. As you would have, if she had lived, perhaps.'

'I don't want to discuss this.'

'Try the dress,' said Poppy gently.

Alice shrugged. 'What's the point?'

'Don't you want to make yourself attractive?'

'What, to males? To *boys*, rather. No.'

'Why not?'

'Of all the ways to waste time, it seems the most pointless. I see girls all around me, some of them perfectly intelligent, pouring out so much energy and imagination – and on what? Not on the things which will really decide their fate, like examinations. On some spotty, boorish bore who will fill her with shame in two months' time if she gets him, and with surprise that she ever found him attractive if she doesn't.'

'But it's all experience.'

'What is the point of such experience, unless it's to inoculate you against the disease of foolishness? And if it's a disease which I have no intention of catching, why bother?'

'With diseases,' said Poppy, 'you may not have much choice.'

A Christmas service preceded the dinner and dance. Held in the vaults of the Assembly Hall, candlelit and garlanded with holly and ivy, it was the only service that was unequivocally Christian. There were hymns and readings of 'The Journey of the Magi' and 'The Burning Babe'; there was an excruciating address by Hart about the importance of children. Here, too, was the one and only performance of Hubert Parry's setting of 'At a Solemn Music' which the choir had been practising all term.

'Blest pair of sirens, pledges of heaven's joy,
Sphere-borne harmonious sisters, Voice and Verse,
Wed your divine sounds and mixed power employ
Dead things with inbreathed sense able to pierce ... '

The words mystified and enthralled Alice as she sang. What did Milton mean, calling Voice and Verse sirens? Did he mean that they tempted you to destruction, like those in the *Odyssey*? Then why was destruction blessed? And then, to what did 'dead things' refer? Did it mean the sisters were dead? That language and music were inert? Or that the things they affected were? Hew had not explained it; she rather doubted that he was capable of doing so. All that mattered to Hew was the music, which he conducted with scowls and grimaces, terrifying as God, his magenta shirt growing patches beneath the armpits.

> 'That we on earth with undiscording voice
> May rightly answer that melodious noise;
> As once we did, 'til disproportioned sin
> Jarred against nature's chime and with harsh din
> Broke the fair music that all creatures made
> To their great Lord, whose love their motion swayed
> In perfect diapason . . . '

Everyone swayed as the music swelled, triumphant. Out of every mouth streamed notes, glorious and insubstantial as bubbles, growing and spreading into a sphere of sound until it could stretch no further, and burst in a shower of sweetness.

Only when singing did Alice feel herself willingly become a part of Knotshead: not Knotshead as it was, but Knotshead as it could be. She supposed that this was the point of depicting heaven as one long choir; even someone like Grub (a surprising bass behind her row of altos) behaved himself, despite all the fooling about during rehearsals.

Grub was in fact thinking of nothing. His mind was completely blank; Tore, grinning and making faces from the males' rows in front of him, gave up in disgust. The more advanced a certain kind of musician, the less he can enjoy or even hear himself performing. All that happens is the music. Grub enjoyed himself no more than a vector or lightning conductor. A few weeks ago, he had come across a Shakespeare sonnet which described it exactly: 'Who, moving others, are themselves as stone.' The poem had been referring to love, but it was the same when he sang or, more particularly, played the piano. To be able to identify the pianist was, he thought, a mark of failure – unless, of course, he was Glenn Gould. Those wankers in the Amadeus Quartet! That tosser Nigel Kennedy! That wittering Petrie! That ridiculous, though enviable, Rostropovich! Perfect musicianship was like Garbo's face, a Platonic blank on to which anything could be superimposed.

Yet, to be a successful performer, you had to project your

personality: something which wasn't even you, but a package, an artefact. Even if he had the sheer pianism to become concert standard – which Hew would tell him soon enough, once he had passed Grade Eight – there was that compromise.

The assembly was over. The choir shuffled our first, passing up the line of shaking hands and wishing the automatons attached a happy Christmas.

Hurrah, thought Grub; time for mince pies and dinner! He loved Christmas dinner, both here and at home. Christmas pudding, he could live off it, and brandy butter – what genius had thought of making butter alcoholic? It was the one time in the year when Knotshead sanctioned the ingestion of alcohol, and he intended to enjoy it to the full. Then at home, there would be the whole business of choosing a tree from Camden Market, the resinous smell of pine needles, and the blaze of little lights and big, coloured balls; his father there without the bimboid Fiona, and all the family together. A sense of immense wellbeing filled him, somehow connected with the red and cream blur ascending the stairs to the Quad just in front. Who is that? he wondered, vaguely. The figure turned sideways, and he saw the short, aquiline nose. He knew, and did not know, Alice.

Her hair was pinned up on top of her head, in a sort of twist which made him think of bread rolls. For the first time in years, he remembered what he and Tore had done to her in Block 3. It had been meant to be a joke, but it had all gone wrong. He remembered Sparks, paralytic with laughter as he danced about, waving her blouse.

She had not tried to conceal herself, after a single, convulsive movement, but had waited for Tore's lunge, stepping aside and punching him straight out like a boxer. Her tits had, indeed, come as rather a disappointment – little blobs, hardly the size of meringues. But it was the defiance which had spoilt it, much more than the fist which had bloodied Tore's nose. Such determination, such contempt. Looking at her as she crossed the Quad, he wondered how they had ever dared. She had been formidable even at twelve. Then he thought of Poppy, and wondered whether Alice knew; whether she, too, was like that underneath. It disturbed him to think this.

All through the Christmas dinner, Grub was distracted, hardly tasting the rubbery white slices of turkey which he shovelled down so absently he spilled more than usual quantities of gravy down his front.

'Fucking hell,' said Tore, seeing this. 'You need a baby's bib.'

'Sorry.'

'So listen, what are we going to do about the you-know-what?'

'What?'

'The fucking record cover, man.' Tore spoke in his hoarsest Darth Vader voice. 'You haven't forgotten? Mrs Fart in her birthday suit?'

'We can't do anything, can we?'

'Of course, we can. Everyone hates him, don't they? Everyone wants to topple him, don't they? It's only a question of which paper we send it to. *News of the Screws? Sunday Sport? Daily Mail?*'

'Won't it embarrass your father?'

'Him? Nah, he'll love it. He likes publicity, my old man, though he pretends not to. That cover caused a scandal then, but now – whooee! Which do you think would pay us the most money?'

'I'll tell you what,' said Grub, desperate to be left in peace. 'I'll ask Sam. My dad. He works for a lot of newspapers, remember?'

Tomorrow, thought Winthrop, I can kiss all this goodbye. Tomorrow, I'll be going – no, not home. Mother and Bunny were spending Christmas on Mustique.

I'm so bored of ski vacations [she had written him the week before]. Bunny and I feel like some sunshine after Thanksgiving. Manhattan has gotten so dull now that everyone has to be austere. However vulgar the Reagan years, at least people like us had some fun. Now every time I turn on the TV I see someone just like your father as President. Come back and amuse me. B. never remembers that I like a dash of orange bitters in my gin.

　　Arrivederci,
　　　　Bitsy

P.S. Yr last ltr. v. funny. I want you to be independent. Take care yrself. Sending Timberland boots.

The thought of seeing blue sky again made Winthrop almost

pass out. Yet, at the same time, he found himself reluctant to leave Alice. He was in limbo, waiting. He did not know what he wanted from her. It wasn't the usual thing. In fact, the idea of even touching her somehow filled him with shame. At the same time, he had an insane longing to do so.

All he knew was that he wanted to *be* with her. Absent, he felt like some kind of zombie. With her, he was tense and in some strange way afraid, but he was also alive. It was she and not the school that had made him think those uncomfortable thoughts about who he was and what he really wanted to become. Before Alice, he had always assumed that everything would continue as it had done for generations of Winthrop Sheens: L. L. Bean, deb dances, Ivy League, country clubs. Now all that seemed almost as weird as the life at Knotshead. When his boots arrived by special delivery, he looked at them and wondered what in the hell was happening to him.

Emerging from the self-service queue with a tray on one arm, he looked for Alice's neat, dark head in the confusion of the dining hall. As soon as he didn't know exactly where she was, he will filled with anxiety, but once he had her pinned down, he had to be careful not to seem to stare. The carol service had been good, just because he had been given an excuse to observe her. He had been astonished, seeing the red dress at the Christmas service; then pleased. It must be a sign, he thought. Something had changed.

He did not attempt to approach her table, but sat at some distance where he could watch without seeming to do so. Occasionally, he raised his eyes and thought he saw hers flicking away from him, but then she was always withdrawn in public. All Rejects were. There was one girl in his block, a scientist nicknamed Crater Face, who had not been known to speak for years, and another, Douche, who could only speak in a whisper.

People bolted their food in order to be in the Quad by the time the music began at 8.30. Both enclosures were galvanised by excitement; tables full of giggling girls tossed their heads pretending not to notice if a male stared at them. The males picked at their spots and looked self-conscious. It was just like a dance back home, and probably identical to anything you saw in the jungle. He did not know whether to be amused or appalled at this thought. After all, dancing was endemic to preppy life.

Just before the appointed time, the raucous start of 'Rock

Around the Clock' boomed out. Grub had made himself sick on
mince pies and Christmas pudding, and was now fortified to endure the worst. Sparks crouched over a mystic, flashing black
rectangle of sound controls. There was a scramble to finish.
Alice and Winthrop were among the last to leave.

'So,' he said. 'Is this the start of a new career as a scarlet
woman?'

She shrugged. 'My sister gave it to me. I wasn't going to wear
it, but . . .'

'It's cute. I like it.'

'I didn't wear it to be, what a dreadful word, cute,' she said
irritably.

'Why did you, then?'

'I – I don't know,' she said, confused.

'I like it. You have great legs, you know?'

Alice said nothing. Bill Haley was in full swing, and the sweat
on Winthrop's skin jumped with every beat.

'Dance?'

'No,' she said, shocked.

'Aw, come on.'

'No, I don't dance. I told you.'

'It doesn't matter if you haven't done it before. I have.'

'I am perfectly aware,' said Alice, almost shouting against the
din, 'that you have done everything I can think of and probably
more, before; and that I have not. But it's neither here nor there.'

'Why?' asked Winthrop in her ear. 'Are you so frightened by
the people you claim you despise?' She turned her face away.
'What does it matter what they think?'

'It isn't what they think. It's that I *do.*'

'Why did you change your image, then?'

'How *can* you be so stupid?' she exclaimed, in a burst of
fright and bad temper. 'Hasn't anything I said made sense at
all?'

'OK,' said Winthrop, amiably. 'You say that to change from
one colour to another doesn't matter, because it doesn't alter
what you are like inside.'

'Yes, I mean, no.'

'So, if what you really are remains unchanged by external fac-
tors, why can't you dance?'

'Because an action is not the same as a piece of clothing.'

'So you could take all your clothes off and still be unchanged,

but not dance for two seconds without some major catas-
trophe? C'mon!'

He had her in check. They both knew it.

'No,' said Alice. 'I won't. Ask someone else.'

'OK,' said Winthrop. 'But in return, you have to stay and
watch.'

Winthrop danced. He did not make the same mistake he had the
first time; but now Olivia wished he had. Dancing was one of
the things he was good at, when not showing off. Consequently,
and unknown to him, his social status rose. Girls who had
ignored him – in so far as any male could be ignored at Knotshead – looked, and looked again, whispering to each other as
they stood around waiting for partners that the American was
really quite sexy, that he could certainly dance, that he was definitely improving his image. Despite the deafening beat, Alice
could hear them, and wondered at the misery that it caused her.

His white shirt and fair head seemed to float in the lights. She
could not wrench her eyes from him. Envy of each girl he was
with rose in her throat, sour as vomit. She was astonished at her
reaction. This is absurd, she told herself, almost laughing as she
felt her lips tremble; that is hateful, cretinous, petty, all that I do
not wish to be. She loathed the music she was listening to, its
crude, repetitive messages of lust and longing; and yet it hyp-
notised as well. Thump, thump, thump, thump. Suffocation. It
would control the beat of her heart and the breath in her lungs
before long. She tried to remember the music she had sung in
the choir, but could no longer even hold on to the right key.

Winthrop smiled – baring his teeth as if flossing them, she
thought savagely – at his partner, who this time happened to be
Fay. She looked appropriately dazzled. He bent his head, and
Fay, who barely reached up to his elbows, almost jumped like a
little dog for the customary parting kiss. Alice turned away.

Looking down from the stage, between tracks, Grub saw her
throw an end of her shawl over each shoulder, and move
through the crowds along the walls to the swing doors. A blast
of cold air as she went out made the others shiver, but only
Winthrop turned his head and followed her into the dark.

It was cold outside, but well above freezing. Steep hills shielded
the school from the cold winds blowing up above on Dartmoor.

The sky was marbled with massy, luminous clouds. A strong blue light, softer than that in the Quad, cast shadows everywhere.

Alice was walking fast up ahead. The twining roses down her back looked like great black stains, or spiders. Winthrop began to run, cursing his stiff new boots; then saw that she was not, as he had expected, heading for the Dower House. Instead, she was walking towards the upper bridge, past Flottage and the Tower of Babel.

Where could she be going? If she stopped on the bridge, he could catch up.

She crossed the Knot and walked along the bank for a while, until he was sure she must be heading for the Librarian's cottage. He hesitated. The fever of dancing was dying down in his blood. Already, he felt the need for a jacket on top of his sweater. If she were going to see Kenward, she might be hours with the old man. Winthrop really didn't like those Yoda figures you found in boarding schools, they were so corny. But she turned up the hill, flitting in and out of the tall trees like a moth. He came to the stream bed, and followed her up it, thankful now for his boots as they kept the water out, thankful too for the noise the stream made, concealing his own passage. The white of her shawl glimmered ahead, always ahead, drawing him deeper and deeper into the wood. It creaked and whispered to itself, as if talking in its sleep. A month ago, the idea of walking at night in the country like this would have chilled him out, but now there was no room for such feelings. Even when he had to scramble up the slimy stair of the little waterfall, sinking in above the ankle and soaking his socks, he didn't care. He wanted ... he wanted ... vague phrases of apology and resentment curdled in his head. She was always so poised, even in anger. There she was, sitting on a tree stump, bent over as if laughing at his clumsiness. He gave an embarrassed grin.

'Hi,' he said, and then saw. 'Oh, Alice, Alice, don't. Sweetheart. Don't cry.'

He was on his knees, his knees were soaking wet, everything was suddenly boiling hot, the taste of tears and wet hair and her mouth. Her soft, soft mouth. When it opened, slowly and timidly, he thought he would just die.

'Oh, Alice. Sweetheart. Nothing can harm you now.'

'No,' said Alice. 'The harm has just begun.'

PART TWO

14

Grub had almost forgotten his promise to Tore to tell his father about Poppy Hart during the Christmas holidays. Absorbed in mastering his wine-making kit (from Sam) and a fiendishly difficult piece of Albeniz (from Ruth), he let school life recede in his mind. When he remembered, he was not at all sure Sam would be interested in any case. Sam was never predictable in his responses.

'I have the lowest boredom threshold known to man,' he would say, with complacency. 'I hate dogs, babies, actors, women, foreigners and the English. If I wasn't a cartoonist, I'd be a mass murderer.'

A leading political cartoonist, he was most bored by politicians; what amused him was stories about eccentrics and lunatics, for whom he might well be mistaken himself. The only cartoons he actually enjoyed drawing was his strip, 'Dum and Mad': the tribulations depicted, he would say with an owlish stare, were all drawn from his own family.

'The fact is that people who want power are not only corrupt but dull,' he said, wriggling his holey socks in front of the fire. 'Thatcher, Major, spot the difference. Politics is just theatre with very bad actors.'

'Are powerful people always boring, Dad?'

'Dunno. I hardly ever meet anyone, pegged out over the drawing board, paying for you lot,' said Sam, irritably and inaccurately. 'Met Mrs Thatcher once, though. I thought she looked like she was on Valium. Either that, or blotto.'

'Have you ever met Tore's father?'

'Old Rubber Hips? Amazing how he still puts it about. When we were all young and dossing around Chelsea. Married the bird next door, Tara something, usual bimbo. I suppose she's the mother of your friend Johnny.'

'Yes. They live in Notting Hill.' Grub did not visit him in the holidays: Tore liked to hang out with some older boys then, and seemed ashamed of his Knotshead friends. 'Jono says she's never got over the divorce, though his old man had hundreds of groupies almost raping him on and off the stage while they were all together.'

'Yes, yes. Usual stuff,' said Sam Viner, yawning. 'Sex and drugs and rock and roll. People are so sodding censorious about the Sixties, these days, but Christ, it was fun. And I don't just say that because I could pull more birds. It was something unimaginable. No fear about lung cancer or AIDS or mortgages, just one long paradise, everything free for all. Ah, God, sometimes I think the ones who OD'd were the lucky bastards after all, you know.'

Grub looked anxiously at him. In a few minutes he would be sloping off back to Lamb's Conduit Street and Fiona. Stay here. Come back to us all, he willed silently. Ruth had never asked her sons to take sides. She had said that every divorce had its reasons on both sides, but that made it worse. He had seen, and felt, such titanic emotions he felt he would have gone mad without music. The simplest words had become twisted and tangled into such complexity. Even now, he was only just beginning to understand them. At thirteen, it had been as if half of himself had retreated from all feelings, and yet had prematurely aged.

'Actually, Dad, you know the fuss about my headmaster's letter that got into the papers?'

'The one about law and order breaking down? Oh yes. Cue for the usual sanctimonious bashing of progressive schools in the right-wing press.'

'Well, we've just discovered something. You know the first hit Gore Tore had, the one with the cover that was banned as obscene?'

'Vaguely. Suppose it was part of my misspent youth.'

'Well, the girl he's having it off with is our headmaster's wife, Poppy Hart.'

Grub's father burst out laughing. 'No!' he said. 'I can't wait to tell Fiona that.'

Grub's heart sank.

The Harts' Christmas was a low-key affair, mostly revolving around the twins. Simon took them to church in Minedale, though Poppy stayed at home.

'I hate God-bothering,' she said. 'If there is a God, he must be bored sick of all the stupid things we pray for. Leave the poor sod alone.'

Lily and Daisy woke their parents every morning before dawn to ask if it was time for their presents.

'It's shocking how young they become greedy, now,' said Hart. He thought about all the theft in the past term, and sighed.

'Chokky, mummy, we want chokky!' said Lily.

'Play with us.'

'Tell us a story.'

'We want chokky.'

'Mummy! Mummy!'

'Yes, darling. Yes, my sweet lambs. Come and snuggle. Which would you like first?'

The passionate love on Poppy's face was almost fanatical. Hart blinked, morosely. She had never once looked at him with even half as much attention, let alone affection. Poppy had discovered maternity late in life, and was enjoying it with all the zeal of any born-again convert.

'Where's your sister?'

'Sulking somewhere.'

'I worry that she spends too much time on her own, you know, dearest.'

'She's just an introvert, like my mother. It's a peculiarly Scottish type.' Poppy always said 'Scottish' instead of 'Scots' because her mother had insisted it was common.

'Ah. You think she's happy?'

'People like Alice and Mama don't have feelings like happiness or unhappiness. They just award themselves marks out of ten.'

'The staff don't quite know what to make of her. Mortmain was quite scathing in his end-of-term report, says her sanctimonious manner is most off-putting. Miranda Jupp is inclined to agree. Apparently there was some row about *Madame Bovary* in which Alice told her she had no sense of irony. Miranda was mortified, quite mortified. She agrees with Veronica that Alice is antisocial.'

Poppy made a rude noise.

'Yes, but she is. Kenward seems to think highly of her, though. Says she's Oxbridge material. I hope so, because it's rather embarrassing for me in my position. You can't deny she's eccentric, all that black.'

'Just showing off. A Hamlet phase. The next thing you'll know, she'll be burning her wrists with cigarette ends. Half the girls at St Crumpet's did it. Heavens, it's good not to be a house-mistress any longer. No wonder Veronica is such a cow. It's just a phase, you know, wandering lonely as a cloud and thinking everyone else misunderstands you.'

'Aha-ha. Yes, I take your point. Tell me, do you think Veronica is doing a good job as a housemistress?'

'How should I know?' Poppy asked, brusquely. 'I never have anything to do with the school. Why don't you ask Alice?'

Hart looked at her and sighed.

Alice threw the red dress into a dustbin and resolved to avoid Winthrop when she saw him again. The decision took most of the holidays to reach, and when she made it, she felt a depression as deep as any she had known.

For it had been very agreeable to be kissed. When she remembered what it had felt like – which she did, in elusive snatches, as one might remember a passage of music – everything in her seemed to faint, melt and become changed. She was acutely aware of sensation – and of herself as feeling these sensations – and of finding them foolish and reprehensible. She blushed painfully even when completely alone and unobserved.

She knew that she was acid, unpopular, ugly, and was mysti-fied by Winthrop's apparent attention to her. Again and again, she tried to concentrate on work for the next term, but would sink into a dream. Print dissolved into ripples of thought. The start of Ovid's *Metamorphoses* rang through her mind end-lessly:

> *nulli sua forma manebat,*
> *Obstatque aliis aliud, quia corpore in uno*
> *Frigida pugnabat calidis, umentia siccis,*

Mollia cum duris, sine pondere, habentia pondus.

With her, too, nothing had any lasting shape, but everything got in the way of everything else; cold warring with hot, moist and dry, soft with hard and light with heavy. At night, before she fell asleep, she would stretch out, as if to pull him to her through thousands of miles of empty air. Then she would wake, her groin pulsing like a second heart, convinced he was in bed with her. But there was nothing, nothing except her own foolishness.

She spent the first week of the holidays sorting the Christmas mail in the Minedale post office. She liked the jolly country faces, full of bad teeth and good sense, and had enjoyed being with them in her quiet, dry way. Until this particular Christmas, it had been agreed that the headmaster's sister-in-law was a nice child, not like the rest. This time, she was so aloof, they thought she had become a snob. She knew this, but could not recall the persona she had assumed before. It was like an epileptic fit: terrifying, tempting, inescapable, blissful.

She told herself that all it had been was one mucous membrane against another: *tongues*, how disgusting, how unhygienic, how animal. What was strange was that she always heard her mother's voice saying this in her head. Then this dour Edinburgh voice would be suddenly blotted out on a wave of abandonment, or rebellion, and she would be back inside that moment, the feel of his arms, everything deliquescing. Mush, she heard her mother's ghostly voice say, pure mush. But I *am* mush, she answered. So is everyone. Why do I always have to be clever and cold and hard? Because, her mother replied, work is the only thing you can trust.

He had said, 'I can feel your heart, like a bird.'

'Birds can fly away,' said Alice, embarrassed by this display of sentiment.

'Don't fly away.'

'It's you who is leaving.'

He had said, 'I'll be back.'

'I can't trust you.'

'You don't really feel that, do you?'

'I don't know.' She rested her head on his shoulder, trembling. '*Da mi basia mille, deinde centum/Dein mille altera, dein secunda centum ...*'

'What are you saying?'

Give me a thousand kisses, then a hundred, then a second thousand, then a second hundred. 'Oh, nothing.'

She had seen the ring of ice round the moon. 'Look. A chastity belt.'

He had said, 'But even the moon was landed on by Americans.'

She was afraid that her imagination was embellishing every instance into something as tritely lubricious as the romances floating round the pink candlewick bedspreads of the Dower House, simply because she knew so little about him. Why had she not asked him more? What were his parents like? Where did they live? How did they live? Did he have any brothers and sisters? Why did he have such a peculiar first name? Because of her shrinking from probings about her own family, she had been so cautious as to appear incurious about his, and now she was consumed by curiosity.

She had come back to the Dower House at the last bell, the red dress soaked almost to her waist. Veronica, who was checking everyone off on her perennial clipboard, asked her sarcastically if she had been swimming. Alice had given her a dazed smile. Veronica's eyes narrowed.

'Did you enjoy the dance?'

'I went for a walk.'

'Alone?'

'Yes,' said Alice, truthfully. She realised she should embellish on this, and began to talk about the ring around the moon. This was acceptable Knote behaviour (nature existed to be gushed over) if uncharacteristic for Alice, but Veronica did not bother to cultivate the acquaintance of Rejects.

'Very well,' she said, dismissing her.

Alice had sprinted up the stairs just before lights out, creeping into her dorm to hear Fay droning on about Winthrop. It was clear she had a huge pash on him. The pleasure of hearing his name was infinitely outweighed by considering the circumstances which had led to both of them becoming transfixed by the same person. It was this, as much as anything, that made Alice decide that love amounted to nothing more than self-hypnosis, and that, after a single lapse, she would reject it.

Winthrop lay on a sun lounger and felt all his foggy Anglo-

Saxon worries evaporate and float away. The sea breathed in and out, the white-coated waiters brought long cool drinks tinkling with ice, some long-legged cheerleader types played Frisbee in the sand. This was how real people lived: not pissing around in the mud like mastodons in 3,000 years BC.

If he went back to Knotshead – and Bitsy had told him there was really no choice – this time things would be different. He had made a bad impression, but that could be changed. He could take on an anorexic like Tore any day.

He should have jumped Alice. Looking back, he couldn't figure out why he hadn't. All that tongue sushi had been rather sweet, it was years since he'd just kissed a girl and nothing more. She had been all psyched up for him, too, in her repressed British way. It would be absolutely awful if he had blown it. He was so frustrated, it gave him a hard-on just thinking about her. The cheerleader types on the beach had given him a lot of encouragement, but for once he wasn't interested. It was weird. He dreamt about Alice every night, lagoons of sperm drenching the sheets, and that was when he was asleep. During the day his dick ached so that he almost hated her.

He had not told Mummy about her. She was so pleased he had gotten a good end-of-term report, she had faxed his father and his trustees right there and then to tell them to restore his allowance as a reward. Bunny asked whether he was dating anyone, and seemed relieved when he said no.

'There are some very pretty girls though, Winkie. We saw a photograph of Lady Olivia Paddington in *Vogue* magazine, and she looked just lovely,' said Bitsy.

'Sure, Mummy. If you like public monuments.' He wondered what Bitsy would make of Alice, if she ever met her. Horrified, he guessed. A gold-digger she could handle, but Alice would faze her even more than Bunny's Scottish relatives. Imagine, Mummy meeting someone poor, smart and probably not top drawer. It must be her worst nightmare. That, and finding Bunny in a male assertiveness course.

He thought of the things Alice had said, and laughed aloud, sometimes. He was not only in lust with her, he liked her, even if at times she didn't have both oars in the water. She was so stiff and strange, like the ultimate Puritan WASP, and yet there was this feistiness, too, that wasn't like anything he had come across before, even in New York. He liked the feel of her, the way she seemed so vulnerable without being delicate. Imagine, hitting that psycho Tore on the nose, and living with the consequences . . .

In addition to Alice's other attractions, there was something else to consider. Tore had failed even to get to first base with her. She was the only girl at Knotshead who had stood up to him, and it was obvious that he had been totally jacked out by this. If he, Winthrop, succeeded in his place, Tore's power base as Big Man on Campus would be shaken. However cute Lady Olivia, she was, as any guy could tell, pretty zoned. Alice was . . . original. Bizarre. Darned sexy, although she didn't know it yet. Winthrop dozed off again, listening to the quiet breathing of the sea, imagining her moving beneath him. No, he was coming back. He had to be the lead goose.

15

Three weeks into the spring term, it began to snow. Fat black specks whirled down from the bleached sky. At a certain, indefinite point, they reversed into white. Light as talc, the snow made everything pure and strange. The old buildings on the estate turned from pale sandstone to canary yellow. Willows turned auburn, weeping over invisible waters. Towering whitely and fragilely above the bare treetops the glass dome of the Quad became a pale sea green, then a gigantic half eggshell. The lake froze black. Even the seagulls disappeared. When people looked away from the windows, their eyes swam with moving specks.

The Quad, already darkened, became so slippery with slush that people did not so much walk as skate across its parquet floors to the dining hall. Light became blurred and downy, so that those moving between classes appeared and disappeared unexpectedly into a fuzz like static. Pigeons roosting around the Males' Flats puffed themselves out into feathered spheres. Wodges of newspaper and cardboard were put down before doorways in an attempt to stem the tide, but rapidly disintegrated into a pulp. Fierce, short skirmishes were fought for places next to the radiators; invariably, these were won by the males. The girls blew on their fingerless gloves and talked in loud, disconsolate voices about how sitting on radiators gave people piles.

'Such a lot of fuss about a little snow,' barked Maggie Brink to the 6i Humanities class. 'In China, they'd have cleared the roads long ago.' She scratched herself miserably. Was it her imagination, or was the psoriasis map of Lithuania on her left lung disappearing from the Soviet block?

'Are you aware that according to the *Guinness Book of Records*, Mao Tse Tung was the greatest mass-murderer in the history of mankind, ma'am?' asked Winthrop.

Maggie's eye met those of Karl Marx. How noble that great head looked.

'Oh, pooh,' she said.

In the staff room, Horatio huddled over an extra two-bar electric fire, polishing off bags of leftover Christmas nuts with morose delicacy. The Librarian dosed them both with slices of orange, pondering again whether he should not return the macaw to the Amazon.

'This sort of thing is all very well at first, but if it keeps up we'll be cut off from the rest of Cornwall,' Hew remarked, gingerly warming his fingers on a cup of cocoa.

'Oh, don't be such a killjoy,' said Beatrice Bassett. 'Half the kids here have never seen snow outside a paperweight, thanks to the greenhouse effect.'

'Or the vigilance of Customs and Excise,' murmured Toby Hindesmith.

'I thought the greenhouse effect was supposed to make us warmer, not colder,' said Pedigree Chumley. 'A threat to Life Itself.' He looked longingly at Helge.

'I've never heard anything so ridiculous in my entire life,' said Pug.

'It says in the *Independent* we're at the start of a mini Ice Age,' said Norman Sproggs.

'Let's hope it freezes his fountains of spit,' Toby Hindesmith muttered to Miranda Jupp, who giggled.

'It says in the *Guardian* that that's all a load of tripe,' Mortmain countered. Feelings were still running high between the arts and sciences over the Arab incident, and the Crumps were not speaking to Pug.

'Good Nordic weather,' said Nicholas Crump, humming a bar of 'Die Winterreise' as he shed his duffel coat.

'Oh, for God's sake,' said Hew irritably. He hated lieder.

'I wonder if we'll get snowed in? Rather thrilling, don't you think?' said Chumley shyly to Helge.

'Every single flake is a different shape,' said Delus dreamily. 'Imagine how many million, million crystals fall, and no two ever alike.'

'Like Life Itself.'

'Individually handcrafted by the blind watchmaker, no doubt,' said Norman Sproggs sarcastically. Sally gave him an anxious look.

'Craft: a fool's brains.'

'Quiet, Horatio.'

'That parrot has more intelligence than some people round here,' said Beatrice Bassett.

'Oh? To whom might you be referring?'

Both the Crumps bristled. Beatrice raised her copy of *New Scientist* higher.

Maggie dunked a digestive biscuit in her coffee and sucked noisily.

'Can't even get the lazy little sods to do gym, it's so cold,' said Bruce Whittaker. 'I don't see the point of trying to teach sport in a school like this. I can't wait to go back to Oz.

'Look at it coming down! Like a, mnyah, mnyah, featherbed, wouldn't you say, Helge?'

'Pah! God's dandruff,' said Hew.

'In my country, this is very ordinary,' said Helge.

And still the snow fell through the wild, cold air.

People began to feel ill. One by one, members of the choir disappeared from practice, pleading sore throats. Hew conducted the opening passages of Constant Lambert's 'By the Rio Grande' with streaming eyes and nose. Eventually, as Grub remarked to Tore, it became impossible to tell where the Day-Glo clothes stopped and the nostrils started. Hew retired to his bed to bellow at his mousy wife. By Sunday assembly, half the congregation was coughing and snuffling; by the following week a third of the school had flu.

Alice was one of the first to go down with it. Happiness makes people more resistant to disease; its converse, less. She had clung to her resolve to freeze Winthrop away with all the stubbornness of her nature, but it made her wretched. She would look straight through Winthrop with the calm face of an icon, but her heart felt as if hot steel wires were wound round it. Three times he attempted to come up and talk to her, waiting on the Library steps, but she refused to speak to him. Afraid to even acknowledge his presence, she changed the pattern of her walks, and spent as much time as possible in the Library.

'I feel so rude,' she told Horatio. 'But there isn't anything else I can do.'

'Fool,' said the parrot, disagreeably.

Feverish and miserable, she coughed so much that the Librarian cancelled her lesson and drove her to the Sanatorium, where, for the next two days, she was too ill even to feel sorry for herself.

By the time she was well enough to read, every bed in the San was full up. Holly the nurse tramped round with grim efficiency, making hot drinks and taking temperatures. For most of the year she lived undisturbed with her little daughter, but in epidemics like these she earned her keep.

Thirty pupils and five teachers were affected. Knotes who were immune tramped round to wave through the windows at their friends. Alice watched them, sealed off in the bubble of companionship as effectively as honeymooners in a strange land, and thought that for these, in later life, Knotshead would always be a blissful memory instead of a five-year sentence in which illness was a respite.

Poppy did not visit; she was afraid of giving the twins flu, she said, in a note accompanying a pile of glossy magazines. Alice was surprised, and grateful even to receive these. She lay wrapped in her shawl, coughing and watching the icicles drip daggers of light. One became so long it reached from the guttering to the ground.

She dreamt of her mother, and all the loss and longing that she kept suppressed rose up until the coughs became sobs and the whole of her face poured salt water. O Mama, Mama, Mama. Everything had gone wrong since then. She had kept expecting the grief to go away, like an illness, fighting puberty to the verge of anorexia in the hope of staying a child . Nothing had been the same. At intervals a viscous red liquid, sweet at first and then bitter, was poured down her throat. Later, she would cough up heavy pale green gobs in a paroxysm of disgust.

From time to time, she heard male voices. Sickness was supposed to segregate the sexes in the Sanatorium, with only a corridor between the various dormitories and isolation rooms. Some convalescent girls revelled in this, dawdling to and from ablutions in their prettiest nightgowns and snogging in locked lavatories when Holly was elsewhere. Alice made cautious dashes when need became intolerable and wished they would go away. Whenever she thought of Winthrop she felt worse. If she could get over the flu, she could get over him, as well.

After a week, she felt well enough to sit up. The day after, she had a bath and washed her hair, which had become a disgusting sticky mess of medicine and tangles.

'Should I go?'

'Not yet,' said Holly. 'I want the doctor to have another look at you. I expect you're missing your friends, like all the rest. But if you're bored, you can get up and have tea in the sitting room.'

Wrapped in a blanket, Alice shuffled reluctantly down the corridor and opened the door. Someone was kneeling on the floor toasting crumpets on the gas fire. He turned as Alice came in. They both became very still.

Winthrop smiled at her.

'Have some. They're almost as good as waffles, with chocolate spread.'

'Where did you get them?'

'Holly.' They both began to cough, partly out of embarrassment. 'I paid her, when she went into town. My trustees have given me back my allowance.'

'Oh. Are you rich?'

'In a manner of speaking. They can always take it away again until I come of age. But my eighteenth birthday is in April, so it isn't worth the paperwork.'

He buttered a crumpet, put Nutella on it, and handed it to her. She looked at it doubtfully.

'I'm not infectious any more.'

'I know. Me neither.'

Still she hesitated.

'It's not, like, the forbidden fruit, you know.'

Alice picked up the crumpet and took a small, irritable bite.

'Good?'

'Have you been in here for long?'

Winthrop made an impatient gesture. With a silk scarf round his neck and a long shot-silk dressing gown over his pyjamas, he looked like one of the male models in the glossy magazines Poppy had sent her. Alice wanted to giggle. He is a ridiculous creature, she imagined her mother saying, and tried to hold on to this thought.

'Why have you been avoiding me?'

'I'd have thought it was obvious.'

'Perhaps I'm really dumb, but it isn't obvious to me at all.'

'I like your dressing gown,' she said politely. 'Where did you get it?'

'Sulka's. Don't change the subject. Tell me. You aren't like the others.'

There was a painful pause. I suppose, thought Alice, the first thing you lose is your sense of humour.

She said, 'It's because I'm not like the others that I decided . . . we're both . . . ' She went bright red. 'Whatever.'

'"Whatever"? Why don't you say it?'

'Oh, for God's sake, I'm only sixteen, I'm not ready for all this,' she said, wretchedly. 'Where would it lead? What's the point?'

'What's the point? What's the point of anything, if you think like that? What's the point of eating, if it's going to end up as a turd in the john?' Winthrop was pale with emotion, part of it surprise that he should still have to try so hard. He suddenly looked all rabbit. 'You know what your problem is? You don't know the meaning of *carpe diem.*'

'Yes, I do,' she said, stung. '"*Carpe diem, quam minimum credula postero.*"'

'It means, "Enjoy life now."' He had heard it in a movie, *Dead Poets' Society.*

'Actually,' said Alice, 'it's from Horace's *Odes*, and it means, 'Seize the present, for tomorrow is not to be trusted.' That's what I worry about, you see. The next day, and the one after that. And so on.'

Winthrop stared at her, his eyes glittering with fury, then began to laugh.

'Oh, Alice,' he said. 'You are so British, and so pedantic, it's hilarious.'

'I meant to be.'

'Come on, lighten up, sit down. Have another crumpet.'

'A crumpet,' said Alice, blowing her nose, 'is a very light woman indeed. Ugh!'

'Do you still feel bad?'

'Frightful.'

'Me too,' Winthrop lied. The Masonic grip of flu, he thought. 'Everything hurts, even after a bath.'

'Where? Here? Or here?'

He put his hands on her shoulders, and kneaded them through the nightdress. She started and shrank away.

'Your muscles feel like stones. Relax. Don't you trust me?'

'No.'

Winthrop laughed. That was progress, to make her admit it. 'Oh, come on! Don't tense when you cough. Relax. Relax.'

'Do, do stop saying that,' she said irritably. 'I can't relax. I'm not a relaxed person. The next thing you'll say is, "You're going to be OK." That's what they always say on television just before someone snuffs it.'

'You're going to be OK,' said Winthrop, in a droning voice.

They both laughed. He put his hands under her breasts, suddenly, as if catching them.

Alice froze. 'Don't.'

'Why not?'

'You know why not.' Her voice came out in a croak. She put up her hands to take his away, and fell back against him. This is worse than the flu, she thought; much. 'Don't.'

He took no notice. It was all part of the game: the girl tried to play goalie, and you had to get past her to score. She put up a good defence, but really she wanted the same as you did. There was no hiding place for lust. Her nipples were like rivets. Really, he thought, it was just like making out anywhere back home: sofa, fire, the possibility of being interrupted by irate authority. His last lay – the school teacher – had been so uninhibited that he had forgotten what a bizarre business it could be to reel in the biscuit. If she so much as brushed against him he would burst.

'Oh, Alice, honey.'

'Please, please, don't.'

He put a hand on her chin and turned her head as easily as a doll's. Her eyes had become huge. He almost felt sorry for her, but then he was also fed up with unrequited lust. Oh, she felt good, fragile and strong at the same time. What a drag his sinuses were . . . He should have done this weeks ago. His hand inched up her inner leg. In a moment he'd have her begging for it . . . A slurp of slippers outside the door. Alice dragged her mouth away from his so violently there was a popping noise in his head. Hell, it was that dork Grub.

*

Grub loved the snow. It reminded him of icing sugar, turning everything outside into celestial confectionery. Wrapped in his big wine-coloured Christmas muffler, he had capered about in an ecstasy of high spirits.

'If this cold goes on, we won't have to do any more lessons, by law!'

'We could just leave you out there, and in ten minutes you'd make a great Michelin snowman,' said Tore. Greatly taken with this idea, they chased Grub in and out of the trees, laughing hysterically, until they caught him and thrust a mouthful of snow down his throat.

'Ow, bog off!' said Grub, putting handfuls of pine needles down the back of Sparks's collar.

'Har, har, har,' the Westler brothers laughed, shaking their heads like bears.

The Lads jostled clods of snow off the trees, kicking the trunks in the orchard. The clods turned to powder as they fell, creating miniature blizzards. Smaller males darted about, moulding snowballs, which they threw at the girls. The girls ran, shrieking, down the icy paths to and from lessons. Most of the balls were so soft they fell apart in mid-air, but those thrown by Tore could draw blood, for they had stones in.

The slope below the main house down to the lake rang with muted shrieks and laughter. Despite Veronica's best efforts, everyone stole trays from the dining hall and used them as toboggans. Whooshing down, they looked like Liquorice All-sorts from a distance. The Librarian glided past on langlaufing skis with Horatio buttoned inside his Crombie. Sally Rupple dug out a pair of skates and did some quick figures of eight. Everyone who escaped the flu had a wonderful time.

Unfortunately for Grub, he was not one of this number. Two days after the snow began, he felt the ominous buzzing head-ache and sore throat. Greatly to his disgust, he found himself occupying the last empty bed in the San.

At first he had hoped he would be joined by Tore or one of the other Lads. It felt, odd, being on his own in termtime. He couldn't play the piano, he found reading a great effort even at the best of times and, worst of all, the flu killed his sense of taste and smell. He lay in bed and for once did not enjoy it, although his exhaustion was so profound it was a relief not to have to do anything.

Despite inertia, he was no longer as fat as he had been the year before. Instead he was growing by what seemed to be an inch a month.

'You're going to wind up just like those tomcat brothers of yours,' Holly remarked, taking his temperature. 'They were just the same. One day they were blobby little kids and the next they were in and out of the Dower House like nobody's business. Jewish, aren't you?'

'Mmm,' said Grub.

She gave a surprising chuckle. 'Always best at it.'

Grub blushed. It was strange to think of his two brothers ever having been anything other than incredibly handsome and wildly successful with girls; at Oxford, *Cherwell* said Josh was 'worth paying for'. He wondered when he would ever know what it was like. It was all so easy in dreams – the seraglio of smiling girls, the effortless parting of clothes, the utter self-confidence. Waking, he knew the smiles to be mocking, the clothes intractable, the confidence delusory. He was stuck inside his mess of a body: fat, red-haired, left-handed, bespectacled, half-Jewish – it was a bad joke. How could anyone like him possibly have a normal love life?

A dozen times a day, he would be overwhelmed with such frustration he thought he would impale anything, even a goat on the estate, to be rid of it. It was like the B Minor, so calm and sane for a few bars and then darker and darker, until lust would seethe through him like a disease, those shivering semiquavers like sperm shooting out between his fingers, followed by such blank weariness that it seemed impossible he should climb out of it, smile, joke, perform. Yet again and again, he did. He even managed to persuade himself that he was nothing more than a clown most of the time. But then the depression would grow in him again, his soul seemed unable to bounce back and stay there. It was a torment which repeated itself like the B Minor – soaring self-confidence tipping over into utter despair, absurd melodrama and real agony, all hopelessly intertwined.

Where was the legato, the connecting thread that would make him able to control it? he thought, coughing and coughing. His head swam with flu and confusion. The mechanics of pianism was one thing, any idiot could grind that out up to a point, like Fay. He thought of Glenn Gould, singing along as he played. Music was something you had to feel, you couldn't sit still like those stuffed shirts in a concert, it was meant to go through you and make you want to dance and cry and shout. But to get behind those swarms of black dots on the sheet and find the music pulsing behind each note, like a beautiful, beating heart, like the tender face of his mother, like the vague voluptuous shape of his desires – that was what took everything, everything and more.

One night, he sweated so much that it went all the way through the mattress; and after that the worst was over. Two days later, he was definitely better. Progress, he thought, was something one was not aware of until one could examine it with hindsight. The difficulty was, one progressed in different bits of oneself, and never as a whole being.

He could smell crumpets along the corridor. He got up, and followed his nose.

16

The moment Grub blundered into the sitting room, Alice fled. Winthrop, in literal agonies of frustration, would have hit him had he not been doubled over.

Grub did not even register Winthrop's presence. The shock of having Alice brush past him in a wave of soap, chocolate and confusion had rendered him speechless. His mind became completely blank, spinning round like a top he had once had, which let out a single humming note when pumped to a blur of motion. That note had stayed with him all his life, forming the key to his perfect pitch, but he was barely conscious of it except in moments of crisis. He had heard it when his mother had told him she and his father were getting divorced; he had heard it once with Tore; and he heard it again now.

'Er . . .' he said, agape. His red hair stood up in spikes. He looked exceptionally stupid. Winthrop began to cough in a paroxysm of rage. Grub's eye fell upon the box of crumpets and the chocolate spread. The dizzy sensation subsided. This, at least, was familiar. 'Oh, brill! Can I have one?'

'Take them all. I hope you choke,' said Winthrop savagely. His lips had gone white. The last time he experienced blue balls like this, he had been thirteen. If I don't have her, he thought, it's going to seriously kill me.

Grub looked at him. 'Did she kick you? he asked, with interest.

'No.'

'Oh. She can be quite an Amazon, you know.' A month ago,

Grub would have said this in quite a different tone. Now, he felt an inclination to laugh.

Winthrop glared. 'I know. We were getting along just fine.'

'What?'

Grub's voice died away as he realised what this meant. Vistas of jealousy opened up beneath his feet.

'You're such an asshole,' said Winthrop, his anger boiling over. 'Haven't you got anything better to do but hang around stuffing your face and treating Tore like he was God instead of some pop singer's kid? Yes, sir, no sir, three bags full, sir. Why don't you wise up and start acting like you were an adult instead of something barely out of diapers?'

He went to the door, flung it open, and disappeared in a swirl of Sulka silk.

Grub stared after him, his open mouth smeared with chocolate.

'Crumbs,' he said.

And still, the snow fell.

Alice was lying in bed, half-asleep, when the door opened. She gave a sigh and turned her face into the pillow, pretending to sleep. She had been crying again. Her misery bored her even more than the flu, but was as difficult to throw off. It seemed to go on quite independently of any rational process.

The figure came to her bed, but instead of moving away again, stayed there. It breathed in a snuffly way. Not Holly, then. It touched her cheek.

'Alice?'

'What on earth are you doing here?' she whispered, sitting bolt upright. 'Winthrop?'

'Shh. Don't be mad at me.' He began to shiver. 'I'm so cold.'

'Do you want . . . ?' She meant to say, a blanket.

'I must – I must – If I could just . . . Oh, Alice, I'm so lonely.'

So saying, Winthrop lifted up the sheet and got into bed beside her. The calmness with which he did this made it seem perfectly sensible. In any case, if she made a fuss, Holly would come and find them. There was very little space unless they both lay on their sides, and she had to put her arms round him to stop him falling out on to the floor. He was indeed cold, but she trembled as if she were the colder.

At first they were both still. She could smell the toothpaste on his breath. Little by little, warmth crept back. It was not, after all, so very strange a sensation; quite comforting, like having a teddy bear, Alice thought vaguely. She had had a teddy in Ayrshire, but Mama had thrown him away when they moved to Edinburgh. She had missed him terribly. Winthrop began to move, very slowly, stroking her as if calming a horse.

'I have to do this,' he said, almost inaudibly. As she made no resistance, he became bolder. 'Don't be frightened.'

Alice was suddenly consumed by fury.

'I'm not frightened, nothing frightens me,' she hissed. 'For God's sake, stop fiddling about and making such a fuss! Just do whatever you came here to do. Then we can both stop thinking about it all the time.'

She sat up and threw her nightdress off with a single movement before shooting back down under the sheet. She was shaking with fright. Her skin crawled and burnt as if the fever had come back. Winthrop laughed, and abandoned the veterinarian approach.

'Oh, Alice! You haven't done this before, have you?'

'Of course not,' said Alice gloomily, 'but I've read *all* about it. There's really nothing I don't know, in theory, if not in practice.'

Winthrop laughed again. 'Alice?'

'Yes?'

'This isn't some sort of power struggle. Stop thinking.'

'But I am thought. There isn't anything else.'

'Yes, there is. Here. And here. And here. That is you.'

Silence. Then she whispered, 'But bodies are such miserable, treacherous, slippery things. It's like being attached to some sort of moron all the time ... Oh, God. Is that the normal size?'

'Quite normal.'

'It's *huge*.'

'Think how much bigger a baby's head is.'

'What if you get stuck?'

'Every guy's worst nightmare. We'd have to be surgically parted.'

'Really?'

'No, just kidding.' Every time he managed to distract her, she relaxed a little.

'It hurts.'

'Alice, what are the five great pleasures in life?'

'What?' She considered. 'I don't know. Reading. Mozart. Privacy. Chocolate. I haven't thought.'

'You can't think about them. They are: sleeping when you're tired, drinking when you're thirsty, eating when you're hungry, pissing when you're full and fucking any time you can.'

'What about banging your head against a brick wall?'

'What?'

'It feels so wonderful when you stop. This really is hurting terribly . . . '

'It's never good, the first time. Even when you've done it before.'

'Does it hurt you, as well?'

'Hell,' said Winthrop, 'I can stand the pain. It's the pleasure that's hard to take.'

'I suppose that's true, about pleasure, at a very basic, animal level, but . . .'

'People are at a very basic, animal level. Everything that's OK about human beings is animal.'

'You don't suddenly abandon everything that you are just because . . . '

'Yes?'

'Just because . . . Oh . . . '

'Alice?'

'Yes?'

'Don't think, now. The bad part is over. Feel.'

'Yes,' said Alice. 'Yes.'

By morning, the snow stopped. Beneath a neon sky, everything was covered with pillows and billows of white, a vast and virginal expanse. Roofs and branches were gilded with sharp silver, fine and blinding. Long flutes of ice hung from the guttering, tinkling as fragments broke off.

'You have a visitor,' Holly said, coming in with fresh sheets.

'Who is it?' she asked.

'Mr Kenward.'

'Oh.' She had resolved to hope for nothing where Winthrop was concerned, but found it hard to suppress disappointment.

'I'll let him in, shall I? You're quite decent.'

Alice nodded.

She felt a quite unreasonable dread of seeing the old man, at the same time as feeling his kindness very keenly. When he came in with Horatio, a bag of clementines and a hyacinth in flower, her eyes pricked with tears. He regarded her beneath bristling brows.

'So. When are you going to be well enough for Ovid again?'

'I don't know. Soon.'

'The judgement of Tiresias awaits your perusal.'

Alice pleated the new sheet between her long thin fingers, and would not meet his eyes.

'Tell me what is wrong.'

She looked at him, then away again. She could feel the blood and semen still trickling out on to a sanitary towel: she had told Holly she had the curse. 'Mr Kenward, were you ever in love with someone?'

'Love: insanity,' said Horatio, who had crawled up on the Librarian's shoulder and was nibbling his ear.

'Of course.'

'What was the point of it?'

'There is no point.'

'Oh.'

'Unless you take the purely natural end of procreation as such.'

'So it's completely silly and useless?'

'Not at all. Art has no point, either, if you like. Of course, people are always trying to give it a moral value, claiming that it ennobles or informs. That's nonsense, in my opinion. Of course, it may do both those things, quite incidentally, as a sort of by-product. But really they are both about the same, utterly useless thing.'

'What's that?'

'Enchantment,' said the Librarian.

Horatio whistled.

'But enchantment isn't always a good thing, is it? I mean, practically everyone in the *Metamorphoses* gets enchanted because they're miserable, or helpless, or being punished.'

'Some of them change because they are brought to life, though. Like the stones which grew into men, after the first flood, or the dragon's teeth which became Thebans. Not all transformation is bad. Ovid says that without it, harmony would never be brought from chaos.

'Think how many metamorphoses go on even before we are born, the way we encapsulate every stage of evolution, from amoeba to fish to mammal. Yet this is nothing to the changes occurring in your spirit or personality. You yourself are going through that most fascinating of all metamorphoses, from child into young woman. A whole future will or will not be possible for you, according to what is happening now. It's a frightening business, but you shouldn't be afraid of it.'

'But you said that we each had to choose what we became.'

'Yes. But metamorphosis is going to happen if you want it to or not. What is in your power to decide is if you turn into a reed or a stone or a woman. Metaphorically speaking, that is. Your inside can change much more that your outside appearance.'

The Librarian sounded so serious, Alice could not suppress a smile.

'I think far too much about myself as it is. It's my worst fault, I think. I hope.'

'Why shouldn't you?'

'Well, all egoism is bad, isn't it? And boring for other people?'

'It may be dull for other people if you drone on about it, but it's worse for you if you blunder along without self-scrutiny, believe me. People, adults, criticise adolescents for being self-obsessed – often, I suspect, because they are ashamed they didn't make a better job of themselves while they had the chance. You have every right to think a great deal about who and what you are during this particular period of your life. Indeed, it is quite essential that you should do so.'

'Mr Kenward, do you still wonder who you are, or do you know by now?'

The Librarian looked at her with his sharp old eyes.

'There are some questions which should not be answered,' he said; but whether he was talking of her, or himself, Alice could not tell.

At teatime, Alice had another visitor. Whenever the door of her sickroom opened, she looked away, afraid of showing either hope or disappointment. Her senses were so stretched, she knew at once it was not Winthrop, and yet she willed it to be so despite the lighter step and the wave of Poppy's perfume.

'How are you? Holly says your fever is down.'

'Down but not out. It's kind of you to come. Are the twins all right?'

'Fine.' Poppy looked tired and strained, but she smiled as she spoke.

'You do like them. Children, I mean.'

Poppy gave Alice a long look. 'How much did Mama tell you about me?' she asked suddenly. 'All those years when you were in Edinburgh, what did she say?'

Alice shifted uncomfortably. 'Only that you had run away to London and not come back.'

'I must have been exactly your age, you know? What a long time ago it seems now, the era of flower power. Everything was so exciting. Sex and drugs and rock and roll. I suppose I had too much of all three.'

Poppy paused.

'Did she tell you I was on smack?'

'You were what?'

'Smack. You know, H-E-R-O-I-N.'

'Oh. No. No, I had no idea at all.'

'Well,' said Poppy. 'I was. Horror of horrors! New Town must never know! I suppose that's why she didn't tell you.'

'I see.' Alice didn't know what to say. She was embarrassed, curious, but not particularly sorry for her sister. Poppy did not, somehow, invite sympathy. She was too poised for that.

'It was really quite an ordinary thing, for my generation. A bit like a war, except that what started out as a war against other people's values turned out to kill us instead. I suppose most wars do.'

'How long were you addicted?'

'I still am. Oh, I don't mean I shoot up. But it's something you never get over. I took it for three years, if that's what you mean.'

'How did you stop?'

Poppy shrugged, and said in her bored, charming voice, 'The usual. Things happened which made me want to stop enough, and I went to a clinic.'

'Oh.' Alice felt slightly dizzy, trying to take all this new information in.

'How beautifully Mama brought you up! If only she'd succeeded with me. The perfect Edinburgh gentlewoman, so polite. I do admire it. You don't know what to say, do you?'

'No,' said Alice quietly. 'Not really. I'm sorry if you suffered.' She closed her eyes, feeling dreadful.

'Does Simon know?'

'Oh yes, some of it. As a matter of fact,' said Poppy, 'he found it a real turn-on when I told him. Like most Englishmen, he puts women on a pedestal unless they've been down in the shit. I told him some of the things I'd done to pay for a fix. And even so, it took a heatwave and a trip to the naturist beach in Brighton to get him cranked up. He's quite weird, in his own way.'

Alice felt a wave of distaste pass through her. This was repulsively crude of Poppy. Often, listening to the conversation in dormitories she had thought that the reason girls were so frightened of male indiscretion was their own betrayals of privacy. The idea of other people ever knowing about her and Winthrop made her shrink inside herself.

'Why are you telling me this?'

'Because it may –' Poppy stopped and shrugged. 'I thought you ought to know. You're old enough to know a few secrets.'

'I see.'

'It's not so very unusual, believe me.' Poppy seemed very insistent.

'No, I suppose not.'

'I'm one of the lucky ones.'

'Yes,' said Alice, politely, 'I suppose you are.'

They sat in silence. Blessed pair of sirens, Alice thought, over and over. The need to see Winthrop again paralysed her like a mild poison.

'Well, now,' said Holly, coming in. 'Had a nice visit, have we? I'm afraid visiting time is up, now. Your little sister'll be back on her feet tomorrow, I expect, Mrs Hart.'

Poppy left, and so, after bringing round the supper trolley, did Holly. With an effort Alice ate and bathed. A sensation of complete emptiness filled her as she lay in the dark. The patter of feet on lino and the roar of water from taps ceased. A few other patients coughed in other rooms. She could hear the wind whistling through the ill-fitting window panes, and the creak of the nylon stuffing in her pillow. When Winthrop came to her room again, she said nothing; and this time, there was no need.

17

Fay was in love with Winthrop. There was no way of remaining ignorant of this information, for she broadcast it before and after the Christmas holidays to everyone but her parents. To them, when asked how her first term had gone, she lied that she was blissfully happy; had she said anything else, they would have taken her away, and then she would not have seen him again. Parents had to be protected from the truth, that was obvious. They might have had just as much persecution in their own schooldays, but time and the acquisition of more civilised manners had clearly erased it from memory. Nobody told parents what they really felt about school.

She had returned from the Christmas holidays full of resolute calculation. Fay was not one who willingly stood out from the crowd: on the contrary, she wished to adapt, survive and rise in the world. She wanted to be in with Olivia and the Lads, not to mope about with Alice, Crater Face or any of the other Rejects. In order to rise, she had to become sexy.

There were other ways to rise in the school, but they took far too long, and were, in any case, run by the usual cliques. Acting, journalism, photography, even playing in the school orchestra – these were uncertain routes to social acceptability, compared to sex. It was the same the whole world over, Fay thought, looking pensively at her poster of Madonna. If you were a girl, you could survive on one of three menu options, on your looks, on your wits, or on your back.

She perceived that any claims to sexiness were politically useless as long as she stuck to her boyfriend in London. What was necessary was to go out with another Knote. The ideal – for a Reject girl to be fancied by a Jet-Set male – was as improbable as the story of King Cophetua and the Beggar Maid, so had to be firmly discounted, but she had observed that even two Rejects who went together were automatically upgraded to a higher status.

Winthrop was by far the most attractive option. Rich, handsome, moderately bright, he was, as it were, a commodity undervalued by poor self-presentation. With different clothes and different manners they could both rise to at least Semi-Groover status, thought Fay, trudging round the sales. Already she had thrown out her sequinned sweaters for Fair Isle and replaced her jeans with trendy Joseph leggings. If only he would do the same!

Her campaign to attract his attention had been moderately successful, although the flu epidemic had meant the loss of some time. She contrived to sit opposite to him most mealtimes, and tried to engage him on the Gulf crisis. When this failed to work, she had offered him some of her pot of Marmite for breakfast. Unfortunately, he seemed not to like it much. Just before St Valentine's Day, she had walked all the way to Minedale to buy him a card. She had even considered visiting him in the San, in the manner of Florence Nightingale – didn't patients often fall in love with their nurses? – but at this, her nerve failed her.

Her actions had been observed, if not by Winthrop, then by the other girls in Block 6i, for no flicker of interest in the rates of exchange between the opposite sex went unremarked. As a result, Fay's status remained very much the same, but Winthrop's began, almost imperceptibly, to rise. Even if his mother did ring Simon Hart every day to make sure her darling had not been blown up by Iraqi terrorists, he was definitely looking more like a Knote and less like an American.

Grub, Alice and Winthrop were released from the San at lunchtime on the same day. A thaw had set in, and icicles were falling with a mushy crash from the eaves. The sky, parchment-coloured for days, turned blue as a thrush's egg. The river had burst its banks, turning the lower cricket field into a part of the lake. Two or three goats, marooned from the herd, bleated distressfully, but the rest were too heavily pregnant to care. All along the path from the San to the main house, spines of daffodils had suddenly appeared. They passed a flotilla of blue and yellow buds ballooning out of the cropped grass.

'Are those actually flowers growing in the dirt?' asked Winthrop.

'Crocus. Don't you have them in America?'

'I don't know. Hell, I guess I never noticed.'

Grub, trailing up the path behind them, snuffled and wondered what the penalty would be if he were to take a rock and bash Winthrop's perfectly formed head in. He had never felt so fat, angry and depressed.

It was obvious – painfully so – that Superbrat had got off with Alice. He kept touching her, and she was wearing that manky silk scarf of his round her neck. They both kept laughing for no apparent reason, completely oblivious to Grub. Winthrop was staggering along, bow-legged as a Mafia don, pretending to try and trip her up in order to rub his bulging dick against her, and Alice, unbelievably, was quite happy for this disgraceful exhibitionism to continue. Grub had always thought her frighteningly intelligent, so why was she suddenly behaving like a twerp? What did Winthrop know of the Sonata in B Minor? What did Alice see in him?

His mind rang with jealousy. For the first time, he understood why people could believe that opera could be real and serious, that you could sing in a moment of crisis because mere words would buckle under the weight of feeling. And yet, in real life, he was struck dumb. He could not say two words to either of them, let alone sing.

Too late, too late! he thought, kicking each puddle in the tarmac behind them with a convulsive fury. He had been completely deaf and blind, swaddled in assumptions – Tore's assumptions. This was the bitterest thing of all. However much he despised Winthrop, saw him as facile, vulgar, stupid in the worst kind of way, he had perceived Alice first. And Alice, Grub suddenly saw, with one of those painful flashes of insight which are never any use, had been longing to have someone on her side, just as he had done in his first year before Tore took him up. If he had had the courage to befriend her then, it could have been he who walked and talked so, now. He had only himself to blame.

Leigh Hunt roared past them in the tractor with a blast of his horn and a clattering of shovels. If he had missed tobogganing while in the San, he had also missed clearing the drive for Outdoor Work, thought Grub, trying to find something to cheer himself with. He was always afraid he would damage his hands doing manual work in winter, but the prospect of jogging was too uncomfortable an alternative.

As they approached the main house, Grub saw Alice move away from Winthrop's encircling arm, saying something in a low voice. At once, he understood. She wanted to be discreet. Winthrop's loud laugh confirmed this. He untied his scarf from Alice's throat, and put it in his pocket. They went into the main house, and across the Quad to join a few late stragglers in the self-service queue. Grub was so anxious to keep up that his plate and glass slid all over his tray, slopping water and gravy on to the floor. He slipped, fell and sent his tray flying. By the time he had collected his wits, and a second lunch, Alice and Winthrop had each gone through into the dining hall, and were looking for somewhere to sit.

Their entrance had not gone unremarked. From where they stood, a silence was rippling out like rings from a dropped stone. Grub saw Alice tense, and Winthrop step closer to her. Then, one by one, the males began to whistle and clap and stamp their feet.

'Whe-hey, nice one, Win!' called one of the younger Lads.

'Right on!'

'Yo, man!'

Alice's tray shook.

'What is it? Winthrop, *how do they know?*'

'Sweetheart, it's obvious,' he said.

She turned round, blindly, and faced Grub. It was indeed quite obvious. Across her neck was a circle of large purple blotches, which had previously been concealed by the scarf, but which anyone who knew anything recognised, could only have been made by Winthrop's large white teeth – without their retainers.

The season of goodwill had not lessened the antagonism between the pro- and anti-Arab camps. On one side, the Crumps, supported by both sports teachers, Pug, Miranda, Norman Sproggs, Kit Ricks and Beatrice Bassett remained adamant that Mrs Crump could have seen Hussein and not Naimh boarding the Intercity. On the other, Maggie Brink, Mortmain, Hew and Delus insisted that – despite the disparity of height – the similarity of jackets, the monitor's tick beside Hussein's name in the lights-out check list and the unswerving denials of both boys cast sufficient doubt on Mrs Crump's testimony. So deep did feeling run that by now the entire staff room had been forced to side with one or the other, with only Hindesmith and the Librarian staying out of it: one because he preferred to be equally spiteful to both, the other because he wished to be equally charitable. The Slythes also remained aloof.

Between these two camps and the Males' Flats rushed Pedigree Chumley with the eager incompetence of a nervous collie. Hardly a day passed when he did not come into the dorms to ask either Naimh or Hussein if they were absolutely sure there could have been no mistake.

'No! No! I swear it on my mother's grave!' Hussein insisted with tears in his large brown eyes.

'I thought your mother lived in Paris,' said Chumley.

'Did I say mother? I mean my father, who died in the Lebanon,' said Hussein.

'Ah, fucking Arabs! They get confused about family,' said Tore, creaking through the door in his black leathers. 'Too many bombs, Pedigree, you know? Too many bombs.'

'Ah, yes, yes, quite. A tragic country,' said Chumley. 'It's just so awkward for the staff, you see. Nick Crump feels very strongly that his wife's word of honour is being questioned.'

Tore and two Arabs stared at him with unblinking earnestness.

'I wish we could help, man,' said Naimh. 'I most truly wish we could.'

'Ah, yes. It's all so muddling. Like Life Itself, I suppose,' said Chumley. He went out, sadly, thinking of Helge.

As soon as Chumley left, they all collapsed into snorts of laughter.

'Cost you a Chinko.'

'Thanks, man.'

'I mean, tonight.'

'Sure, sure.' Hussein picked up his portable telephone and switched it on.

'What d'you fancy, Grub? Duck pancakes? Spicy fried seaweed? Sweet and sour pork?'

'I don't mind,' said Grub listlessly.

'Ah, for fuck's sake, you can't still be down with the flu!'

'Sorry.'

Tore shrugged, and stood over Hussein as he dialled the Chinese restaurant in Knotsmouth.

This accomplished, the Arabs rang off, and wandered down to the Quad to eye up any girls hanging around. Grub wondered why the taste of grief was so like stale cheese and onion crisps. He had completely lost interest in food, and even found the grinning teeth of the piano induced a violent wish to smash it up.

What did it matter whether he got the B Minor right or not? Who except he would ever care? What was the point? He would never be recorded playing it, the examiner would listen to him once, and even Hew would hear only the faults.

'Try to get more control, boyo,' Hew had told him at the start of the term. 'Nobody plays like Horowitz any longer.'

'But that's all fashion. When Beethoven played his pieces, he stompfed up his pianos, bits of wood flying about all over the place. He didn't mean them to be played as Pollini does.'

'He was deaf. And didn't have more than a primitive piano-forte. You do. It's like talent. It's not enough to have the fantastic range – ' here Hew played two chords, one pianissimo and one triple forte – 'you have to learn to control it.'

Oh, God, control! It was so boring, people only noticed you had it when you lost it. Why did he put himself through this monotony of misery, this trapeze act over the abyss, when it would all be gone, gone, as soon as the notes had left his fingers? Nobody would know the dreadful, wrenching effort with which each phrase was dragged up out of him. And if they did, why the fuck should they care? People hated you if you had talent. Even if you shut up about it, they thought it was unfair, as if it were some undeserved gift that made everything magically easy, not a great bruise that spread over everything, and then made you scared that you didn't have enough of it.

That was what he liked about Tore. They shared the psychotic quality of – whatever it was that made him a musician. Tore was an outsider, too, albeit of a different kind.

'Christ, this is so fucking boring,' said Tore. 'You slothing about like a dollop of lard, Pedigree popping in and out all the time, nothing in the papers about Poppy fucking Fart. Where's

Superbrat?

'With Alice, I expect.' He could no longer bear to call her by that silly nickname.

'God, what a slag!' Tore began to kick the leg of Winthrop's bed with concentrated fury. 'I'm going to get Sparks to wire his bed up at night, all right. See how he gets off on a few hundred volts when we switch it on, eh?'

'Oh, shit. Why bother? What's the point?'

Grub got up and went to the window, looking down at the lake. It reflected a scene of exquisite beauty. Clouds slid across the blue bowl of a spring afternoon, coagulating into creamy peaks of whipped white. Far away at the end of the peninsula the milky domes of the Temple of Venus shone like two breasts. Sheep and goats grazed, lamenting, with their new born young. Delivering these in the barn, hands slippery with lanolin and hot blood, was usually one of the highlights of Outdoor Work. It always made the Lads laugh, the way the ewes were so stupid they would gallop to the feeding trough in the middle of their labour. But this year he had seen the ewes' slobbering orifices with a sick horror. The cunts in skin mags always looked so clean and plump, like old roses, but when you saw sheep, you knew that was the real thing, just slime and ugliness.

Everywhere he looked, some blinking bird was getting its end away. It was quite incredible. Even the fat black flies on the windowsill were at it. Furious, Grub raised his copy of *Viz* and splatted them dead.

'Fucking awful, nature, isn't it?' said Tore beside him in his Darth Vader voice. 'Nature fucking.'

Oh, Alice, Alice, thought Grub.

'Or is it just a hand job? We should ask Mortmain.'

'It pisses me off, the way he's swaggering about massaging his cock, with that big grin on his face.'

'Who, Mortmain?'

'Don't be fucking stupid. Superbrat.'

'Oh, him,' said Grub, as if he had been thinking of anyone else.

'He's got a giant stonker on him *all the time*.' Tore began to laugh, in his high, hysterical screech. 'It's fucking unbelievable.'

'Don't we all?'

'Yeah, but I mean ... What is she *doing* to him?'

'Perhaps she isn't,' said Grub hopefully, pushing his spectacles up his nose.

'Oh, come off it, stupid! Of course she is. You've only got to look at her, she can hardly walk, he's shafting her so often. When I think of the way the little slag behaved before, I – '

'Yes?'

'I should have fucking well raped her before,' said Tore. 'It makes me look so soft, doesn't it? Authority has no power without recognition. Even Olivia fancies him.'

'She's just having you on.'

'No, I think she means it.'

He began to stab at the soft wood in the window frame with his knife. There was an electric heaviness about him, like the air before a storm. Grub knew him in these moods and was frightened of him, but was too depressed to say anything.

Sparks Delus put his head round the door.

'I got half a gram of coke, Jono. Can Jas and I come to the Chinko tonight?'

Tore brightened and began to negotiate, when the telephone on Hussein's locker rang. The Lads looked at each other.

'Dare?'

'Yeah.'

Tore picked it up, and said, 'Hallo, Saddam Hussein speaking.'

Sparks and Grub began to laugh.

Tore covered the mouthpiece and said, 'Shaddup, it's his bank manager. Yeah. A bounced cheque? At Tramps?'

The voice quacked on.

'How should I know?'

The voice on the other end became very agitated.

'Listen, you old git,' said Tore, trying not to give himself away although the other two were by now snorting against their arms with tears running down their faces. 'Why don't you take it and stuff it up your arse?'

He rang off. They all rolled on the floor, howling.

'Oh, Christ!' said Tore. 'I can't wait to see what his bank manager'll do.'

'I wonder why it bounced,' said Sparks.

'Ah, those Arabs, they talk big but they're always having cash-flow problems,' said Tore.

The bell for afternoon lessons clanged. Grub mumbled that he had to practise, and went out.

At this time of day, the music rooms were usually sufficiently deserted for him to stand a chance of practising on the only semi-decent piano there, the American Steinway. Grub was suspicious of Steinways; their glassy brilliance of tone never sounded quite right, particularly playing anything earlier than Beethoven. If you were really good, you had your own specially customised; Grub's hero, Glenn Gould, had got Steinway to gut a piano so that it sounded like an 1895 Chickering he had once heard in Boston, and nobody else, famously, could play Horowitz's bucking bronco. But at Knotshead it was a good day if you even got hold of a Broadwood.

The usual discordant taps and squeals of different instruments being played seeped from the Tower of Babel. A parttime music teacher, one of the many losers hanging round the school, was playing Britten's 'Young Person's Guide to the Orchestra', a piece which must have made more young people hate classical music than any other, in Grub's opinion. A good Block 3 fiddle near the entrance was being taught by the violin teacher, whose career had been ruined by a massive 52-inch bust like balloons filled with water. Jean-Paul was thundering out the 'Appassionata' on the Steinway, probably after another long-distance row with his alcoholic father on the Cayman Islands. Grub sighed. Someone was playing Schumann's sickly 'Scenes from Childhood' in the Broadwood room. Grub's spirits rose as he saw Fay. Here was someone he could easily get rid of. She stopped as soon as he came in. He stood there, grinning and leering, until her nerve broke.

'Bog off.'

'Bog off yourself.'

Her monkey face contorted. 'Why can't you ever treat me like a human being?'

Grub said, 'You don't go to boarding schools to have people to be nice to you. You go to them to learn to see people as they really are.'

Fay glared and looked mutinous, turning back to the piano. She was obviously not going to budge.

Accidie overwhelmed him like a wave. He shrugged, slammed the door and mooched back through Flottage. Through the window of the physics lab, he could hear the scrannel voice of Norman Sproggs demonstrating the law of motion with a stroboscopic light. As always during such lessons, there was a constant ripple of giggles because Sproggs showered his audience with spit, so that fifty fascinated eyes watched the saliva dive back into his mouth. In another prefab classroom, Pug was seated like a Buddha on top of his desk, massaging his flab, while a luckless Block 3 with a perfect French accent read a passage of *Le Petit Prince*. Pug's own accent was execrable, and he picked on anyone who constituted a possible threat with unrelenting sarcasm.

A banana-shaped moon ripened in the sky. Grub drifted past the budding apple orchard towards the Library. It always reminded him of a ship – Kenward like Captain Hook with his parrot, the cargo of books. Becalmed in a swaying pool of hyacinths and narcissus, this likeness would have been perfect but for the fact that the Librarian was crouched down inspecting the ground below the windows.

'Viner,' he said imperiously, before Grub could bound up the steps, 'come here, please.'

Grub instantly feared that he had been discovered as the perpetrator of the rotting kipper joke two years ago, but it appeared the old man had other ideas.

'Tell me, do you see that crack?'

'Yes,' said Grub.

'And these ones here?'

'Yes.'

'Ah. Tell me, have you noticed any others around the school on your perambulations?'

Grub stared at him. How could he be expected to notice anything like that? Horatio, observing them both from a creeper, made a rude whistle, then squawked, 'Love: delusion.'

Grub jumped. 'No!' he almost shouted. 'Absolutely not!'

The Librarian stood up to his great height and looked down at him.

'Ah,' he said.

18

Mrs Godwin had always told her daughter that the relations between men and women were those of appetite, but it soon became clear to Alice that this definition could not be condoned. She regretted this. She had genuinely hoped that if she slept with Winthrop once, the distractions of emotion would be dissipated. In retrospect, this had been naive; but then, naivety was no prophylactic.

'Given the choice between sex and chocolate,' she told Winthrop, 'most honest people would choose chocolate. It's just that you can buy the latter cheaply, openly and at any age over the counter.'

He gave an indulgent laugh.

'Oh, Alice! I've known girls who hated going the max and pretended they liked it, but never the other way around. Listen, you can't repent sin and will it at the same time. Why be embarrassed by something everyone does? How do you think you came into the world?'

'Not, I'm afraid, as a consequence of pleasure.'

'Well, hell, that was just someone's major bad luck. You should be pleased you're different from your mother, not ashamed. Look, you're making a face, like I'm saying something really gross, but why be a hypocrite?'

'Things unsaid are sweeter.'

'No, they aren't,' said Winthrop. 'Things unsaid means that everyone fumbles round in the dark, trying to be smart. Things unsaid are for dumb assholes. Why do you think something so natural is bad?'

'I don't equate nature with goodness. The Founder believed that. He thought he was making an ideal world here, where people would grow up without greed or hate or lust. But he failed, didn't he?'

'What do you think is good, then?'

'The laws which *stop* people from being natural. Nature is cruel and horrible and amoral. People are born worse than animals. They have to be taught how to be human.'

'The law! That's just an invention for the weak.'

'What's wrong with that?'

'Well,' said Winthrop, shrugging, and smiling whitely, 'I'm not one of the weak, am I? And neither are you.'

'It's fatally easy to mistake a strong character for self-confidence,' said Alice.

'Oh, come on! Weak people are passive. You don't lie down and let things happen. You stand up and hit back.'

'I let you happen to me.'

'Only because you wanted it.'

She said nothing. The idea that love might stem from loneliness rather than lust clearly never occurred to him. Winthrop touched her breasts, smoother and darker than the rest of her, then her thin ribbed sides and long boy's legs. It surprised him, still, how intensely he went for her.

'Didn't you? Don't you?'

'I can't breathe.'

'Yes you can. Don't give me that broken-glass look.'

'But I'm weaker than you. So I need the law.'

'Laws can be broken by the strong,' said Winthrop, smiling. 'You are strong, aren't you?'

'Sweetheart, I could break your neck if I wanted.'

'Why don't you? It would be the best time to go.'

He grinned as if she were making a joke. 'You could never hit me like you did Tore, could you?'

'I could box your ears.'

'Not while I'm on top.'

They were lying on the grassy ledge where Alice had gone before in more lachrymose moods. It was astonishing to her that she had never been unhappy in such a place. Far away, the sea was a soft huge haze of blue. Every time the warm wind rustled up the hill, it brought delicious scents. A gauze of new leaves surrounded them like a screen, and knots of primroses and periwinkles braided the bright trickle of water splashing out from the cave.

'Wow, it's like Bambi,' Winthrop said, after a fawn paused on the edge of the clearing, sniffed, and bounced away towards the moor.

'Oh, not Disney again!'

He wriggled out of his tartan boxer shorts. Alice still found these terribly funny.

'Would you prefer to make out in the bike sheds instead?'

'I prefer Virgilian clichés to boarding-school ones.'

Winthrop thought it was time to raise his own cultural standards. 'Yeah, I always did think Hemingway sucked. This grass seems to get wetter and wetter. It really jacks me off that we can't use the Stagehands' Hut. It's wasted on that asshole Tore.'

'The temples would be worst of all. Constantly patrolled by the Slythes. At least nobody else comes here.'

'And you taste *so* much better in the open air,' said Winthrop, parodying the soulful Knotshead voice. Alice made her snorty little laugh. 'It's a pain we don't get study-bedrooms for a year.'

'Actually, it's much harder to ... misbehave then, because they're so jumpy we might abuse the privilege. Although, of course, people do. It's a rule, you have to keep one foot on the ground all the time, just like in old films, or you get expelled. Even to have a red lightbulb hanging from your ceiling is a serious offence.'

'Why?'

'It's supposed to induce lascivious thoughts,' said Alice with the rustle of laughter in her voice that he liked.

'The British libido is just so weird,' said Winthrop. They were silent for a time.

Overhead, a thin, inhuman voice exclaimed, 'O, the horror, the horror!'

They both froze; parted, and started up, staring.

'Who – who is it?'

'I don't know.'

'Wealth: impunity.'

'Oh,' said Alice, 'it's only Horatio. Look.'

The parrot screeched deafeningly.

'Hell, does that mean Kenward's around?' Winthrop started

pulling on his pants. 'He really gives me the creeps.'

Alice felt a shock of dismay. She was at that stage of love which seeks identity of opinion in all things.

There was a cracking of twigs below in the woods.

'Shit. He's coming up here. Is there any other way down?'

'No, just the streambed. This whole hill is supposed to be out of bounds. It's riddled with shafts.'

'We'd better hide in the mine.'

'I'm frightened of it.'

'We can go just inside. Come on!'

They picked up their clothes and ran barefoot over the mossy turf to the cave. Once inside, each burst into nervous giggles.

'Hell, it's cold. I can hardly see you.'

'Shh!'

'I can feel your –'

'Winthrop, don't. We'll make a –'

'Only chocolate does that,' said Winthrop. They both shuddered, and were still.

'I wonder how long he'll be. I can't hear anything above the stream, can you?'

'You know, it's not as dark as I expected. There must be shafts coming down from above.'

'Don't go in any further.'

'Girls never have any curiosity about exploring. This must go some way back into the hill, you know.'

'Winthrop, I'm terrified of this place.'

'So there are some things even you are scared of?'

'Besides, I think he's gone.'

So strenuous were Pedigree Chumley's incompetent but well-meaning efforts to heal the rift in the Knotshead staff room that they bore fruit in quite an unexpected direction. At long last, the junior housemaster succeeded in softening the heart of the pneumatic Helge. She decided to herself that though puppyish, he was quite *gemütlich*, and deserved a little springtime diversion.

By a dozen small signs, she indicated that she was prepared to receive his advances. Alas, so low had Chumley's self-esteem fallen that when she finally gave up the subtle approach and invited herself round to his rooms in the Males' Flats, he assumed she had come to discuss the Arab problem.

'At least Helge's on your side,' he confided to Naimh and Hussein. Unmistakably one of Them to the males, he felt himself to be far closer in age to his charges than to any of the other staff, most of whom were in middle age, and ate every meal, including breakfast, in the school dining hall. 'We're going to discuss what can be done in my rooms tonight.'

All the males exchanged mocking glances.

'Whehay, Pedigree!' said Tore. 'This is your lucky day!'

'Shall I lend you my bootleg video of *Body Heat?*'

'Oh, you do have such one-track minds!' reproved Chumley, going very red.

'Dirt track,' Grub muttered. Winthrop had just come in, whistling 'American Pie'. The flies of his Levis looked encrusted with – Grub couldn't bear to think what – and he was covered in grass stains. He ignored all of them, shrugging out of his clothes and stripping for a shower before afternoon lessons. Meathead, Grub thought, watching the muscles of Winthrop's arms ripple. Fascist. Killer rabbit. I bet you fuck like one, too. I bet you never struggled with a bullworker in your life.

'Hey, Superbrat,' said Tore, jeering. 'I hope you're practising safe sex.'

An immaculate white towel round his narrow waist, Winthrop swivelled and swept the dormitory with a blank blue stare.

'There's nothing about sex that is safe,' he said, and went out.

Tore said, 'Fuck, how I hate people who deliver lines like fucking actors,' and threw his Zippo lighter against a window, smashing it.

To say that Chumley lacked the feminine touch was like saying Gore Tore was just a rock star. Having drifted through school and university with a minimum of contact with the opposite sex, he had retreated to Knotshead with the vague idea that it would be of psychological benefit. Terrified of women, he spent the holidays under the thumb of his mother, who periodically sent him food hampers as she had done all the way through Sherbourne and who kept nagging him to get married.

His ideal was to have a small sports car and a life style which included wall-to-wall shag carpets and black leather sofas. The reality consisted of enormous yellowing Y-fronts dripping from the bathroom radiator, a college photograph of himself in a mortar board and numerous cartons of sour milk in the fridge. His sole contribution to improving his rooms as housemaster had been to hang a very small pink Chinese lampshade from the ceiling in his living room.

All this had been easily ascertained by the males over the monthly mugs of tea and biscuits which constituted pastoral care at Knotshead. Further information, gleaned by Lads night wandering past his windows on the parapet, had revealed him to be boringly inhibited in his private habits. He did not even read the pornography he confiscated, like Pug.

Had it not been a fine spring night, it is possible that Helge's visit might have gone unobserved. As it was, Grub was woken by Tore, shaking with demonic laughter at around midnight.

'Come out on the roof.'

'What?'

'Come on! This is going to be a laugh and a half, mate.'

'Why? What are you on about?'

'Pedigree and Helge. He hasn't drawn the curtains. I've been watching the whole thing.'

Tore's whispers woke everyone in the dorm. Gradually, Grub became aware that all the other Lads – in fact, what looked like half the Males' Flat – were climbing through the window.

'What the hell?'

Winthrop's sleepy drawl made them all stop.

'Pedigree's bonking the German teacher,' said Grub, unwillingly. 'You can come and have a grandstand view.'

Winthrop yawned. 'I'll pass,' he said.

'Afraid he'll get caught,' said Tore in a sneering whisper.

'Hell, there's nothing he could teach me that I don't know already,' said Winthrop.

There was an unpleasant silence. Suddenly, everyone else wondered whether they were not exposing their own inexperience.

'Come on, come on, or we'll miss it,' said one of the younger Lads. The illicit thrill of night wandering suddenly took possession of them, and they began to shove each other to climb out on the parapet.

'Grubbo, we need your torch. The moon isn't out.'

Grub rose, put on his dressing gown and followed Tore, shining the pencil beam along the parapet. Arriving first at Chumley's rooms, he had a good view of what was transpiring through the dormer windows below.

The first thing he noticed was the number of aluminium cartons from the Chinese takeaway scattered round the room, not all of them empty. A pity, this. Then he became conscious of Helge and Pedigree staggering around the room in an awkward kind of dance. Pedigree kept making wild snapping dives at the German girl's breasts while at the same time trying to get out of his trousers. Helge had other ideas; with the result that they were both hopping about among the cartons wrestling with items of clothing entangled round their legs. A ripple of sniggers passed along the line of watching males. The expression on the housemaster's face was one of intense anxiety.

Piece by piece, the two teachers struggled out of their clothing. Buttons popped, elastic snapped, and Helge's bra sank down to her stomach before springing open with a click at the front. One of the males began fisting himself, and was nudged sharply in the ribs. Wanking was supposed to be done in the bogs. Grub began to feel very uneasy. At last she was stark naked. Pedigree was left wearing only his pimples and a pair of black socks.

They smiled at each other, embarrassed. He really was very shy, thought Grub, suddenly appalled. What if it was Pedigree's first time? Completely oblivious to the twenty pairs of eyes following his every movement, the housemaster flung himself on to Helge, and proceeded to almost throw her, impaled on his dick, about the room. Everything wiggled and jiggled grotesquely. Helge was flung from the sofa to the carpet and back on to the sofa like a rag doll, both of them panting and scarlet in the face. The watchers on the parapet shuffled their feet like awkward cattle, trying not to touch each other. This was not the way it was supposed to be; this had a horrid similarity to their worst fears of looking like complete and utter prats. Grub felt himself blushing all over in hot misery. It wasn't even funny, just tasteless and grotesque and somehow pathetic. Poor Pedigree, he kept thinking. I bet Winthrop doesn't do it like this.

The end came quickly, but not soon enough.

Chumley suddenly froze, rolled his eyes like a dying ox and collapsed. After a few seconds, Helge patted him kindly on the head.

'What a gas,' said Tore, when they climbed back through the window. 'What a gas!'

Now that it was all over, the males began to laugh and slap each other on the shoulders.

'God, that was the funniest thing I ever saw!'

'Cor, she's a real goer, isn't she?'

'That bit when he had her all squashed against the sofa!'

'Waving her legs in the air!'

'And when she tried to – '

'That pin-sized dick!'

'And he didn't even take off his *socks*!'

'Oh, God, those *socks*!'

'Those black socks!'

'Did I miss anything?' Winthrop asked.

A roar of laughter went up like a wall around him.

'Oh, Lord, if only you'd seen!'

When Chumley came down for breakfast the next morning, he walked with a pained and timid step. His entrance was greeted by a chant:

'Black socks, black socks!'

'Black socks, black socks!'

The males banged on the tables with spoons and fists, and most of the girls were giggling. On every face, the young man saw a gloating knowledge of what had happened. He shrank, like a snail dropped into salt water, and ran out.

Hart received his resignation before lunch.

19

Chumley's resignation cast the staff room into a frenzy of uninformed speculation. A broken man, he left on the same day as his meeting with Hart. Those who had seen him go said that his face wore such an expression of acute misery that the art master's supposition of his being discovered in some flagrant act of gross moral turpitude, comparable to the time when the former pottery mistress had a lesbian affair with the head girl, was altogether untenable. Maggie Brink was convinced that the call of 'black socks' had a political, and possibly Fascist, connotation. Beatrice Bassett put it down to the essential volatility of the male species. Mortmain believed his junior to have had some kind of nervous breakdown as a result of teaching *Kes* to Block 4, and wondered aloud whether his own A-level classes on Margaret Drabble's early works could possibly have the same effect. Helge very sensibly kept her mouth shut. She was leaving at the end of the term anyway, to go back to her country, and did not see why the English made such a fuss about sex. Pug was beside himself with fury. 'This is absolutely outrageous,' he gobbled at the headmaster.

'It was his own choice,' said Hart.

Pug snorted. 'We all know that's a euphemism for being sacked. I don't care what he's done, I can't be left to cope single-handed. It was different before Quirk abolished prefects, but now it's impossible.'

'Everyone else is married,' said Hart wearily, in his flat, grey voice. 'I do a thirteen-hour job myself.'

Pug looked at him, glowering. What precisely headmasters did do, apart from puffing themselves up in the national media and irritating pupils with their fatuous opinions at Jaw, was something of a mystery. Long ago, when he had thought of his position as a stepping stone to a headship, he had perceived that the greatest single quality demanded by anyone who rose to the top was a simple capacity to survive change. Hart's predecessor, Quirk, had tried to win over the pupils by being terribly chummy and giving lectures on liberal politics, but Pug knew that it was not the pupils, but the parents, who really mattered.

True, once locked into the Knotshead system, they were, like honeymooners on a cruise, most reluctant to admit they might have made an expensive mistake. But it was the parents who were stumping up the cost of a Rolls-Royce to pay for their child's education, and it was they who had to be placated, toadied to and generally congratulated for making their choice. Unfortunately, Hart had come to very similar conclusions in his own career. He was popular with parents, or at least enough of them to retain a good public image – remembering the names of their offspring and making flattering remarks about their progress. Even the fact that he had been educated in a grammar school and was clearly lower middle class made the liberal-minded hesitant to complain about him for fear of seeming snobbish.

Despite the internal promotion of Veronica as deputy head, Pug still cherished hopes that, if Hart's contract should fail to be renewed, he himself would land the plum. With the exception of the Honourable Mrs Kenward, the governors were all men in late middle age, and no coeducational public school had, as yet, been known to appoint a headmistress. So Captain Wash still conceived of his chances with a hopeful eye. It was, after all, the natural progression – housemaster to headmaster – and one which Hart had made himself.

'Hew tells me theft is even extending to musical instruments. I think we should call in the police again.'

'Have you forgotten what happened when we last did so?'

They were both silent, remembering the unpleasantness in the autumn after Hart's letter.

'There's a bad atmosphere in the Males' Flats,' said Pug, in a truculent tone. 'Very bad. Feels like a ship about to mutiny.'

'There always is, this time of year. It'll pass. At least 6ii are kept clear of it.'

'I preferred it when we had prefects.'

'No doubt. But such hierarchical systems are really not in keeping with the Knotshead philosophy, and are a distraction to those in the final year.'

Pug looked at Hart, unable to see his eyes behind the blank reflection of his large, square spectacles. Grey anorak, grey trousers, grey hair. How could the governors ever have thought such a man would command respect in a school like Knotshead?

'I want my unease made a matter of record for the next board meeting.'

'Very well,' said Hart.

Alice loathed the Dower House increasingly. The continual reek of deodorants and charring sanitary towels made a silent hysteria well up in her. The rows of beds with their pink candlewick covers, the clutter of clothes and face creams, even the disgusting floral wallpapers seemed designed to induce a repulsive femininity, a mentality in which women could be allowed only to be passive and decorative. Tore might be, in Winthrop's phrase, a freewheeling psycho, but at least he had more spirit than Olivia.

She compared the freedoms the opposite sex took for granted with those timidly grasped by the girls. Males relished eccentrics like Grub: girls ostracised Fay. Males swooped round the estate on bicycles: girls went for timid walks to Minedale and Anstey for specific purposes. Males were not self-conscious about their bodies: girls would spend hours worrying about their figures in front of full-length mirrors. At least two girls in every block were anorexic or bulimic.

Previously, her disdain for the rest had not been so absolute as to cast out her fear of them. A year ago, she had walked into a bathroom where a Groover in the block above had been wallowing, and had been ordered to squeeze a pimple on the girl's back. Revolted, Alice had lied that it had not come to a head; today they knew she would have openly refused. But today, nobody would ask her to do so.

Everything had changed since Winthrop. She had been mortified by the incident of the love bites, and had told him that if he ever, ever breathed any detail of what they did together to the

Males' Flats, she would never speak to him again.

'Why would I want to spoil their imagining it instead?' had been his response.

Winthrop's star seemed to rise by the day. Week by week his status had climbed, so that he was now within an ace of being one of the Lads. Rumours of the Sheen wealth suddenly became legion; it was discovered, probably by Olivia, that a cousin of his was married to a Yorkshire branch of the Paddingtons themselves. His peculiar pink and green wardrobe was said to be that of the American aristocracy, not some brash nouveau hallmark. Girls who had dismissed him on the grounds of unfashionable muscularity now sighed longingly as they stood behind him in lunch queues. One or two had even given up smoking because he was open in his dislike for the habit.

'It's such a banal admission of social inadequacy, don't you think?' he said, to a fuming Tore.

Everything he did was cool. It was the sex that did it. Unlike the other couples who openly canoodled in the Quad, he never even touched Alice in front of them. There was no need; even without the stupid incident of the bites on her neck, it was obvious to everyone but the staff that they were doing it. Such discretion added to his image of sophistication. Knotes suddenly discovered he was witty, and now he only had to say a word in class for laughter to break out.

For Winthrop had a sense as rare as Grub's perfect pitch. He could see power: the connections between people, who was trading off what. Every new school he had been to was like a code he had to crack, but once he had gotten on to the same wavelength it was easy to manipulate people. Knotshead had been particularly difficult because of the difference in so many things, but now he was fully operational again.

'Less is more,' he muttered to himself, jogging along the wood-chip paths. 'Less is more: that's how Win'll beat J. Tore.'

Only Alice continued to call him Winthrop. Everyone else knew him as Win.

Without having the faintest interest in the matter, Alice, too, had left her Reject status behind. As Winthrop rose, so she was dragged up in his wake as a 'happening' person. Her rating in the factory line after Jaw had gone up from zero to five, and then to six. This bemused her. Nothing about her dress or appearance **had** changed: she was still too tall, thin, sallow, and did not go to school dances, but this was now fashionable. Girls told her they envied her legs, her nose, her eyes with the same frankness that they had mocked these very features six months ago. Males whistled instead of shouting 'Ugly' as she crossed the Quad. The other members of her dorm covered for her when she was late for lights out, and asked her if she would like to come home with them at half-term.

Alice thought them all fools.

However, if her position had changed for the better in relation to the pupils, it had undoubtedly worsened in relation to the staff. By mid-March, every adult, including Veronica, had reprimanded her for idleness. She seethed at the injustice of this: after all, people like Tore and Olivia were allowed to get away with a minimum of prep, so why attack her for the slackening of a month? Why persecute her simply because, for the first time, she was enjoying what it meant to be young?

Much of this resentment was compounded by guilt. She knew that she attended Knotshead on sufferance, because of Simon. She knew that, as a result, she was one of the pupils expected to keep the school's examination marks looking respectable. She knew that she was betraying all her mother's feminist principles. Yet none of these stood a chance against the thrill of Winthrop. She was sick of carrying the burden of her personality like a snail's shell, of inching forward so painfully over tracks of text. Why suffer, when it was so needless? Why choose hate instead of love?

She dreaded going into the Library. The distinctive smell which emanated from it, once the incense of a temple of civilisation, now fell into its component parts of old glue, old leather and old Horatio droppings. Alice found herself slinking past the Librarian's office on the rare occasions when she spent her prep periods working. She had been stuck on Echo and Narcissus for nearly a month, until she felt that she, too, was wasting away into a shrivelled reflection of the Librarian's own passion for Latin.

> 'Quae simul adspexit liquefacta rursus in unda
> Non tulit ulterius, sed ut intabascere flavae
> Igne levi cerae matutinaeque pruinae
> Sole tepente solent, sic attenuatus amore
> Liquitur et tecto paulatim carpitur igni.'

The Librarian looked at her over his half-moon spectacles.
'Translate, please.'

'But as the flame ascends – '

'Look at the case ending.'

Horatio ground his beak.

'But as the morning sun ignites – '

'No.'

She said, guessing wildly, 'But as the morning melts like wax,
so love consumes him like a liquid fire.'

'"*Non tulit ulterius*"?'

'He can bear no more?'

'That, at least, is correct. "He can bear no more."' The
Librarian paused. 'It reads:

'As soon as he sees this, when the water has become clear
   again,
He can bear no more; but, as the yellow wax melts before
   a gentle heat, as morning frost melts
Before the warm sun, so wasted away by love,
Does he pine and is slowly consumed by its hidden fire.'

'Love: delusion.'

'Thank you, Horatio.'

Alice felt very like crying. 'I'm sorry.'

The Librarian took off his spectacles and polished them
thoughtfully.

'Is this going to be a temporary aberration or a long-term
one? I ask because if your enthusiasm for Latin has been altogether dissipated, there are still a number of other subjects you
could take instead, even halfway through the course. But unlike
most of the subjects on offer here, you really cannot expect to
pass this particular board without adequate preparation.'

She stared at him.

'Oh *NO*!' For an instant, her will blazed up again, pure and
strong. 'I swear not. It's nothing to do with Latin. You really
mustn't think that.'

'I see.'

'I don't care about beastly *Madame Bovary* or the early
works of Margaret Drabble, but I do, do love Ovid. And
Horace and Catullus and even Virgil. It's just that nothing sticks
in my mind any more.'

'I see,' said the Librarian. 'You are in love.'

Alice went scarlet.

'Were I a woman – a fate which, thanks be to God, I happily escaped – I would put off falling in love for as long as possible. It is so very bad for the intellect. Not to mention the rarest of all properties, common sense.'

'I *did* try,' said Alice miserably. 'I tried really hard. I've been in love with Rikki Tikki Tavi and Robinson Crusoe and Mr Darcy and Hamlet and Catullus, and none of them – '

The Librarian burst out laughing. Horatio uttered a long, mocking wolf whistle.

'You don't see, do you? said Alice, losing her temper. 'You think love is all books and words, but when you feel it – when you really *feel* it – nothing that's ever been written or said measures up.'

'Oh dear, oh dear,' said the Librarian, mopping his eyes. 'I do apologise, I didn't mean to be unkind. Of course, it's simply overwhelming, and nobody has ever, in the history of the world, felt love as you do.'

'That isn't what I said.'

'No, but it's what you believe, in your heart of hearts, isn't it? Well, my dear Miss Godwin, nothing I can say will make the slightest bit of difference. It is an absolute disaster for you, academically, but you must try very hard to overcome the consequences.' He paused, and polished his glasses again, sighing. 'I have always thought that the best possible education for young women was to be at a single-sex school with an entirely male staff of outstanding intellect and no interest whatsoever in sex. Those who taught science and mathematics would be particularly handsome. There's nothing like a colossal crush on a teacher to develop the feminine mind.'

'Oh?'

To herself, Alice considered the possibility that age had leached the calcium from the Librarian's bones only to put it into his head.

'My great-niece, Emma, showed every sign of becoming a complete flibbertigibbet until conceiving a hopeless passion for her tutor at Oxford. The fact is, young people are like goslings: they become imprinted by the nearest available object that roughly corresponds to their biological drives. Even if that object is a plastic bucket.'

'Winthrop is not a plastic bucket.'

'Did I say he was?'

'Aark!' said the parrot, rocking back and forth on his pole. 'Fidelity: hope.'

'No, Horatio,' said the Librarian, 'hope: fidelity.'

With the advent of spring, the stench of fungus had become overwhelmingly strong in the headmaster's house. Spots of black mildew dripped across the beige carpets like the spoor of a wounded animal. Hart sometimes wondered whether it was not his own. In the drawing room, the white baby piano left by the Quirks had become completely untuned, even to his own ear. Plates were piled high with festering scraps of TV suppers and baby goo. What went on in the nappy bin was simply not worth contemplating.

Poppy made no attempt to clear up the mess. Never especially fastidious, she had abandoned all pretence of interest in running an orderly household since the birth of the twins. The more Hart thought about this, the more resentful he became. What else did she have to do all day? Didn't he try to help, with his drip-dry shirts and pyjamas? She always looked so charming, he'd never have guessed she was such a slattern on the domestic front; but apart from throwing out his nice fluffy pink toilet cover, she had done nothing at all to the house.

She was slumped apathetically on the brown corduroy sofa, as usual, when Hart came in at the end of his day. Even with her hair in a dirty tangle, she looked lovely, but he found he was no longer moved by it. The curtains were not yet drawn over the picture windows, and the living room was full of soft, thick blue light.

'Hallo, dearest,' said Hart. 'Where are the twins?'

'In their room.'

'Ah-ha, ha, yes. Well, what's for din-dins?'

Poppy remained staring at the ceiling. 'There isn't anything for supper. Sorry. I didn't have time to drive to Knotsmouth today. Simon, there's something I absolutely have to tell you, a journalist rang me up – '

'You didn't have time? *You* didn't have *time*?'

All Hart's anger and frustration suddenly boiled over.

'What is it, do you think you're too posh for that sort of thing, is that it? It's beneath you, going round a supermarket with a trolley like the hoi polloi?'

'Simon, I – '

'Lady Muck!' said Hart. 'Oh, the Godwins are such an old Scottish family, oh so very upper class! I should have known better when I married you. A meal ticket for life, that's all you wanted.'

'Oh, for God's sake, Simon, stop talking such snobbish drivel!' Poppy shouted. 'When have I ever said that? When have I ever, ever discussed my family?'

'And your sister looks down her nose at me, and winces whenever I say "toilet",' said the headmaster. 'And you despise me for wearing an anorak and driving a Ford Cortina. Don't think I don't notice.'

'Oh, come off it!'

'And you think you're so clever, sneering at me, sneering at this house, but without me, where would you be? Stuck in a girls' boarding school for the rest of you life!'

Poppy began to laugh hysterically.

'Go on, laugh,' said Hart, furious.

'Don't be such a pompous prick. What is it about headmasters that always makes them so full of themselves? You carry on as though you're God in your little world, and it's only a school, for God's sake!'

'But it is a world,' said Hart. 'Don't you see? I didn't make it, but I can try to sort it out, to make it work. It's my great chance to really do something, to be someone.'

'If schools are worlds, they're of a sort which disappeared along with Cro-Magnon man and the dinosaur.'

'You forget, dearest,' said Hart coldly, 'this is a progressive school.'

'That,' said Poppy, 'is a contradiction in terms.'

20

Spring swept up the valley of the Knot. Almost overnight, trees became half submerged in glittering leaf, the nests of birds floating along in the branches like little lifeboats. Streams of white narcissi stretched up the slopes of the lake, foaming and bobbing this way and that. The avenues up to the temples crawled with life: miniature cork-skinned toads, flea-bitten hedgehogs, neurotic squirrels. It became hard to tell which noise was the waves in the Sound, and which the wind in the woods.

Exhilaration and frustration fermented through the pupils like yeast. It was unbearable to be kept in, the day chopped up into forty-minute sections as if it were meat on a butcher's block, when everything else was going on out there. Easter was a fortnight away, and it seemed as if the holidays would never arrive.

The day after Poppy and Simon's quarrel, spring fever reached such a pitch that both the Dower House and the Males' Flats were seething with unfocused excitement. The noise in the Quad and dining hall changed pitch, becoming higher and louder. That evening, it took almost ten minutes to command silence for Jaw before Veronica, with icy stare and folded arms, succeeded.

Under the hiss of showers a whispered message was passed round before lights out.

'Dorm riot! Dorm riot!'

'Get ready for the dorm riot!'

There had not been a dorm riot since Hart's arrival. Periodic

attempts had been made by bored pupils attempting to whip up
trouble, but had always failed because of a lack of general enthusiasm. If the chemistry went wrong at the last moment, all
that happened was that a group of cowering Knotes were confronted by Veronica and Pug in full Stalinist fury, and the ring-
leaders made to do outdoor work in every free period for the
rest of the term.

This time, the rioters were not to be quelled. Everyone knew
that Pug would have no way of coping with a hundred males on
the rampage; even 6ii were going to join in. As the bells were
rung at ten to ten for lights out, even the most abject Reject
clutched his or her pillow and let out a yell.

'Dorm riot! *Dorm riot! Dorm riot!*'

Feet in slippers thundered down every corridor and staircase.
At the foot of the Dower House staircase stood Veronica, with
Miranda Jupp giggling nervously beside her.

'Go back at once!' Veronica shouted, drawing herself up to
her full height and looking uncommonly like Mrs Siddons as
Lady Macbeth.

'Yah, you cow!' shouted Nicola boldly, and hit her on the
head with a pillow.

'Yah!' shrieked Fay, besider herself with excitement.

'Yah!'

'Dorm riot!'

'Yah!'

Veronica disappeared beneath a flail of thudding pillows.
Miranda Jupp, being despised instead of hated, was thumped
more gently: the main aim was to get out of the Dower House.
Out they ran across the wet grass in their nightdresses, beneath
the star-prickled sky. Yells and shouts from the Males' Flats indicated that a similar rebellion was in process.

Through the swing doors of the Main House they streamed,
and into the Quad, where a furious pillow fight was in progress.
Males were thumping everything in sight – girls, each other,
staff, and even, in the case of the Westler brothers, themselves.
Several pillows had burst, and the air was full of swirling brown
down, which got up everyone's noses and made them sneeze.

Grub yelled and swung his pillow with the rest, but he
strained the edges of his spectacles to see where Alice was. Just
as he caught sight of the familiar rose shawl, a wadge of white
descended on his nose, wrenching the metal frame half off his

ears. Holding her pillow in both arms, she was watching the melee, and the expression of ironic detachment on her face made Grub think of his mother. Part of him perceived her chosen isolation with hopeless adoration, and part with intense irritation. Why was she so unnaturally grown-up? He wondered what it was like to bonk her: probably like watching St Theresa receive the stigmata, he concluded, with gloomy longing.

'Yah!' he shouted, raising his pillow and advancing on his newly gangling legs.

He was brushed aside by something that felt like a small tractor. Winthrop's broad Sulka-clad back retreated rapidly in the direction of Alice. They promptly disappeared together into the Quad telephone booth.

Grub's jaw fell open.

Tore materialised by his side, his eyes glittering with excitement. 'Hey, Grub!'

'Yo!'

'Come on, if any of us hang back they'll punish the rest.'

'Superbrat and Alice,' Grub hissed.

'What?'

'They're having it off in the Quad telephone booth.'

'What? *Now?*'

Grub nodded.

'Then for fuck's sake shut up about it,' said Tore through gritted teeth. 'If you tell anyone, I'll never live it down.'

'Why?' asked Grub, bewildered.

'Because *I've* never fucking done it under the noses of the whole staff, that's why, you stupid fucking git!' Tore shouted. 'Get them out!'

'But Jono – '

'Now! This'll all be over in another minute.'

Dubiously, Grub edged towards the telephone booth. Tore's observation was true. Unused to prolonged physical exertion, both sides were running out of breath and starting to get a bit jumpy about the consequences of the riot. Like the Rape of the Sabines in reverse, the girls were preparing themselves for flight back to the Dower House.

There was a small pane of glass set in the booth door. Nervously, Grub tapped on it. Nothing happened. Perhaps, he thought, he had been mistaken. He took hold of the handle and opened the door. His stomach churned.

'Hurry up,' he said through the crack, before closing it again. Winthrop's drawl. 'We'll be through in twenty seconds.'

For the rest of his life Grub thought he would remember the nakedness, not of Alice's body, but of her face.

Hurrying over from his house after an alarmed phone call from Miranda Jupp, Hart watched the mayhem with dismay. This was not self-expression, this was utter loss of control. His lips drawn in a tight, humourless line, he tried not to feel overwhelmed by fear. The brutish, acned faces shouting with open mouths, the big, clumsy bodies lurching blindly around in the downy air were like something out of a nightmare.

Ineffectually, he tried going up to particular groups and saying, 'Stop this! Stop this at once!' but they took no notice of his bleating voice. Only four adults to two hundred and fifty adolescents on the rampage: how on earth were they to cope? Wash was making no attempt, standing there with folded arms and the expression of a captain watching another ship's mutiny. Miranda Jupp was twittering and getting tangled up in her wrap-around Indian skirts. Veronica was calmly ticking off names of female miscreants on the register for the Dower House. No need to ask what she would have been in the Eastern Bloc, Hart thought sourly.

It could not have gone on for more than ten minutes, but they seemed the longest of his career. Eventually, at some invisible signal, the girls gathered together like starlings and took off again back to their own dorms, still babbling with excitement.

'A disgraceful scene,' said Hart furiously. 'Quite disgraceful.'

It dawned on him, suddenly, that here was the weapon he had been seeking against Veronica, and the pleasure this thought caused him made it hard for him to keep a smile of malice off his face. 'If you cannot keep control of the Dower House, I must ask the board to reconsider your appointment, both as housemistress and as my deputy.'

Veronica gave him her basilisk stare. 'Do,' she began to say, when suddenly the Quad was filled with a deafening clangour of fire alarms. A flaming wastepaper basket fell down from the Males' Flats, narrowly missing both adults.

'There can be only one democratic solution,' said Maggie Brink. 'We must have a vote of no confidence in the man. The governors can't ignore that, surely.'

'They supported him after he sent that stupid letter that got into all the papers,' said Martin Mortmain. 'It could look as if we were failing to, ah, mnyah, come to the aid of the party.'

'The scene last night was monstrous, quite monstrous,' said Pug. 'I've never seen anything so ridiculous in my entire life. Things cannot be allowed to continue in this manner.'

Delus sucked on his pipe. 'Oh, come, old chap. Surely it was just an explosion of youthful high spirits.'

'A Molotov cocktail, more like,' said Philip Slythe. The bursar had been dragged away from watching *The City Programme* to come to his wife's assistance, and was still seething.

'We've had dorm riots before, in Quirk's day,' said Hindesmith. 'All those fetching little boys running about in pyjamas. It was really rather charming, I thought. "What mad pursuit? What struggle to escape?" Rather in your line of business, I'd have thought, Mortmain.'

'That is as may be,' said Veronica coldly, 'but when it escalates to arson it endangers pupils' lives. I vote that we vote for or against.'

'Who votes that we vote?'

Maggie ticked off the raised hands.

'The Librarian isn't here,' someone objected.

'Oh, he never gets involved in school politics anyway.'

'We'd better hurry up. Hart'll be due down from his office any moment now.'

Miranda Jupp giggled.

'Oh, dear, this does feel wicked,' she said.

'Right,' said Maggie. 'We now vote on whether or not we continue to give our support to Simon Hart as head. Those in favour?'

Toby Hindesmith yawned ostentatiously and picked up *The Times*. He saw what was underneath, and stiffened.

'Nobody in favour.'

'Hang on just a minute, Maggie.'

'I do hope, Toby,' said Maggie, annoyed at being interrupted, 'that you aren't going to turn fifth-columnist. Those against?'

'Wait, wait!' the art master burst out, jumping to his feet. 'No wonder we haven't seen him all morning. Good God, look at this!'

He held up a copy of the *Daily Mirror*, the only tabloid

allowed in the staff room.

They crowded round.

'SEX PICTURES OF SCANDAL SCHOOL WIFE: EXCLUSIVE.'

'Good God!'

'He doesn't exist,' said Veronica, automatically.

'It's Poppy!'

'So it is.'

'"SIR'S WIFE WAS NUDE 'MODEL'. Sexy public-school head-master Simon Hart" – I must say, I've never thought he was much to write home about – "is lying low today after proof that his beautiful wife Poppy, 40, is a former sex model. This explicit picture, taken 15 years ago for the cover of Gore Tore's hit record *Bulldancer*, was withdrawn by Pineapple Records after being banned as obscene, but the lovely Poppy went on to feature in many other magazines, including a soft-porn film *King Dong* – Turn to Page 2. More Exclusive Pictures inside",' Mortmain read.

They all crowded round.

'I wonder if Simon has seen this?'

There was silence in the staff room.

'He's probably being besieged by the press at this very moment,' said Beatrice Bassett. 'Pigs, the lots of them!'

'Male chauvinist, or the other kind?' asked Toby.

'We'd better close the school gates, or they'll be running all over the estate like weasels.'

'One scandal after another! This really is bad news,' said Daphne Crump, showing the *Mirror* to the Librarian, who had just walked in. He looked at it, then at the circle of faces: some gloating, some shocked, some indifferent, some amused.

'O, the horror, the horror,' said Horatio. All the staff burst out laughing.

'It's odd,' said Mortmain. 'That phrase can be made to apply to almost any situation.'

Horatio gave him a wicked glance and added, in Chumley's voice, 'Like Life Itself.'

21

Easter came and went in a daze of misery for the Harts. Surrounded by journalists, they took the telephone off the hook and hardly dared venture outside the gates. The *Sun* tried to sneak into the grounds and take photographs with a telephoto lens of Poppy inside the Headmaster's Lodge, but was discovered in time and ejected by the police.

In an attempt to rid the school of further embarrassment, Simon was persuaded to give an exclusive interview to Fiona Bamber and the *Daily Mail*. The fact that Fiona was, in effect, Grub's stepmother gave him more confidence that she would present his image in the best possible light.

'I want to be completely honest,' he told *Mail* readers. 'All schools have problems like ours. All schools have scandals. Every school is a private place, presenting a public face. But it's only because I've been open about the difficulties we face that so much attention has been focused on Knotshead.'

The Harts were photographed toasting their marriage with a bottle of champagne, which, along with the cut-glass flutes in their hands, had been bought by Fiona. This upset parents more than anything. The story appeared under the headline: SCHOOL FOR SCANDAL MASTER – 'NO REGRETS' ABOUT WIFE'S SEXY PICTURES.

'My wife's sexuality is her own business,' Simon was quoted as saying. 'People criticise her for not fitting the usual twinset and pearls image of what a headmaster's wife should be, but like Knotshead itself she challenges stereotypes and does not hide beyond a hyprocritical façade of outdated morality.'

Poppy, described as 'a bubbly Julie Christie lookalike', was quoted as saying, 'We have a very modern relationship, based on complete honesty and trust. My husband knew about my past, but as it all happened fifteen years ago, he didn't think anything of it. I have no regrets about my past behaviour.'

Whether this was true or not, Simon had no means of ascertaining. An impenetrable silence had descended since the row. Both were meticulously polite to each other before Alice and the twins. Lily and Daisy, like seismographs, registered every rise and fall of emotion, and howled themselves scarlet in the face. Their innocent misery distressed Hart more than anything; more, even, than the idea of his wife's image being pawed over by sniggering millions.

The exposure of something so intimate made him feel as if the skin had been flayed off his own body. He would stare at the reproductions in the tabloids – for Knotshead subscribed to a cuttings service, and the newspapers were doubly inescapable therefore – until the photographs dissolved into specks of grey. There was a sexual presence in those pictures which he himself had never sensed. She had always been beautiful, charming, kittenish, but never the thing on the record cover. Even someone as timid and anxious as he could tell that.

He wondered what she felt about having Tore's son in the school. She had not been there, the one Parents' Day that the singer had come down: some crisis with the twins, he remembered. Now he wondered.

After a while, the journalists drifted away. But the school knew it was being watched, and kept its gates closed, now.

In an agony of suspense, Alice counted the days until Winthrop returned. Nothing else mattered. She felt dreadfully sorry for Poppy, of course, but it was as if she were under a kind of anaesthetic. She knew rather than felt compassion. Nothing really penetrated the sphere which she inhabited with Winthrop. Unable to read, she went for walks along the Knot with the twins. Its banks were crowded with dense, acrid rhododendrons, their flowers garish even in shadow. Lily and Daisy were fascinated by them, as by all bright colours, playing endless games of hide-and-seek. They were at the paradisial stage of childhood, their little bodies seeming to bunch and stretch into new and more beautiful shapes every day.

'After this, little nieces, it'll all be downhill: lessons and spots and self-consciousness. *Carpe diem.*' But they took no notice.

Her breasts itched and tingled as if continually subjected to a mild electric shock. The three weeks to the summer term seemed to go on and on.

The swan, too, had found a mate. She watched the female sitting on its nest of twigs and fluff.

'It's all very well for you,' she told it, throwing bits of bread. A flurry of mallards raced forward with a whir and splash, and the twins shrieked with joy. 'You're bound together by inertia.'

She wondered if the same was true of Poppy and Simon; or, indeed, of Winthrop and herself. She made herself think these painful things, as if probing a wound.

'Do you know what Stendhal says?' she told the swan. 'He says that in Europe, desire is whetted by constraint, but in America it's blunted by liberty. Which do you think applies to school?'

The swan hissed.

The staff were almost as embarrassed as the Harts themselves. On the one hand, they loathed Hart and longed to be rid of him as soon as possible. On the other, they could not now call for his resignation without appearing illiberal and acting in concert with the minions of the capitalist press.

'I can't understand why it didn't come out before,' said Beatrice Bassett. 'I mean, I know absolutely bally sod-all about pop music, but if it is such a famous album, why did nobody spot the likeness?'

'Oh, God, Bea, it's nearly twenty years old, and you know how much women change. If anyone noticed a passing resemblance, they probably just put it down to coincidence. Those *Daily Mirror* hacks must have spent weeks tracking down that appalling-sounding film.'

'*King Dong.* The title has a certain panache to it, like the lovely Mrs Hart,' said Hew.

'I do wish we could see a copy, don't you?'

'Oh, come off it, Mortmain, that sort of thing is terribly dull, really. I mean, how many times can you watch a piece of gristle going into another piece of gristle?'

'As well as being grossly exploitative of women.'

'In any case, who cares? We're not living in the Victorian era, however much Simon wishes to turn the clock back,' said Toby Hindesmith. 'The English are so hypocritical about sex. The fact is, they think it's all terribly filthy and disgusting and only for foreigners. Just think of the archetypal Englishwoman. That sprigged dress! That appalling flowery scent! Those lycra tights! Really, Poppy should be congratulated for injecting a note of lust, albeit of a dreary hetero kind.'

'Alternatively,' said Sally Rupple, 'just think of the average Englishman. That plucked-chicken appearance. That dislike of personal hygiene. That belief in clashing colours and cat-re-pellent aftershave.'

'Oh, shut up, both of you! They're just using it, yet again, to attack the principle of progressive schools. It's contrary to this government's dictatorial concept of a national curriculum to have a place like Knotshead even exist.'

'Oh, come now, Maggie, I don't think Fleet Street takes its orders from Downing Street quite yet. They just knew a good story when they saw one.'

'Don't you dare patronise me! Of course they're out to get us. This school represents everything the Tories want to destroy.'

'What's that?' said Hindesmith. 'The idle rich having a good time?'

'It's timing of it that is so appalling,' said Pug. 'We cannot now exercise our democratic right to remove a man plainly in-competent to be headmaster, and replace him with another chap.'

'A man, you think?' The bursar's voice seemed without in-flection, but suddenly Pug started to sweat. Someone rose, and opened a window.

'Or woman, of course,' he said, not daring to look at Veron-ica.

'There never has been a woman head of a progressive coedu-cational school, has there?' Maggie mused.

'I've never heard of anything so utterly ridiculous in my entire life.'

'Mnyah, you may have a point there.'

Mortmain's discomfiture spread throughout the arts staff, and was therefore enhanced by the scientists.

'An excellent idea!'

'Most unusual. We should be proactive, not reactive,'

Sproggs agreed in a burst of enthusiasm and saliva.

Nicholas Crump sucked on his moustache. 'Mustn't rush things, you know.'

'I wonder,' said Dai Delus meditatively, 'how long we can keep control over the wilder elements in the school now that the loss of authority is so plain for all to see?'

Grub threw himself into practising for his Grade Eight as if casting himself off a cliff. For two terms now, he had neglected the set pieces he was supposed to be doing for the impossible Everest of the Liszt. There was the Bach fugue from 'The Well-Tempered Clavier'. Grinding his teeth, Grub thought the title alone was provocation. The Mozart K333 in B flat was described on one recording as 'a life-enhancing stream of gracious melody'. Oh, pass the sickbag, he thought.

Ruth, hearing him performing these in his best Richard Clayderman style, sighed.

'Heavens, Grub, I know you yearn for *Sturm und Drang*, but I do wish you'd grow up. Why are you satirising those beautiful pieces? Can't you take your aggression out on something else?'

Grub went on thumping his hands down savagely, then swerved into another piece.

'What's bothering you? Is it something you want to talk about?'

'Don't treat me like one of your fucking patients!' said Grub, in a tone of such fury and misery it was hardly rude.

'I've been thinking,' said Ruth, after a pause, 'it really is time I got you some contact lenses instead of your glasses. I know you're still growing, but they only last for a year anyway, so what the heck?'

'Wouldn't do any good,' Grub muttered.

'Have you fallen out with Johnny, or Jono, or whatever he calls himself?'

'No!'

'Oh. Why don't you go over to Notting Hill?'

'I've told you, Tore doesn't like people visiting him.'

'Maybe you could meet on neutral territory. Like, in the cinema?'

'Just leave me alone, Mum.' He swerved into another piece.

'Ah, jealousy,' said Ruth, with one of her alarmingly clever flashes of intuition. 'He wrote them when he thought Clara was having an affair, didn't he? Very different from the usual thing one associates with Schumann.'

Grub thought of Fay playing the 'Scenes from Childhood', and grunted.

'Hey, I think we've got a Glenn Gould recording of that Bach somewhere. Maybe your hero can enthuse you better than I can.'

Ruth's Americanisms grated on Grub horribly. Throughout the holidays, he had been afraid to go out of doors, the sight of any tall man with blond hair roused such murderous fury in him. Even Belsize Park Village, as it was now known, seemed to be teeming with Winthrop lookalikes.

The intensity of his jealousy was such that he dreamt, night after night, of terrible revenges: knocking the American to the ground and stamping on his ribs until they broke, one by one; or smashing his large white teeth open and peeing into his mouth. Tore had done this, once, to a new boy, while the other Lads had held him down on the ground, unzipping his flies and letting out an arc of steaming yellow liquid which seemed to go on for ever. It hadn't been quite as funny as some of the Lads' pranks, but when Tore got into one of his psychotic moods there was nothing anyone could do to stop him. Tore had seen through Winthrop from the first, whereas Grub had been in-clined to dismiss him as a pain.

The story about him shafting Alice during the riot had got round, even if was totally inaccurate, and now he was a hero. The cool of doing it right under the noses of the staff had cap-tured everyone's imagination. Sparks Delus had offered Win a tab of acid the very next day, and the Arabs had invited him to share in their end-of-term Chinko. They were always quick, in the interests of self-preservation, to spot a new power baron, thought Grub. It had not been an enjoyable occasion for the Lads. Winthrop, accepting their offer, had promptly wielded his own credit card, and when the taxi had arrived from Knot-smouth, he invited everyone in the corridor to share in his two huge eighteenth-birthday cakes.

The squeals of piggy delight had caused Tore to remark, 'Greed is a hologram of fear,' and mooch off to the Stagehands' Hut. For the rest of the week he had worked ferociously on his crossbow in the workshops, until the news about Poppy had been splodged all over the tabloids.

Grub did not dare ask his father what part, if any, he himself had played in this. The Bimbo was not one to let slip any snippet of information which could lead to a good story, but on the other hand Sam was such a cussed, unpredictable man that he could easily have forgotten what Grub had casually mentioned. Or else, he could have remembered it, one bored moment (and Grub hoped there were many) in bed at Lamb's Conduit Street.

Yet it was too much of a coincidence to believe that the *Mirror* could have turned up that lead on its own. To catch out that old prune, after all his pontificating Christianity, married to a former tart should have been a priceless joke.

He wondered why he felt so miserable about it.

One thing you could say about England was that the water that came out of the faucets didn't taste like it had been piped straight from a swimming pool, thought Winthrop. Nor did England make him feel like an ant crawling along the bottom of a cliff. There were no trees, no views and a buzz he could almost shave himself by. A psychopath was stalking the streets at every change of the zodiac, and the noise that came through if he opened the windows was like the end of the world.

Manhattan had swept him back into itself within moments of his lifting the telephone. Everyone was around, what with the aftermath of the Gulf War, and, having been absent from the scene for nearly a year, Winthrop found himself something of a celebrity among his friends. The scandal surrounding his expulsion from the last school had been transmuted into part of the rolling saga of Poon Man Sheen, and the teacher in question had dropped out of sight.

He went dancing at Nell's, attended two Rites of Spring parties and mooned out of a car while being driven past the Trump Plaza. It was great to be back with people to whom he did not have to explain the way things worked all the time. But he still didn't go for any of the girls who flocked around him. They were pretty, nice, athletic, rich, and one day he would probably marry one of them. But meanwhile, they were all so deeply unsexy, as well as far too well connected. There was no question of deploying the old line of 'find 'em, fuck 'em, fight 'em and forget 'em.' You played around with your own class at your peril: that was one thing the prep-schoolteacher incident had taught him. Of course, life could not be a chain of

mountaintop experiences, but whenever he was asked how he
was getting on in England, he took pleasure in answering,
'Better than Henry James.'

It gave him great satisfaction to think of this. When his daddy
had left him for another family, he had realised that personal relationships were shit. All sex was about power. He had used his
knowledge well. He hadn't planned his response to Alice, but in
retrospect he had really lucked out on that one. It was just like
being a dealer: you found something that was undervalued, and
bought it. Then, when everyone looked your way, you sold.

The scandal surrounding the Harts trickled across the
Atlantic, but when asked about it by Bitsy, Winthrop shrugged
and pointed out that it was a very old story.

'Besides, Mummy, those Norman Rockwell types always
have something tacky to hide.'

'Oh, Winkie, you're so cynical. I just worry about how per-
missive Knotshead is. I mean – '

'Yeah, yeah. "Controlled and disciplined living can lead to a
greater sense of personal freedom," and all that shit. Mummy,
believe me, I can handle anything that place throws up. Who
cares if the head's wife dabbled in vice? I don't have anything to
do with it. And I like it there. I'm setting up a film club to teach
them American culture.'

'Well . . . ' said Bitsy.

'No way,' said Winthrop.

22

The start of the summer term brought a resurgence of interest from the tabloid press. For almost a week, men with vulpine faces and expensive cream mackintoshes attempted to stop pupils on the way to the village shop to elicit or solicit quotes as to their opinion of the headmaster and his wife. They were particularly keen to get hold of Johnny Tore, to ask him whether his father had had any further contact with Poppy. As a result, Hart suddenly found himself more popular than at any time since the suicide.

'Really,' pupils like Nicola went round saying, 'what Poppy did only shocks the bourgeois middle classes. There are more tits in *Tatler*, any day.'

'If she got laid by Tore's dad all those years ago, then good luck to her,' said a Lad in Block Five. 'The one time he turned up for Parents' Day, he had all the tarts drooling over him.'

Many parents were far more shocked than their children, and when term began it was discovered that twenty pupils had been withdrawn. One of these was Olivia.

'She shows no sign of being interested in academic work, and has been invited to take up modelling instead,' Lord Paddington wrote to Hart. 'As I'm sure your charming wife must know, it can be a very lucrative career.'

Hart had crumpled the letter up in a convulsive gesture, and thought bitterly of revolution. He knew his position was increasingly in danger. Those who had written already to complain about his performance as headmaster now redoubled their efforts. On the plus side, others sprang to the defence not of him but of the school. One OK, now an influential columnist, wrote a long piece reminiscing about what a happy time she had enjoyed at the school, 'apart,' she added, 'from the compulsory sex'. Others thought it best to keep their heads below the parapet. People who had never heard of Knotshead now bandied its name about as a place to which it was, or was not, desirable to send children. The received wisdom had always been that it was good for girls but less so for boys: but how could anyone be sure? Dark doubts swelled in every mind.

The children and staff reacted predictably. If parents were against Hart, they were for him. At the first Jaw, Hew played Blake's 'Jerusalem', and for once even the most unmusical of Knotes bawled it out without using hymn books as a means of scribbling messages to each other. Suddenly, Hart had become interesting.

It filtered out that the governors were considering dismissing him on the grounds of unsuitable conduct. This was felt by staff and pupils alike to be monstrously unjust. Why should he be made to go because of something his wife did? Of course, he was a disaster. Every time he opened his mouth and that flat voice came out, they all cringed. They cringed when he wore a grey suit with pads which rose and fell like amputated wings when he moved his shoulders, and they cringed when they were made to sing hymns like 'Lead Kindly Light'. His remarks that his wife had been free to express her sexuality had been subject to much sniggering when pictures of her in shiny black corsets and long hooker's boots had been reprinted in *News of the World*.

On the other hand, to condemn people for what they did in private was universally felt to be illiberal. Not since the issue of whether Shit Horder should ban all non-biodegradable cleaning liquids from the school had debate raged so furiously.

'What does Poppy think, Alice?' asked Fay, when they were alone in the dorm.

Alice shrugged. There was too much malicious curiosity in Fay's voice for her to be trusted. When she returned from being with Winthrop, Fay would look at her as if devouring the sight. It was a most distasteful feeling. Yet she pitied Fay. More and more, she saw the similarity between their lives: both of them pushed by parental will as well as inner compulsion to exceed at all costs.

'We don't discuss it. She's too proud to talk to anyone. It's pretty awful.'

'Do you really think Simon knew?'

Alice moved restively. 'Yes. In part.'

'It seems incredible that he thought she'd get away with it.'

'Why not? Morality was different then, and it was such a long time ago. It seems so cruel that something she did two decades ago should come back to haunt her and Simon.'

'You don't really know each other at all, do you? I suppose it's natural, with such an age gap.'

'My parents had a difficult marriage,' said Alice. 'They separated when Poppy was a teenager, and hardly ever saw each other. I was an afterthought. A mistake.'

'My parents didn't get married until they were in their thirties,' said Fay. 'Everyone seems to have gone off having children in the Seventies. Not like grown-ups now. My cousin Izzy was desperate for years, and now she's got one you'd think Gabriella was one of the wonders of the world.'

Alice said, 'I suppose it depends at what stage in your life you get pregnant. I mean, it would be an absolute disaster if we did at our age. But it might be just as horrible if we couldn't in ten years' time.'

She scratched her breasts absently. Winthrop had hugged her so tightly at their reunion, she thought she would explode with pain as well as happiness.

'Yes,' said Fay, pensively, 'it would.'

The days lengthened and brightened. In the Library, those taking GCSEs and A levels scribbled nervously, many wearing triangular paper hats which were popularly believed to concentrate beneficent cosmic rays into the head. Quarrels broke out among those taking music examinations over the allocation of rooms, before the Tower of Babel became too hot to endure. Those racing to finish pieces of woodwork or jewellery for Parents' Day were officially excused Jaw for three nights a week.

May came late, in a froth of blossom, after a cold start. Beech trees flushed crimson with new leaves, oaks yellow. The sky above and the ground below were a wash of blue.

Winthrop's meetings with Alice became less difficult. It was not necessary to go all the way up to the mines now, for the big field between the Dower House and the school San was thick with grasses growing waist-high. Here couples would retreat, completely invisible once they sank down into the rippling, wind-muscled green. Rejects would give this field a wide berth.

Winthrop did not believe in public displays of affection, but he was satisfied with the way Alice had become submissive to him. He had gained the upper hand, and often spent the afternoon playing tennis on the courts across the lake to emphasise this, while she waited for him. He set her to do his French prep, as well as her own, explaining that his film club took up a lot of time, and that he was blown out. The school had no computers, so he had to copy it all in his own handwriting.

All the same, he became annoyed with the way she tried to keep being the good-attitude student. Of course, he believed Latin built a sound vocabulary, but it really was not key to modern existence. Sex was.

'If mothers had any sense, they'd teach their daughters how to give good blow jobs,' he said, lying back in the flattened circle made by their bodies. 'It's the most useful asset any girl can have.'

Alice hated it when he talked like this. It was, she supposed, a joke; but it was so crude, as when he talked of her 'losing her cherry'. Such language had nothing to do with the things she felt, but she supposed it was the way males came to terms with the whole business. She asked him, once, what went through his head when he was inside her, and he had looked very surprised.

'Nothing.'

'Oh.'

'Isn't it like that for you?'

'No.'

'Do you think of someone else, then?'

'No.'

'Not Tore?'

'*No!*'

'Well, that's OK. What do you think about?'

'How much I love you,' said Alice. 'Idiotic.'

'I think it's nice.'

'No. It's horrid. It makes me sick, sometimes, I feel it so much.'

'What, literally?'

'Yes. Isn't it silly? Just sometimes. When you're . . . late.'
'Oh. The afternoon. Not in the morning?'
'Oh, no,' said Alice.
'Good,' said Winthrop.

In the fetid fastness of the Stagehands' Hut, Grub was crouched over his wine-making kit, unused since Christmas. He had discovered on a recent expedition to Minedale that the supermarket now stocked a kind of grape juice which, with proper fermentation, could be turned to wine. Further experiments had followed.

'The fact is, you can turn any fucking thing to booze if you have the right equipment,' Tore said, watching him. 'Look at Russians, getting pissed on beetroot. This lot should be much better than the time we tried smoking nutmeg.'

'How long do you think it should be left to mature?' asked Grub, looking at the bubbling liquid. 'It says here two or three months is the minimum advisable.'

'Oh, crap. You can try some as soon as it's done. That's what they do on my old man's château.'

'Not with my Grade Eight coming up.'

'You think the moving fingers might get the shakes?'

'I can't risk it.'

'Well, tell you what. It looks pretty crappy now, so let's wait until after, OK? Then we can celebrate by getting pissed out of our heads.'

'OK.'

Gestures like these made Grub ashamed of having wavered in his faith. It was like the Liszt: he had been forced by temporary expediency to abandon it, but it was still there, waiting for him.

The weather became hotter. The moors all around and above were stained by heather. The swans' cygnets hatched and floated awkwardly upon the waters. Everywhere, girls in sprigged cotton dresses picked armfuls of sappy flowers to put in jugs and jam jars. All the Lads who were not taking exams went night wandering, as much out of restlessness as bravado, and stomped through the fields thwacking off elderflower heads with big sticks.

'What is it that makes boys so destructive?' asked Miranda Jupp in the staff room.

'Testosterone,' Beatrice Bassett answered shortly.

Tore was ensconced in the workshops, sweating over his crossbow.

'Strictly speaking,' said Delus, 'we should get a licence for that, as soon as it's finished. It's a lethal weapon, you know.'

'Yeah,' said Tore. 'I know.' To Grub he said, 'It has the power of two hundred pounds. When I've finished, a bolt from this could go through a suit of armour.'

'But you wouldn't shoot anyone, Jono, would you?'

'Just think,' said Tore dreamily. 'It was the invention of cross-bows that won the Norman Conquest.'

'I thought it was the stirrup?'

'Ah, bog off!'

Grub pushed his spectacles up his nose and said, 'Perhaps you should try it on Sally. Now she's married Norman Sproggs. Like, Cupid's dart.'

He mimed an arrow going into the gym teacher's heart, falling to the floor dramatically.

'I have a few possibilities in mind,' said Tore.

Knotshead came into its full glory during the summer term. Trees all around shimmered with shifting leaf: a green so fresh it made Grub wish he were a slug. People played croquet and tennis on the lawns, and went swimming in the lake during gym. As was traditional, no pupil was allowed to wear a swimming costume, except during mixed bathing in the free period after lunch. Of course, the sexes were supposed to be segregated during the official swims, but the Lads always managed to sneak up and whistle at the girls before being chased away by Sally.

Swimming without clothes on felt wonderful, thought Grub. There was something unreasonably sensual about the touch of cold water, quite different from the steamy fug of the bathrooms in the Males' Flats. He floated vertically, looking at the smooth stripes, pale green and dark green, tracking up to the big house. Already the sprinklers were in motion, moving backwards and forwards like the tails of ghostly peacocks. Where they could not reach, cracks of drought appeared, both in the lawns and halfway up the dining-room walls. The Assembly Hall, being subterranean, was worst affected: one crack was big enough to hide comics in. The scent of mown grass, he thought. Waterweed and lilac. A mallard quacked past his nose followed by two ducklings bobbing in her wake. It was only when they were little that you could see the frantic motion of their webbed feet paddling beneath the water; when they grew up, all that was visible was the smooth glide across the surface. He wondered whether this was the same with humans.

Turning, he squinted across the glinting waters and looked at the five temples shining at the end of their long avenues. Love, chastity, wisdom, music and booze. They looked very pretty, so cool and white above the mass of rhododendron and camellia. But the Venus parties weren't the same without Olivia. She had split up with Tore in April, soon after joining Models One, and had sent him a letter telling him that she was going out with someone else. It was the only time Grub had seen his friend cry. Since then, various school factions had tried to curry favour by getting him interested in another girl, but he wasn't interested any longer. He spent all his time working on his crossbow. Dai was pleased with his application, promising to exhibit it on Parents' Day, when Gore Tore was going to make one of his rare visits.

He was seriously worried about the situation between Winthrop and Tore. Yesterday at lunch, Tore had started baiting Fay again.

'D'you know what Fay needs? A Boy Snout. Oink, oink!'

Fay had sat there with tears in her eyes, while the others shifted uncomfortably. Somehow, these jokes seemed less funny than they had been, especially to Grub. He thought of what he would feel like if Tore had made them about his mother, who had shared the Viner family picnic on successive Parents' Days with Jono, and knew he would never have forgiven his friend. But it was too embarrassing to stop him. The rest of the table smirked and whispered to each other.

'Fay, Fay knows sweet FA,

Hard to shake off but an easy lay,'

Tore chanted, his black eyes glittering, when Winthrop and Alice sat down.

Alice overheard him, and suddenly lost her temper.

'Tore, Tore, he's such a bore:

Too thick to pass exams like his daddy Gore,' she said. 'Why don't you pick on someone your own age, for a change? And you, why do you make such a fuss about easy things, like South African oranges, and sit here grinning while he spouts this sick spite?'

There had been absolute silence at the table, and the sound of knives and forks clinking on other tables had become unnaturally loud. Everyone felt her remarks had been in very bad taste. Fay was scarlet.

'Sounds to me like you're pretty sick already,' said Tore.

'Why don't you shut the fuck up?' said Winthrop.

Tore bared his pointed greenish teeth at him. 'Why should I? This is my table.'

The hatred between them had been almost visible, like lightning. Winthrop didn't know what Tore was capable of, Grub thought. He was completely fearless, that was why everyone was so frightened of him. Grub had watched expectantly as Tore fingered something in his pocket, smiling.

'You'd better watch out, Superbrat. It seems to me you're getting a little bit full of yourself, fucking Louse and setting up your film club. If you don't watch your step, you could find yourself in a most unpleasant situation. Geddit?'

'And you could find yourself fishing your teeth out of the toilet, asshole. Geddit?'

How matters would have resolved themselves, Grub had no idea; but at that moment Nicholas Crump had come and sat down at their table.

'Ah, Johnny, I've been meaning to have a word with you,' he said. 'About that Hussein affair. You're quite certain you ticked him off on the list that night?'

Tore glowered at him, then rolled his eyes.

'Not again! Look, we've been through all this before. Your wife made a mistake, right?'

'If so,' said Crump, smiling behind his toothbrush moustache, 'how is it that Hussein's bank manager has written to the headmaster complaining about a bounced cheque written out in Tramps, and dated that night?'

23

Both the Arabs and Tore got into serious trouble for lying about Hussein's London expedition. Confronted with the bounced cheque, the latter had confessed at once.

'For nearly three terms, your calculated dishonesty has caused the utmost discord and unpleasantness in the school. The staff have been at loggerheads over your lies, and Daphne Crump has had her honour impugned. It is small satisfaction to reflect that, if you hadn't been so insolent to your bank manager as well, he would never have taken the step of complaining to me,' said Hart. 'You should learn from this, I hope, that bad behaviour always meets its punishment.'

Tore thought it best not to mention the call he had taken on the portable telephone.

Condemned to planting a hundred trees each, Naimh and Hussein were boiling with resentment. Normally, they managed to skive out of any physical labour, but enjoyed a languid game of tennis in the summer months. To be denied this and made to work the land was a terrible blow to their pride. Blaming Hart, they spent hours plotting how to get their own back.

'We send him a Strippogram,' Naimh suggested. 'She kisses him in front of all the parents.'

'No,' said Hussein. 'That will just make them feel sorry for him, man. He's such a spastic. Like a Swiss banker.'

Grub was suddenly visited by a vision of a practical joke so glorious that it almost took his breath away. 'Are you serious about this? I mean, would you spend money?'

The Arabs looked dubiously at each other.
'How much?'
'Probably no more than five hundred.'
'If it's real good,' said Hussein.
'Well, then, listen.'

The highlight of Parents' Day was always the concert in the evening. This year, Hew had chosen Mozart's Requiem. Week by week, the singers learnt each part. Much as Grub resented having to do Mozart for his Grade Eight, the hair on his scalp rose up from the first stave of the Introitus and did not come down again until the last note of the Communio died away. He did not understand the Latin, but the terror and beauty of the vision which was erected, piece by piece, shook him.

'*Dies irae, dies illa*
Solvet saeclum in favilla:
Teste David cum Sibylla.
Quantus tremor est futurus
Quando judex est venturus,
Cuncta stricte discussurus!'

So they thundered, while the orchestra beneath them burnt; fire from heaven, or from hell. Of course, all Knotes were atheists, but when they sang it became rather difficult to remember this. Even singers in 6ii, by now increasingly jumpy about their revisions, came to practice religiously.
'It helps relieve the tension,' said one.
In the middle of June, a clumsy arrangement of scaffolding and stepped wooden planks was put up for the choir to stand on. Here they would stand, as the sun beat down on the glass dome overhead, itchy with sunburn and sexual frustration. Grub would stare longingly at Alice, who had, for the first time in her life, gone a deep shade of brown as a result of all the hours spent lying in the fields with Winthrop. Against the black of a sleeveless cotton dress her flesh glowed. Oh, thought Grub, the painful pleasure of being joined in music with someone you loved . . . Standing jammed up behind the girls' smooth, tanned backs gave most of the males colossal erections – including, Grub noted, Mortmain singing solo in the tenors. He wondered how the old goat still managed to be so randy now that he had

taken on a double load of English teaching. Since Pedigree's departure, the Males' Flats were running wild. Pug was looking quite grey.

The heat wave made everyone fretful. Looking down from the dorms in Males' Flats, Grub could see the cubes and curls of the uprooted parterre, square after square of a three-hundred-year-old pattern, like that on the back of a playing card, coming through the parched lawn. The lake itself was sinking dramatically, since a national and regional ban on hosepipes meant that it had become the only means of watering the farm and the Venus Vale. It was no longer safe or pleasant to swim in. Dark green algae were growing over the surface, and as the lake sank lower in its shores, pieces of old masonry poked through the floating shoals of dead fish.

'It's the old village,' the pupils said to each other. 'The old Anstey that was moved.'

Croquet became impossible on the bleached and prickly stubble of the lawns, and the girls took up the ouija board at night, with inevitable fits of hysteria. The situation regarding Hart affected everyone; it was rumoured that he and Poppy were close to either divorce or nervous breakdown, or both. Sprinklers whirled day and night, but the need for rain was so great that the water evaporated even as it fell. The great trees on the peninsula spread heavily, their boughs dull and weighted by dust. Deer crossed the pebbly trickle of the Knot to crop anything they could find. The Librarian guarded his herbaceous borders and muttered darkly about sending off for lion droppings from Howletts Zoo.

Both Flottage and the Tower of Babel had become unbearable for lessons. Knotes taking exams sweated it out in comparative comfort in the Library, where the only creature which seemed happy was Horatio; but Grub, with the Grade Eight coming up, was in despair.

He had left it too late to work up the three pieces to an adequate standard, because of his obsession with the Liszt. Dripping with sweat, he attacked the Ravel Sonatine, the most difficult of the three, with miserable persistence. No more spoofing around being Clayderman now. His fingers slipped on the ivories and his toes on the pedals as he went over the three movements. Grub liked Ravel, but never had any sonata seemed to him so precious, so mincingly miniature. Fay was also practising for the same examination, a John Ireland piece which was as difficult. They were the only two pupils taking Grade Eight a year early. As the weeks went by, this drew them into a grudging alliance.

'If I don't get this, my parents are going to take me away from here,' Fay confided, one afternoon. 'They're worried about my marks slipping.'

'Don't you want to go?'

'Well,' said Fay, 'yes and no. On one hand, people can be pretty beastly. On the other, it's like that at every school, because I'm always two or three years ahead of the rest.'

'Have you always been the youngest?' asked Grub, suddenly curious.

Fay nodded. 'I've got two sisters older than me, at Cambridge. But they're not that bright.'

'My brothers are at Oxford.'

'Are you going to try for it?'

Grub shrugged. 'I'd prefer the Royal College. Hew thinks I might be good enough to, well . . . '

'Play professionally? It's a hard life. You could end up just being a music teacher, like him, if you fail.'

Grub thought of times he had listened to Radio Three lunchtime concerts featuring someone attempting to scale the slippery peaks of Chopin or Scriabin, and Hew's racecourse commentaries on whether they succeeded or, as inevitably happened, came unseated during the hairpin bends of an allegro. This had always made Grub laugh, but now he saw how much frustration must lie underneath the sourness of Hew's criticisms. Hew had had his chance as a performer, and something had gone wrong. It was failure that distorted a generous spirit, not success, he thought. Perhaps that was the real battle: not just to realise talent, but to keep some spring of hope, liveliness or courage unstoppered. And if you failed, you failed not only as a musician, but in some essential way as a person.

'That's a thing I have to risk, then,' he said, aloud.

He practised; and when the time for his examination came, he walked into the stony bowels of the Assembly Hall without a tremor. A deathly calm descended on him, so much so that despite the stuffy air the tips of his fingers went blue.

The music examiner, a middle-aged man in a bow tie and shirtsleeves, said, 'I would like you to start by playing me staccato thirds.'

'That's not in the exam!' Grub burst out.

The examiner looked at him. 'I'm afraid it is, Mr, ah, Viner.'

Oh, shit, thought Grub. I've blown it already. Shit, shit, shit. He played, thumping them out with a concentrated fury.

'Now the three pieces, in any order you want.'

Grub gathered himself into himself, breathed deeply, and started to play. His display of temper had done him good, releasing the worst part of nervous tension. In the part of his conscious mind which floated above the music like a cork in a stream, he heard it going well with a remote satisfaction.

'Ah, yes,' said the examiner, when Grub came out of his trance. 'Lovely piece, that Sonatine. I remember when I played it before the High Commissioner of Rhodesia in 1963.'

'Thank you,' said Grub, slithering out. He put his thumb up to Fay, who was waiting outside for her turn. She gave a weak grin. He could hear her begin to play almost at once, as he went up the steps to the Quad. As soon as he got to the top, his knees collapsed, and he had to sit down for a bit.

Poor Fay, he thought, for the first time. It must be awful to have pushy parents. I hope she passes.

'Well, whehey! Have you got it?' said Tore, outside.

'They don't tell you for a few weeks.'

'Fucking arseholes.'

'But he said something about it being a lovely piece, which I think is a good sign.'

Tore pulled some leaves off a twig and shredded them in his filthy fingers. 'I wish I were like you,' he said suddenly. 'I wish I had some real gift for something.'

Astonished, Grub reddened, then shook his head.

'It isn't like that.'

'But you know what you want to do with your life. Like my dad. You can play in the orchestra, and sing on Parents' Day, and make everyone – '

'But you've got lots of things. I mean . . . '

'Nothing of my own.'

'There's your crossbow,' said Grub, pushing his glasses up his nose. 'That's good. I mean, Dai thinks so, and it is. And your father's coming to see it on Parents' Day, isn't he?'

'Yes,' said Tore bleakly, after a pause. 'There's still that.'

*

Alice kept being sick. It happened in the afternoon, as she had told Winthrop, but she felt dreadful all morning, too. She ate practically nothing, but her stomach seemed full all the time, even when she could face no more than a piece of toast. In the back of her mind a hideous question had begun to form, but she told herself it was the heat which had made her unusually sensitive to food poisoning.

She dragged herself from lesson to lesson, hating them all. What had she ever done but learn and learn and learn, and what good had it done her? The scholarship her mother had prized so was no more than second best, like winter apples, compared to the real thing. When she was with Winthrop she might be confused, embarrassed, hurt, but she felt herself to be alive in a way that she had not been since she was seven, on the Ayreshire farm.

Even Latin was a misery. They were doing Sallust's *Jugurthine Wars*, which she thought must be the most boring piece of Roman propaganda ever written. The Romans kept trying to scale the city walls, and she was too fed up with Sallust's interminable pedagogy to find out if they ever got to the top, even in translation.

The Librarian was endlessly patient and gentle with her as she struggled through the fog in her head. Such kindness, in one known for impatience and irascibility, made her more guilty.

'Never mind,' he kept saying. 'It's just one of those things you have to get through. I know you don't think so, but it really is a very good piece of prose, even if it doesn't have the allure of the poetry. Such a pity you haven't learnt any Greek; it would be fun to do some Herodotus in tandem.'

Alice shuddered, privately. She found in herself a great loathing for stories of strife and violence. Winthrop's American film club, a huge success, showed nothing but people being ripped apart by monsters and machines; after cowering in the Assembly Hall with her eyes shut and her fingers in her ears through the screening of *Alien*, *Predator* and *Terminator*, she decided her nerves would not take it.

Several times, she made an effort to go and see Poppy and help with the twins. Her sister was more listless and depressed than Alice had ever seen her, and a web of wrinkles had appeared like cracks in her skin. Lily and Daisy clung to Alice's legs when it was time for her to go. She would play with, and cuddle them for hours; and if it was because she missed Winthrop so much, at least they seemed more receptive to simple affection than he did.

'Is Simon all right to you?' Alice asked Poppy, on one occasion.

'He doesn't say anything. That makes it worse.'

'Can't you talk about it?'

'What is there to say? I've ruined his career.'

'It was something that happened such a long time ago.'

'Scandal has a long memory. Wherever I go, now, they'll never let us forget it. There'll always be someone pointing out that I used to be a tart.'

'Oh, how I hate newspapers!' Alice cried. 'The misery they cause, with their poking and prying and distortion!'

Poppy shrugged. 'They have to earn a living, like everyone else.'

'I wonder how they found out.'

'I expect,' said Poppy, 'that someone in the school tipped them off.'

'Who?'

'At a guess, Veronica. She wants Simon's job very badly. It isn't just ambition: she thinks he's ruining everything Knotshead stands for. But I expect we'll never know.'

A surge of nausea went through Alice. To distract herself, she asked, faintly, 'Are you going to stay together?'

'I don't know.'

'Are you . . . in love, still?'

'I never was.'

'Oh.'

A weight hung on Alice's tongue. She said, with effort, 'Were you in love with Gore?'

There was a long silence.

'Oh, yes,' said her sister, almost inaudibly. 'Very.' She cleared her throat. 'Everyone was who met him. Girls and blokes. He had, even before he became famous, that thing, I don't know what it is, not looks particularly, though he has that still – just. You couldn't think about anything except sex when you were with him. And he wanted me.

'I was very beautiful when I was your age. I knew it – God, it would have been hard not to. It gives you such power. I couldn't wait to get my clothes off. I wasn't on smack then, that came later, and I knew I was perfect. I had no shame or fear of anything. I lost count of the number of blokes I slept with before Gore. Dad was very wild, too, you know . . . I didn't give a toss about the record cover. If you want to know, I enjoyed it, having what we did together recorded. I thought it was beautiful.'

'But didn't it cross your mind that it was something very private?' asked Alice.

Poppy shrugged. 'Everyone did things like that then, from Lennon and Yoko down. Morality has changed now, people have gone back to being mean and scared and conventional again, but it was different. We didn't believe in sin, and we didn't have AIDS or . . . I loved Gore. He was the love of my life. Nothing mattered except him. Until the heroin . . . You can't regret a thing and yearn for it at the same time.'

'Yes,' said Alice. 'I do see that, now.' She bounced Lily on her knee. 'What about Simon, though?'

'I married him,' Poppy said, wearily, 'because I was sick of being stuck in a dead-end job as a housemother, and I wanted to be a real one. It's so ironic . . .'

'Wasn't there any other way?'

'What, be a single parent?' Poppy shook her head. 'You've got to be very thick or very rich to cope with that. No, it was a bargain. He needed a wife – a bachelor headmaster always looks iffy – and I needed a husband.'

'Wasn't there anyone else?'

'Oh, there are lots of blokes who'll still screw you when you're thirty-six,' her sister said bitterly. 'But marriage? No. It's the great fallacy of contraception, as far as I can see. All it's done is free men from responsibility. Any really desirable man who wants to marry is still going to look for a wife who's young, rich and conventional – not ageing, unsuccessful and with a dodgy past. No, Simon was the best I could get.'

'You have too low an opinion of yourself,' said Alice. 'I think it must be a family trait.' It surprised her to say this: she had never seen herself and Poppy as being remotely alike before.

'And besides,' said Poppy, with a trace of defiance, 'he's a *good* man. Gore wasn't. Even if he'd been interested in marriage. Or free from that bleached cockatoo, Tara. God, how we hated each other! She was wild with jealousy at every girlfriend he had, she never saw that you couldn't own him any more than the wind. Simon may not be particularly handsome or intelligent or what Mama would call well-bred, but he means so well. Even that stupid interview, which he insisted on doing – he did it to help me.' She began to cry. 'That's why I feel so bloody awful about the whole thing. It's all my fault. I thought I was doing him such a favour, marrying him, and I've been such a cow. Every time he's opened his mouth I've done my best to undermine him, and he has so little self-confidence anyway. That's why he believes in all that crap about marketing and self-presentation. If only he'd be relaxed, like he is with the twins, it would all be so different.'

Alice closed her eyes, unable to speak for fear she would be sick. It hadn't happened for two days, and now it was back again. Oh, please God, no, she thought.

'The thing about love is that it's just as dangerous as smack,' said Poppy. 'People think that if they haven't had the big one, they've missed out on life, not avoided having it ruined. It destroys you.'

'You sound like Mama.'

'Well,' said Poppy, 'one of the things about growing older is that sometimes you see what your parents meant.'

24

Parents' Day dawned the hottest day of the year. Not a breath moved the black clouds over the moors, where it had begun to rain at last. The line of cars glittering back through the twisting, sunken lanes leading to Anstey moved slowly, packed with parents in wilting hats and suits. Tempers were short and the queue for parking was long. When they approached the gates and went up the drive past the Headmaster's Lodge, they all began to laugh uproariously.

For the Harts' house had, overnight, been painted the colour of a giant toadstool, with a lurid red, white-spotted roof. On top, and all around it, sat thirty grinning garden gnomes, pulling their little trousers down, swigging out of bottles or smoking what, even at a distance, looked like fat brown rolls of marijuana. Every one of them, beneath its scarlet cap, looked just like Simon Hart.

The Arabs' money had done the Lads proud. The crates arrived two days before, unnoticed in the muddle surrounding the other preparations, and had been stored away in the Lads' Hut. The night before, every Lad from every block had crept out to drag the crates down the drive and climb up, silently, on to the headmaster's roof, which was sprayed with quick-drying paint. The joy when they saw their own handiwork in the full light of day was intense.

There was no doubt about it: it was an inspired practical joke. As word spread around the school at breakfast, Knotes streamed out of the dining hall to applaud it and roll around the stubbly grass in glee. Grub, revealed as the brains behind it all, was caught with Naimh and Hussein, and thrown up and down in the air as if it was their birthdays.

The cache of Grub's home-made wine was brought out to celebrate. Nobody could get into trouble for drinking alcohol on Parents' Day. Bottles passed from pupil to pupil.

'Christ, what the fuck have you put in this?' Tore asked, coughing and spluttering as he took a swig. 'It tastes like neat meths.'

'It's all according to the recipe,' said Grub, in a portentous tone.

'Hmm, a dry, spry little vintage,' said Nicola, passing it on.

'With a very good head,' said Winthrop.

'Where's Alice?' Grub asked Fay, longing to have her witness his moment of glory.

'In the Dower House. She's not feeling well.'

'Oh.'

By the time half-past ten struck and the parents started rolling up, the entire front lawn was covered with reeling, retching teenagers, some of them so drunk that they lay insensible in the boiling sun. The laughter that erupted as each parent passed the Headmaster's Lodge either died on their lips or redoubled. The conclusion, however, was identical. Simon Hart had completely lost control of the place. There could be no question, now, that he must go.

'Oh, my God, the little bastards!' said Maggie Brink.

'It's just like the proletariat: give them an inch and they'll take a yard,' said Nick Crump, nastily.

Toby Hindesmith, elegant in cream linen and a panama hat, giggled unstoppably.

'You haven't drunk any of the bloody stuff too, have you, Toby?'

'Heavens, no! I took one sniff, and it practically bit my nose off.'

'Where the hell did they get it? It smells like paint remover.'

'Someone seems to have had a home wine-making kit, from what I can gather.'

'Who?'

'Dunno, but I bet it's in the Stagehands' Hut. That place really ought to be closed down. Veronica's going to investigate tomorrow.'

The strains of 'The Four Seasons' throbbed out of the school stereo system and wafted over the Venus Vale.

'Not that bloody syrup!' Hew snarled. 'My nerves are shot to pieces already.'

'Oh, but they're such nice tunes,' said Miranda Jupp.

'Remember Beecham, Hew: "the English may not like music but they absolutely love the noise it makes",' said Hindesmith.

'Keep pouring coffee down those blighters,' said Beatrice Bassett grimly. 'That'll sober them up.'

Groaning, the pupils came to their senses. One or two were sick.

'How are you, darling?' asked a mother, bending over her son. He took one look at her hat, and slumped back.

'Awful.'

'You are naughty!'

'This school is a disgrace,' said Fay's father. 'I'm not letting my daughter stay here another day. Not another day!'

'Oh, Dad!' Fay wailed.

'Your marks have been going steadily downhill, and now I hear you've failed your Grade Eight.'

'What I've always said is, character is more important than brains,' said an OK loudly, overhearing this.

More and more parents thronged the lawns.

'Look at them all,' Mortmain muttered. 'Every profession in the country represented. Including the oldest one.'

'Oh, for heaven's sake, stop making such a fuss about it. I think it's jolly brave of Poppy to turn up at all,' said Sally Rupple.

'Just look at the way the Slythes are oiling round. You do realise, don't you, that they're what we'll get if Simon goes?'

'Come on, darling, I want to see what you've got on exhibition.'

'I say, frightful pong coming from the lake, isn't there?'

'It's this awful drought. The West Country always gets it worst.'

'The bloody water board is useless. There's been a hosepipe ban even in the middle of winter.'

'I heard they're thinking of lining the rivers with rubber.'

One by one, the parents picked their pallid offspring off the parched lawns and drifted away to look at the workshops.

Tore's crossbow, completed at the eleventh hour, had pride of place in the 6i selection. Its copper-bound frame and fletched arrows drew many comments, especially when parents read the surname on the label. They all knew that Johnny Tore was Gore Tore's son.

'I like your style,' said Ruth Viner, shaking hands with her son's friend gravely. 'Hallo there, again. You should come and see us in London.'

Tore blushed, and pulled nervously at a cigarette. 'Hi.'

'Is someone here for you, or would you like to join our picnic like before?' Ruth asked, with the easy mixture of tact and directness which made everyone trust her.

'My old man's coming,' Tore muttered. 'I think.'

'Oh, great. Well, if there's any problem, we'll be over underneath that tree with Grub's brothers.'

'Th-thanks,' said Tore.

Ruth went over to where Grub was wrestling with Josh and Tom.

'Ow, ow, bog off!' Grub shouted as, despite his increased height, Josh got his head under his arm and kept it there while Tom tickled him.

'Boys! Boys!'

'Hey, Mum, we're men now, or hadn't you noticed?'

'Not particularly,' said Ruth dryly. 'Why don't you help unpack the hamper?' To Grub she said softly, 'Is Jono's father really going to turn up?'

Grub shrugged. 'I suppose so.'

'Tell me,' said Ruth, 'is there anyone else you'd like to invite, particularly? We've got so much here and I notice there are some kids who look as if there's nobody with them.'

She looked at Grub with her bright, dark eyes. He flushed.

'Yes.'

'Why don't you go and find her?'

Grub was halfway up the lawns when he wondered how his mother had guessed it would be a she.

Alice hated Parents' Days, and would have gone off and hidden in the woods like a cat during a thunderstorm had it not been for the concert at the end. To avoid envy of those who had parents, even divorced ones, was one of the silent, unending battles which she fought, and Parents' Day always made the contrast between herself and the rest hard.

One reason why she did not retreat from the milling lawns was curiosity. Winthrop had informed her that his mother and stepfather were in London for a month, staying with the new American ambassador in Regent's Park; they would be dropping in on their way to another social event. Alice wondered what they would be like, and hoped she could observe without being observed herself.

Poppy and Simon were coping, however ill-matched they appeared. Poppy was dressed in bright Indian muslins, and Hart in an ill-fitting grey suit, but they stood side by side, shaking hands and smiling as if nothing in the world could be wrong. Mama, Alice remembered, had been very hot on noblesse oblige, and evidently the training had stuck. There could be little doubt that a number of parents had turned up solely because of the scandal surrounding her sister. She was furious about the gnomes, and wanted very much to do something supportive but was afraid that her presence would crack Poppy's apparent composure. From where she stood, uncertainly, by the Library, she could see them coming up to the Harts with bland and cordial smiles, then turning away with the avid expressions of gossips. Pity and anger made her clench her fists.

'You aren't about to hit anyone again, are you?' said Grub, coming up. Alice gave him a cold look.

'Only thinking about it.'

'Your sister?'

'No. You, among others. It was you who had the brilliant idea about painting their roof and putting gnomes on it? Tell me, how do you think Poppy and Simon feel, being made even more of a laughing stock? Don't you realise how wretched they've been all term? Didn't it ever cross your mind that he'll get the sack if he's made too ridiculous?'

'Oh.' Guilt, an increasingly familiar and unpleasant sensation, filled him. 'Sorry.'

'Sorry! Why don't you ever *think* about other people, for a change?'

'It's not the end of the world if you lose your job,' said Grub, defensively. 'Jobs are boring.'

'Oh? And what are they to live on? Air? And what do you think will happen if they get divorced? Well done, Grub. You've probably just made another broken home.'

This was dreadful.

'All right, all right, I'm sorry! I've said I'm sorry, haven't I? Shall I go to him and confess?'

'What's said can't be unsaid, and what's done can't be undone,' said Alice grimly. 'Just grow up.'

He wanted to ask whether she was feeling better, but was too embarrassed. Blushing, he blurted out his invitation. Alice looked at him with suspicion, and he realised, painfully, that she had no idea of the change that had taken place in him. It seemed incredible that she could not have noticed, could not read his mind as clearly as he now read hers; but then, he reflected dismally, she was in love with Winthrop.

'Why should I?'

'Mum thinks you're interesting.'

Alice's face froze. Evidently she suspected Ruth was after some inside gossip.

'She's a psychotherapist, you know.'

'No, I didn't. I – it's really not relevant. Why don't you find someone else to annoy?'

Grub felt like crying. 'Really, it isn't a tease, I promise. And she doesn't want to poke about your head, that's not what – She's not at all like most grown-ups.' He had an inspiration. 'More like Mr Kenward, in a funny sort of way.'

Alice hesitated. A long black car, which could only be that of a pop star, swept up the drive. Parents turned as first the chauffeur, then a bodyguard, then a woman so smart she could only be a secretary, and finally Gore Tore stepped out. He was wearing a bright red jumper slung across his shoulders, and very black sunglasses.

'Dad! Dad!' called Tore, in the high, cracked voice of an excited child, running towards him. 'It's me!'

Gore put up a thin, sallow hand and swept the crowd with his Ray-Bans, as if looking for someone else. He came to Poppy, and stopped.

'Hey, *Dad*!'

Tore put an arm round his son's shoulders, briefly, then dropped it. They began to walk towards the Harts. Parents and pupils turned and talked to each other with the ostentatious animation that being in the presence of international celebrity commonly evokes. Alice wondered what on earth Poppy and Gore would say to each other, after so many years. At that moment, a noise which had been fretting the edges of everyone's ears became very much louder. People looked up and began to point.

'A helicopter!'

'A chopper! It's going to land!'

'Good Lord! Where?'

Skirts and bits of straw flew up, hats were clutched or went spinning away. The helicopter made two or three passes across the lawns, swooping lower and lower.

'Bloody disgraceful! What a show-off!' Fay's father shouted, but most of the watchers were thrilled. This was style! This was glamour! Who on earth could it be?

The helicopter settled gently as a feather on a flat piece of ground and the noise of its whirling blades died away, pock-pock-pock, leaving a ringing noise in all ears. Then the door opened and a man and a woman got out. Impeccably dressed, elegant in every movement, they surveyed the crowd, like gods newly descended to earth and certain of immediate worship.

Winthrop strolled forward.

'Hi, Mummy. Hi, Bunny,' he said calmly.

'Hi, Win. Hi, Winkie,' said the two Americans. 'We're staying at the new ambassador's, and thought we'd drop by.'

'Glad you could spare the time,' said Winthrop. His heart swelled with satisfaction.

Winthrop took his mother's arm and steered her away to meet Hart, who was hurrying forward, sweaty palm outstretched.

Alice turned to Grub. 'Thank you,' she said. 'I'll come.'

The sky was increasingly dark with cloud, pressing the sultry air closer. Those who had drunk Grub's wine were still headachy and hung over. Wandering from the workshops to the Library to the art rooms to the cricket game of the staff against the pupils, the parents fanned themselves and exchanged the deep baying noise of the upper middle classes in congress:

'Ah rah-rah-rah! Ah rah-rah-rah!'

Pimply faces which had seemed unique were revealed to be a mere shake-up of a limited genetic code, repeated with slight variations in siblings. In Monsoon cottons and Liberty silks, in safari jackets and sarongs, they proclaimed their sympathy with ethnicity and the exclusivity of their eccentricities.

'Ah rah-rah-rah! Ah rah-rah-rah!'

Hart made a mercifully short and surprisingly graceful speech in the shade of the Temple of Apollo before curling canapés and disgusting petit fours were handed round.

'Every year, I forget how cheapskate the catering here is,' said Ruth, biting gingerly into a cucumber sandwich.

'You should taste the food they give us,' said Alice shyly. She was surprised at how easy it was to talk to Grub's family. Her timid entry into their circle had been instantly accepted; next to their higgledy-piggledy garments, her own dowdy black did not feel nearly so conspicuous.

'Very chic,' said Ruth, 'If I didn't get waylaid by junk, number 1 Belsize Park would look a great deal better.'

'Hey, Mum, I thought you didn't believe in looking after number one,' said Josh lazily. 'Arf! Arf! Ow.'

Grub kicked him. He was furious his brothers kept giving him nudges and approving winks, as if they were no more than fourteen. As soon as they set foot in their old school, they regressed into Laddism, he thought.

'Belsize Park,' said Alice, looking furtively for Winthrop. 'That sounds very grand.'

'Oh, it's not really,' said Grub hastily. 'Our house is all falling to bits and only kept together by the ivy.'

'Typical Hampstead,' said Tom. 'It could be amazing if we had any money.'

'But we don't. And I like it just the way it is,' said Ruth. She turned, smiling, to Alice. 'You must come and visit us when you're in London.'

'I'm afraid I don't go there very often,' said Alice, blushing. She had seen Winthrop approaching.

'It's a terrible nuisance, having three big boys crashing around the place,' said Ruth. 'I always longed for a daughter.'

'Oh no, Mum, not that old chestnut again! She keeps inspecting our girlfriends with a greedy eye,' said Tom.

'Shut up! Shut *up*!' said Grub.

'Boys, stop teasing. Oh, hallo, Who's this?'

'Oh, hi, there you are!' Winthrop said easily, casting his dazzling smile round like largesse. 'I've been looking for you everywhere. I want to introduce you to my mother before they take off again.'

Alice rose, made her apologies to the Viner family, and thanked Grub, who blushed miserably. They all looked at her retreating back, then at each other; and then, with typical tact, Ruth began to tell a story about a patient of hers with a cosmic persecution complex who carried an umbrella everywhere, convinced that acid rain would dissolve him, and who had instead been struck by lightning on Primrose Hill. The noise of the helicopter ascending drowned out much of her words, but Grub still loved her for it.

Josh said in a low voice, 'Whatever she is, I think she looks like Jane Birkin,' which was his highest form of praise.

It became more and more stifling. The sun sank behind looming black clouds.

'Oh, how I wish it would rain!' people exclaimed.

The bell for the concert was rung, and people began to file, reluctantly, towards the Quad. Grub broke away from his family and caught up with Tore.

'Hi, Jono! Did you have – ?'

Tore turned, and Grub saw he was incandescent with rage.

'That fucking evil bastard!' he hissed. 'That fucking Yank! He did it deliberately.'

'Did what? The helicopter?'

'No. That too. The fucking bastard! The fucker! The fucker!'

Grub drew his friend aside. Families streamed past them, incuriously. The orchestra began to tune up.

'What is it? What did he do?'

'He saw the jumper. My dad's red jumper. The one I gave to him for Christmas.'

'So what?'

'He saw that it was his. And my old man wore it, specially.' Tore began to cry, harshly. 'I stole it. To give to him. And now he's telling everyone.'

'Oh, God. I'm sure he won't.' Grub was appalled. 'Why on earth did you do it, Jono?'

'Why the fuck d'you think?' said Tore, smearing snot all over his hand. 'Why the fuck do you think I wear these cruddy clothes and things? He doesn't give us any money. So I steal. I'm a thief.'

'Oh, Jono, Jono! It doesn't matter,' said Grub helplessly. 'Just stop doing it.'

'That bastard, that fucking bastard!' said Tore.

'Hi, Tore.' Winthrop's drawl made them both start. 'Feeling the pangs of conscience, Tore?'

He stood there, flanked by Alice and Fay, his immaculate white clothes brilliant in the setting sun.

Tore's eyes seemed to glow with hatred.

'Hallo, Winkie,' he said. 'That's what your mum calls you, isn't it? Winkie, Winkie, wee willy Winkie! You probably can't even get it up.'

Fay stepped forward. 'Oh, yes he can,' she taunted. 'He's made Alice pregnant.'

The others froze. She smiled maliciously at them, then dissolved into fright.

'Is that true?' Winthrop asked Alice in a dry voice.

Alice swallowed, and nodded slightly.

'Oh, shit!'

'She's a slag, Winkie, just like Poppy. What did you do, pay her?'

Winthrop dropped back a pace, and kicked. His foot knocked Tore to the ground.

Inside the Quad, the shuffling audience fell silent as Hew raised his baton.

There was a sudden, sharp click.

'You shit,' said Tore softly. He had the flick knife in his hand. 'You shitty shit.'

'You don't know shit from shit, you sick fuck.'

The orchestra began to play, one, two three long curling notes.

Winthrop and Tore, oblivious of everyone else, circled each other. The music swelled, oboes to horns to strings. They were smiling now, gently, as if they were the best of friends. Round and round, and then, as the choir joined, Tore stabbed at Winthrop with a sudden jabbing motion.

'. . . *et tibi reddetur votum in Jerusalem* . . .' sang a rich alto voice. '*Exaudi orationem meam, ad te omnis caro veniet.*'

The hair on Grub's scalp crawled.

Alice said, 'Oh, no, no.'

Blood soaked the side of Winthrop's shirt.

Fay shrank back and, when she was far enough away, ran inside the swing doors.

Tore jabbed again, but his knife met empty air. Winthrop had leapt back with all the spring of his athlete's frame, turned, and was running like a deer for the woods. Tore sprang after him, the knife like a dull red flame in his hand. Grub and Alice followed.

25

Winthrop ran. The running was Winthrop, and Winthrop was running. This was what he had been made for. That was all that existed. If he stopped for a moment, the fear at his heels would send him mad.

The world was crackling cellophane, and his mouth was full of metal. Things whipped across his face, stinging. He was barred, clawed, tripped, ripped. Air thickened. Now there were faces grinning at him out of the rock, big ones and little ones, with slime for eyes, and then blackness, cold musty black. Perhaps he was going blind. He put out a hand, and realised that he had come all the way up the hill and into the mine. The ghost of daylight faded behind him. The whole tunnel was full of a clanking swishing creaking mutter, as if an army of the dead was waking. How had he come so far without thinking?

A footstep behind him, unmistakable, and the acrid stench of his enemy. You had to kill or be killed, that was the rule. It was the axiom of male existence. Tore's breath sounded, raspingly.

Winthrop began to run again, further and further away from the light. For a few paces he managed to keep going, and then uncertainty made him lose confidence. At once he fell, jarringly, against the hard rock. The tunnel floor had a surprisingly smooth surface. He found a metal bar. A weapon? He felt it going foward, and then his leg hit another bar, two feet to the left. A railway track, then. It had to be going somewhere. He crawled on hands and knees. Yes, there was light ahead. He stumbled towards it, panting. Further away than he thought. It might be a hallucination, or phosphorescence. Then it became a funnel of green brightness, a wavering shaft coming down from the world above. He ran forward, reaching out. Nearly there.

Darkness fell like a blot on his back. It was trying to stab him and strangle him at the same time. Horror made him shriek aloud, and at the sound of his voice, echoing and re-echoing down the mines, some cold drops fell, patter, patter, patter.

> '*Confutatis maledictis*
> *Flammis acribus addictis:*
> *Voca me cum benedictis,*'

The voices belled up to the great glass dome.

Winthrop braced his legs as his karate teacher had taught him to do against the tunnel floor and somersaulted backwards. The knife flew out of Tore's grasp. They both groped for it.

The rain started to come down as Grub and Alice laboured up the hill. At first Grub had been ahead, but after the bridge he slowed, unable to see. Alice had overtaken him without a word, scrambling up the paths on all fours like a black animal. They were both in sandals, and their feet were torn by thorns. Grub could hear Alice panting, and opened his own parched mouth for drops. It became darker and darker as the heavy black clouds, which had been over Dartmoor all day, moved over the valley. They started to slip and slide, bruising hands, knees and ankles, choking on their own wet hair. By the time they had reached the little stair on the ledge, the path was a rushing waterfall. Alice scrambled up, then collapsed. Grub hauled himself up past her sprawled body.

'There's nobody here,' he said, looking round the clearing.

Too exhausted to speak, she shook her head and pointed.

Grub, purblind from the rain streaming down his lenses, saw the mine entrance, half curtained in ivy, and the blackness beyond wavering in the downpour. A dread came into him, but, at the same time, the idea that if he copped out this time, he would be lost for ever. Alice staggered up and ran towards it. The shock of coming out of the rain made both their ears ring.

'Listen!' she said.

At first, he could hear nothing except the storm which was

now raging overhead. Water was gushing out of the mine, babbling faster and faster as it escaped into the light, but above it he could hear a mechanical thudding and creaking. Alice clutched his arm with the cold grab of fright, and he jumped.

'What is it?'

'I don't know. Wait! If it's not too wet, or broken ... '

He felt in his pocket for the pencil torch on his keyring and switched it on, broadening the beam. They blinked and looked around. The rock was not a sooty black, as expected, but a rich red, like the inside of a body. In places it was streaked and marbled with blue and yellow. As the beam moved, the whole tunnel glittered with minute flashes of copper ore.

'He's in here. Look!'

There was a smeary handprint on the wall.

'Oh, God,' said Alice. 'We've got to find him. Come on, come on!'

She seized the torch from Grub's fingers. He followed, groping. The tiny beam of light rapidly disappeared.

'Alice! Wait!'

Grub blundered into the icy stream rushing down either side of the tunnel. Nothing. He pushed the metal frame of his glasses up his nose, terrified they would drop off and leave him doubly helpless. The clanking noise grew louder. He thought of all the films he had ever seen which featured nasty things in dark places, then wished he hadn't. Swish, creak, splash, groan, swish, creak, splash, groan. Something was advancing and retreating in the darkness. A machine. It was coming for him. Aliens had visited the planet in 2000 BC and left a homicidal android patrolling the – Of course, he thought suddenly. The miners. It must be a piece of machinery too big for the mining company to have taken away. A current of damp air fanned his face. Water-driven. A water-wheel! He felt his way past, gingerly. So this must be the source of the strange noises that were sometimes heard on the estate. How far beneath it did the mines go? Surely Tore and Winthrop could not have come far, without any lights? But Tore had his Zippo lighter. There were holes, now, along the tunnel walls where presumably men had once crawled and blasted; ledges and shafts sloped down and away. They could be anywhere, hiding from each other.

'Jono!' he shouted. 'Jono! It's me, it's Grub! Where are you?'

There was no answer above the rushing waters. The weight of

the hill on top began to crush him. He thought of all the tons and tons of earth and rock and trees that must be on top of him; the sheep and rabbits and people wandering freely on the surface. Perhaps he was lost. Perhaps he had already gone miles under Dartmoor. Panicking, he groped forwards a few steps. Once, in biology, Beatrice Bassett had made them all put blindfolds on and walk. Their journey seemed to go on for ever, through sticky swamps, jungly hills and steep valleys, until she told them to take the blindfolds off. All were astonished to see that they had all walked barely twenty feet across a cricket pitch.

'Now you know how much humans depend on eyesight,' she informed them.

'Stupid old cow,' said Grub aloud. A cry came down the passage, as if in echo, but it was not.

He groped round a corner and saw the dim luminescence ahead.

'Alice! Jono!' he shouted, and ran forward.

'*Oro supplex et acclinis,*
Cor contritum quasi cinis:
Gere curam mei finis.'

A gust of wind whined through the swing doors of the Quad, and the audience shivered.

Alice was kneeling beside Winthrop, who crouched in a corner, muttering. Grub caught fragments of what he was saying.

'Reality checkpoint . . . keep your snorkel above the water . . .'

'Winthrop!' Alice kept saying. 'Wake up! What's happened?'

He was filthy, his white clothes spattered with blood, but the wound did not seem to be too bad. In the middle of the muddy island at the centre of the shaft lay Tore.

'Jono!'

'Winthrop, what happened? Are you all right?' asked Alice, shaking his shoulder.

'Yeah.'

'Oh, Winthrop, I've been so frightened for you. Are you still bleeding?'

'No.'

'Jono!'

Tore's thin face was livid, but Grub could see no mark on him other than dirt. He opened his eyes wide. They were not dark, as Grub had always thought, but grey like shattered glass. Grub looked into their rings of emptiness, as if seeing them for the first time.

'I can't feel anything, Grubster,' said Tore. 'My legs, arms – gone.'

'His spinal cord's broken,' said Winthrop. 'I broke his neck.'

There was a dreamy satisfaction in his voice. Alice turned her head away.

'Is he going to die?'

'He'll never walk again, that's for sure.'

Tore looked up at Grub.

'Are you in pain?'

'I can't feel anything.'

'I guess that's been your problem all of your life,' said Winthrop.

'Oh, God.'

'Imagine being visited by Jimmy Savile, I'd sooner die,' said Tore, with a faint grin.

'Oh, Jono.'

The muddy island where they crouched was shrinking. Funnelled by the three hills, all the rainwater of the day was coming down in gallons from the moors, and the parched earth was too hard to absorb it.

'Help me,' said Grub. 'We've got to get him out.'

Winthrop made a violent gesture, rising to his feet. 'Fuck off! He tried to kill me.'

'Winthrop! You must help. You can't leave him here.'

'Yes,' said Winthrop, 'I can.'

He pushed Alice to one side and blundered through the curtain of water, back into the tunnel. Alice hesitated, cast Grub a despairing glance, and followed.

Grub shouted after her, 'You pair of dirty, stinking – '

'You'd better bog off too, Grubbo.'

'Shut up,' said Grub angrily, wiping the mist off his spectacles. His mind buzzed, persistent as a trapped wasp. 'I'll get you out on my own.'

'You can't. If you move me, it might – '

'Yes I can.'

Tore said, 'I'm frightened of the pain.'

Grub touched him gently. 'You can't stay here, you'll drown.'

He picked his friend up in a clumsy fireman's lift, staggering. Tore was limp, and a dead weight.

'I don't want to go in the dark,' said Tore.

'But we've got to get out, Jono!' Grub was almost crying with fear and frustration. 'The whole place is flooding.'

'Bog off, then.'

'Don't be stupid.'

'I am stupid. Don't you see?'

The water was coming down all around now, hammering Grub's head and back as he bent over Tore. Tons and tons were shooting down. He could hardly see or hear. The last of the mud had gone, and he was standing in an icy pool of seething water.

'You'll drown, Grubbo. Like those poor sods did before.'

Tore's voice was fainter and fainter. Grub bent over so his ear was next to Tore's mouth.

'Alice,' he said.

'I know. I guessed just now.'

'Tell my old man . . . What a pile of shit.'

Tore's eyes closed.

'We can float,' said Grub desperately. 'Look, it's almost a river now. I'll go on my back and keep your head above the water. Just keep breathing. Jono? Jono! Don't be frightened.'

He knelt down in the churning pool, seized Tore's head in both hands so that it rested on one shoulder, and began to do a clumsy back-kick out of the light.

Instantly, the current seized them. The shock of its cold strength almost took his wits away. He kicked out strenuously, as he had been taught to do by Ruth, years and years ago, when she showed him and Tom and Josh how to lifesave. Tore's body floated straight down above his own torso and between his pumping legs, as was correct. If only he wasn't so heavy. It was hard to keep them both afloat.

'Keep breathing, Jono,' he said, but could not hear any reply. The noise was deafening. He swallowed some water, and began to splutter and gasp. Already, each breath was becoming a struggle. They were banged this way and that with dizzying force.

Grub thought his heart would stop if he didn't keep moving. He kicked rhythmically, feeling hot blood suddenly shoot through his veins. Good old heart, he thought affectionately, good old heart. Sentiment for his own organs made him want to weep, absurdly. He remembered when he had thought of his body as being a whole world full of little people, just like school, with armies and workshops and cleaners and menders, all working day and night to keep him going. He shouldn't have let himself blob out. A line floated into his head: 'Let your mind go, and your body will follow.' It was something the school yoga teacher used to intone, but now it had a more sinister import. Suddenly, he banged his head against a rock. Light jagged across his eyes. He sank, and lost Tore.

'Jono! Jono!' he shrieked, coming up. 'Where are you?'

His knuckles scraped against the wall, skinning them. Nothing. Nothing. He spreadeagled all his limbs, searching the current. Nothing. On and on and on, through the pitch dark. Pictures formed rapidly in his mind's eye, bright and tiny as a far-off slide show: his mother, Knotshead, his father drawing, the wicker pattern of a dirty laundry basket in which he had been thrown downstairs his first term, Alice's neck, his bedroom in Belsize Park. Snuffed out in a blink. They were lost in a labyrinth of tunnels, they were going to die here in the dark, and nobody would ever find out. Everything was closing in. There was no hope. He was lost, lost. Oh, let me live, let me live, he prayed. Nothing else. Forgive. There was no longer any sense of time or space or touch. Forgive, and let me live. He sank again, for the last time. Then there was a roaring and a grinding and a shuddering, as a great wave came down the tunnel and spewed him out into the dazzling air. And then he was falling, falling, falling through darkness.

'*Benedictus, qui venit in nomine Domini,*' sang the choir, but hardly anyone was listening. There seemed to be a whispered row going on near the entrance, as a small girl pulled urgently at the sleeves of first Veronica and then, on being repulsed, the Librarian. Parents turned and hissed reprimands, and pupils, when they saw Fay, rolled their eyes to each other expressively. Rain drummed on the Quad roof, louder and louder, as if a troop of cavalry were riding across it. The Librarian bent down to hear what Fay was trying to tell him.

A tremor went through the ground. Horatio, shifting about uneasily on the Librarian's shoulder, took flight with a sharp cry of alarm, as did the various sparrows and pigeons roosting in the glass roof. Hew, about to conduct the last movement of the Requiem, looked up in anger, but nobody laughed. They saw the brown froth of water seeping through the swing doors seconds before the main body arrived, and the quicker-witted had already started up from their seats in dismay. Many more were rooted by shock, and more still by disbelief that anything untoward could possibly happen at Knotshead. This comfortable disregard did not last long.

The wave gathered speed and force as it travelled down the hill, barely dissipating its force by knocking Flottage down like a house of cards. By the time it hit the main building, it was sweeping along all in its path. It poured through the Quad in a solid mass until it met the windows at the far end. Here it rebounded momentarily, churning round people, chairs, plants, spars, planks, glass, musical instruments and paper likes pieces of meat and vegetable in a stew.

Discordant shrieks and cries filled the air. Some, like the Slythes, were overcome by panic, and pushed people off in desperation to ascend the stairs to the Males' Flats; others, like the Librarian, held on to the loggia pillars and formed a human chain to help children and the more elderly to the common rooms.

The water rose. One foot, two feet, three feet.

Miranda Jupp screamed, 'Oh, Martin, Martin, save me!'

Mrs Mortmain slapped her across the face.

'Oh, dry up, you silly little bitch!'

'Hormones, hormones,' Beatrice Bassett muttered. 'What a lot of trouble they cause.'

'At last the collapse of the bourgeois structure,' said Maggie Brink, striding out and seizing Lord Paddington by the arm. 'Do not attempt to withstand the march of history. Workers of the world unite!'

'Oh, pooh,' said the Earl.

'I've never seen anything so ridiculous in my entire life,' said Pug.

'For once,' said Toby Hindesmith, 'I happen to agree.'

Then the pressure on the big windows at the end of the Quad became too great, and the water smashed through the glass like a giant fist, and poured in a roaring cascade down the parched lawns to the lake. But even as it was released, the main house juddered to its foundations.

A cry went up.

'Get out! Get out! The roof is coming down!'

'You bloody fool, Veronica,' Hart cried, seeing her white face on the Males' Flat above him. 'You told me it was safe!'

'You should have checked it yourself!' she shouted back.

A pane of glass fell like a guillotine blade to the floor, and shattered.

'Woman,' said Hart, loudly and clearly, 'you are fired.'

Where was Poppy? Where were the twins? The ground shook beneath his feet, and a crack zig-zagged across the Quad floor, splintering the parquet. What was happening? Could it be an earthquake? All along the sides, people were scrambling to get out through the common-room windows, or jumping from the Males' Flats above, but he couldn't leave until he was sure everyone else had escaped.

The house shrieked, and one wall suddenly subsided by three feet. Sweating and trembling, Hart looked around.

'Poppy!'

He caught sight of her at last, bent over a prostrate figure, her muslins sopping from the receding floodwater.

'Who is it? Where are the twins?'

'They're quite safe. I left them with Mrs Blacker.'

'Oh, Poppy, dearest, I've been so stupid!'

'Poor old Simon. Poor everyone.'

'I'm going to get the sack for this, and then you'll leave me.'

'Actually, you know, I think I'd like you more.'

'Who is it?'

She turned over the body, gently.

'There's nothing we can do for him now, is there?'

26

'Basically,' said Winthrop, 'we have gone from a win-win situation to a lose-lose one. The only viable strategic option is to cut
our losses.'

The car, which belonged to the Librarian, juddered through
the wide pools. He was not used to driving without automatic
gears, and only a dim recollection of his outdoor work session
on the tractor kept him from burning the engine completely.
The suspension of British cars was unbelievably bad, he
thought; no wonder the old jerk had left his keys on the dash-
board. Nobody but a masochist would want such a beat-up
heap of shit as this.

The M4 was flooded, and rain was still coming down in torrents. Ribbons of orange and ebony squiggled across the windscreen. An articulated lorry sat solidly in the middle of the road,
throwing up sprays of blinding mist until Winthrop put his fist
on the horn and forced it to one side, overtaking.

'Don't fuck with the leadership class, dickhead!' he shouted
as they passed the blurred, gesticulating figure of the driver.
Beside him, Alice went even paler.

She had almost stopped being frightened now, although tre-
mors of shock still made her teeth chatter. From time to time,
Winthrop would hear these tiny castanets and glance at her,
saying nothing. A pain in her abdomen was going through her
like a blunt needle, stitching her navel to the small of her back.
It was debatable whether she felt worse with her eyes closed or
open. Whatever alternative she tried seemed more painful than

the one just abandoned.

Grub swirled across her eyelids when she closed them. It was a face she had disliked for so long that his expression of almost adult gravity as he knelt beside Tore was strange to recollect. She had not known he could be like that, without the gross gargoyle mask of mockery. Of course, if she had to choose between two people who had made her life misery and the one she loved, there was no question.

What Winthrop had done was heroic. He had had no weapon, like Tore. If someone tried to kill you and you killed them instead, that was manslaughter: justice, even. Yet Tore had not been killed, and they had left him there, completely paralysed and helpless, with Grub. Was that just? What had Grub done, really, in the past – except be a moral coward? If he was a coward, what did that make her?

All through her schooldays, she had consoled herself with the fact that, whatever else she might be – however plain, impoverished, priggish and unpopular – she was not craven. Others might give in to the system: not Alice Godwin. Other girls would fawn and charm and play the game: not Alice Godwin. Buried in her books, immaculate in her virginity, unshakeable in her certainty that she was right, she had suffered for probity. But when it came to a real test, Grub, that epitome of Knotshead values, had stayed and she had run away.

If only she could have passed the responsibility on to someone else, it would not have been so heavy. But she had not even stopped Winthrop from stealing the Librarian's car.

'Don't leave me, you can't leave me,' she had exclaimed as he started the engine.

'Only if you have an abortion,' he replied.

Then the pain had begun, wave after wave, as if she were on a ship moving up and down across the sea.

'Where are we going?' she asked eventually.

Winthrop shrugged. Beneath the panicky knowledge that he had made a big mistake yet again in his school career, a vague plan of action began to form.

'London. There's an A-Z beside you. Read it, and tell me where Regent's Park is.'

'Oh. Are we going to your parents?'

'That's none of your fucking business.'

O Mama, Mama. But even that had lost the power to help

her.

'I see.'

'You see! You see! No, you don't see zip.'

'But Winthrop, it was self-defence. Anybody would say so.'

'I'm not talking about Tore. Tore got what was coming to him. I'm talking about you.'

'Oh.'

She had actually forgotten about it.

'Jesus, Alice, you're supposed to be the brains around campus. I can't believe you'd be so fucking dumb! I told you to get yourself fixed up.'

'Where? With the school doctor? What do you think he'd do? He's paid by the school, I'd have been reported to Veronica like a shot! Besides, I'm hardly the only one responsible.'

'How many months?'

'Three, I think. I don't know. Maybe two. It's never regular. I kept hoping it would just be a mistake.'

'So it might be four! Oh, my God! Why does this kind of shit keep happening to me?'

'What do you mean?'

'Why do you think I got tossed from my last school?'

'I assume,' said Alice, in a moment of dreadful clarity, 'because it happened there, too.'

Silence confirmed this. Winthrop ground his teeth. The car swished past Salisbury, then Chiswick.

'If my trustees find out,' said Winthrop, 'I've really had it. So what am I going to do?'

Alice wished she could feel frightened again, but felt too ill to move.

When Grub shot out of the tunnel like a cork from a bottle, the flood carried him rolling and tumbling down the hill and left him jammed in the branch of a beech tree. In this precarious perch he lay, bruised and half drowned, while the water poured out of the mine in torrents. Then it stopped, and the rain stopped, and the sinking sun came out beneath the band of black cloud, pure and warm and golden.

'Mum?' said Grub.

The sounding of wailing sirens brought him to his senses. He looked around and saw a haze of unfocused colour, mostly green. Of course, his glasses had fallen off. A confused recollection of what had happened swam into his mind. Where was everyone? Had they all been drowned? He knew he had not dreamt about the wave, for his clothes were still wet, and the ground beneath sparkled with running water.

'Mum! Jono!'

He moved an arm, then a leg. They were full of pins and needles from the awkward position into which he had fallen, but seemed OK. Feeling returned, and with it a headache. He touched the top of his head. It was damp, matted, and slightly sticky. Blood. He coughed, felt himself slip from his cradle of branches, and blacked out.

An image came into his mind, a beam of light leaving the present, hitting a plane at an angle of forty-five degrees and bouncing off it, making a perfect mirror image. It gave him immense satisfaction. He contemplated it, swaying between heaven and earth, for a long while, knowing it was the Liszt sonata. It didn't reach its peak at the end but in the middle, falling into exact halves like two butterfly wings. It was about making a journey from a certain line, and then coming back to it, but in a different position from where you started. So that was it, he thought.

Time passed. Dimly, he heard the sound of more sirens, and then cars, fading away like the light. It would be nice to sleep, but his head hurt too much. Sooner or later, he would have to come down. The ground seemed an immense distance away, and then no space at all, heaving up and down. Frogs croaked. He let himself fall, slipped in the wet. The pain shooting up his leg was the last straw. He sighed like a collapsing tyre.

'Youth: possibility,' said a voice in the twilight.

He looked up and saw the Librarian with his parrot.

'Ah, Viner. I'm glad to see you safe and sound.'

'What happened?'

'A flood,' said the Librarian succinctly.

'Is my mother all right?'

'I believe so. A most admirable woman. When I last saw her, she and your brothers were helping others into ambulances.'

'Have a lot of people been hurt?'

'Only superficially,' said the Librarian. 'Apart from one.'

They hobbled along towards the cottage.

'Jono's dead, isn't he?'

'I'm afraid so.'

'It's my fault, he didn't want to go back into the tunnel, but there was no choice. The water was coming up so fast, it's all my fault ... '

'Don't worry, now,' said the Librarian. 'That will be taken care of. We must let your mother know you are alive and well.'

London was closing in on all sides. The rain stopped, and a strange, livid light fell on the dark, hurrying crowds of people. Cars glittered like the carapaces of insects, droning past the old Volkswagen. Alice stared through the windscreen. So much concrete, so few trees, it was almost suffocating. She was filled with fear and dread. Everything in this big, brutal place crushed her. Her first desolate journey with Poppy from Edinburgh to Paddington came back, riding on waves of nausea.

'Winthrop?'

'Shut up, I'm concentrating on the road signs. Where did you say Park Road is?'

'Could you stop. Please?'

'Why?'

'I'm not well.'

'How d'you think I feel?'

'Please.'

He sighed loudly, and stamped his foot on the brake. 'This OK?'

She nodded, opened the door and collapsed, retching on to a grassy verge.

'Women!' said Winthrop. 'They really gross me out.'

Traffic roared past her, round and round. After a while, she lifted her head, and said, 'Winthrop, I'm bleeding.'

But Winthrop was no longer there.

'It's always been a sad place, this,' said the Librarian. 'Built by folly and greed on suffering, century after century. I suspected the mines extended beneath the peninsula when I saw all the cracks opening up at the foundations. Hold still while I put some Dettol on your head. I seem to have been up half the night doing this.'

Wrapped in a blanket, drinking hot cocoa, Grub felt drowsy.

'It's amazing nobody was badly hurt,' he said. 'You'd have thought with all the glass falling, somebody would have been chopped.'

'It'll be the end of the school, though,' said the Librarian.

'The foundations are too shaky for any rebuilding. There's a limit to how much even the kind of parents who believe in the Knotshead ethos will put up with. The sad thing is that Simon Hart saw that.'

'Hart the Fart. That's what we all called him. Poor Simon. In Hebrew, it means hearing, but do you know the saddest thing? He's tone deaf. Hew told me it was one of the worst things about doing hymns in Jaw beside him. He's so stupid, trying to force us into doing things we hated, and not being any good at it himself.'

'How do you survive in a political situation?' said Kenward. 'For all human relations, both in work and out of it, have a strong element of the political. Do you play the game, and try to beat the other players by being tougher and more ruthless than they dare to be? Or do you turn your back on it, even at the cost of being completely vulnerable to the players who remain in the game. Because the game will go on all around you, whether you want it to or not, and when some weak spot is found, as it was in Mrs Hart's case, it will be exploited.'

Grub thought of Tore, and Winthrop and Alice.

'Is it always that extreme? Isn't there some way of carving an individual path?'

'That is the most difficult choice, because both sides will dislike you. Although it seems to me the only choice that sense and conscience allow.'

'I don't know if I'm strong enough for that,' said Grub. 'My brothers, Dad, Jono, even Mum, they all know so clearly who and what they are. I don't know what I think about anything properly. Not even music. I feel things moving in me, but I can't put them into any shape. I don't even have a proper name. I'm a joke.'

'You can't have been christened Grub.'

'It's so awful. Denis.'

'Denis. Not so bad, to a classicist. It's a contraction of Dionysus. The god of wine –' Here Mr Kenward gave Grub a sharp look. 'Though not, I hope, of the stuff you brewed with your kit – and the life force. It's nothing to be ashamed of.'

'I still hate it. Denis. I mean, it's like Mrs Thatcher's husband, or Denis the Menace. It's a family name, or I'd never have been lumped with it. I prefer Dan, my middle one.'

'A wise judge.'

'I don't know whether I'd be any good at that,' said Grub uncomfortably.

'Oh, I think so. You can learn from the mistakes of those close to you. That's why the third child always turns out best.'

'I didn't expect to find you telling my youngest son stories at midnight, Mr Kenward,' said Ruth, coming into the cottage. Grub started up and hugged her tightly. 'Hey, don't strangle me, child, though it's good to see you, too. Are you OK? I think we'd better be driving home.'

Alice had no idea where she was, but it seemed better to try to keep moving. Blood was trickling down her legs. She had nothing to absorb it, not even tissues. Every month she had prayed for this, and now she remembered why her mother had called it the curse. Pain, embarrassment, stench, mess, the monthly indignity of being a woman. The spasms of her womb increased. She was too unhappy even to cry. It's going, she thought, just like love, no wonder people talk as if love were a third thing between two people. She hadn't wanted to admit to herself there could be anything, and now she had no chance to accept that the little homunculus Winthrop had planted in her was dying.

She crossed a bridge and went through the gates of a small park with a big hill on the left. The park made her think of the only address she knew in London, Ruth Viner's. How on earth could she go to that nice woman and tell her she'd left her son in a flooding mine? At any rate, she would tell her, and not run away from it all again.

At the other end of the park, there was a street sign pointing up the hill for Hampstead. One of Grub's brothers had teased Ruth with living there, so she turned left and started to toil up the road. It seemed to take hours and hours. Pain bent her almost double. The blood was coming faster now, sopping into the folds of her black dress. She was ice cold. When she got to the top, the road went down, and then up again. Her heart fainted, but she kept walking, like an automaton.

A bird sang maniacally in the false dawn of a street lamp. The road forked left, right, and ahead. The one ahead was called Belsize Park Gardens, so she took that.

Big houses were floating past her now. They had Ionic colmns, like temples. On and on, under the pale lamps, through the long tunnel of big trees to the end. There was a car grating up the hill behind her, as if it, too, were very tired and getting ready to stop. She sat down on a low wall, and watched Grub and his family get out.

27

The asthmatic calls of wood pigeons came and went. Snatches of London noise were blown in on the charred air: a police siren, voices, a door slamming, the constant electric hum of city traffic far away. Alice lay in a spare bedroom in the Viners' house watching the feathery branches of a tall ash tree at the back move across the sky. Every chink of blue between the leaves was like one of Winthrop's pale eyes, appearing and disappearing.

She felt drained by her miscarriage. A week had passed since she had returned from hospital, but she had no interest in anything. All vitality, all capacity for feeling seemed to have gone out of her, so that she could think of nothing better to do for the rest of her life but stay under the white sheets of her bed, with the cats Leo and Pard curled at her feet. For the past week she had hardly stirred.

'It's awful, Mum, all she does is lie there and stare,' said Grub.

'She's had a shock. You did too. It takes time to get over.'

'Can't you help her? I mean, professionally?'

'Only if she wants me to. At the moment she just wants to be still.'

One day, Ruth came up the stairs with a cardboard box full of children's books.

'I think you could read now,' she said.

'What's the point?'

'What's the point of anything?'

Alice considered this. 'There isn't, much, is there?'

'If you choose to look at it one way. But there are other perspectives.'

So Alice read about enchantments and quests and riddles; of talking beasts and disguised magicians; of dying parents, wise fools and deluded princes. She learnt that there was a price to be paid for subversion, but there were also rewards beyond it.

'I never had any of these in Edinburgh,' she told Ruth. 'Only myths.'

'A pity. Myths are about gods and superheroes: tough acts to follow. The great thing about fairy tales is that they're just ordinary people who win through by luck and kindness and courage. Much more likely, if you're at all optimistic. Shall I tell you one of my secret beliefs? I think that myths were made up by priests, who want to keep people cowed; but fairy tales were invented by mothers, who want to make people grow up and be able to cope with the world.'

'I'm hopeless at coping, though,' said Alice, in a small, tight voice. 'No amount of . . . Scheherazading is going to really make any difference. I've made such a mess of everything.'

'Well,' said Ruth. 'You haven't had much help, by the sound of things. It's pretty hard, trying to grow up on your own. Even in the stories you've been reading, the heroes need assistance.'

'Yes, but everyone has to do it alone, sooner or later. It's not something you can achieve by proxy.'

'The question is whether it is sooner or later. What worries me most about Knotshead, from what you and Dan tell me, is that it seems to have been so much sooner.'

Alice thought about Winthrop. It seemed to be getting easier to do so without the whole of her being clenching itself up in desolation. He had gone back to America. She only knew that because Ruth had made enquiries of a friend at the embassy, and told her. Apparently, he had made a dramatic entrance at Winfield House, covered in dried mud and blood, and his mother had instantly decided to put him on the next flight home.

Alice had received no word from him; and gradually the hope and dread with which she waited for the post to arrive or heard the telephone ring had been replaced by a dull acceptance that he was out of her life for ever.

She thought about the way he had appeared to her: first

funny, then godlike, then as someone as muddled as herself.

'I don't know if it's not being grown-up that makes it worse,' she said slowly. 'In some ways, I can see that people get more complicated as they get older, so that it's worse when you get dumped then, because there's more to get hurt. But I'm not surprised he left me. I'm just not very lovable.

Ruth looked at her and smiled.

'There's someone here to see you.'

Poppy looked very tired. However exhausted Alice felt, she knew as soon as she saw her sister that her own debility would pass, whereas Poppy's would only increase. She had come to some decision which had no room for prettiness. Her face was full of long lines, as if the earth was slowly, inexorably, drawing her down to itself.

She told Alice about the flood and its aftermath, which Alice had already picked up, patchily, from Ruth. Knotshead was being closed down.

'There simply aren't enough pupils staying on to make it a viable proposition any longer,' Poppy said. Alice noted the echo of Simon in her choice of words and wondered whether this was a good sign. 'Odd, isn't it? It wasn't the baby bust or the crime wave or the scandal about me that did it, but an act of God. And Johnny Tore's death. There's going to be an inquest, you know.'

'I know. Will I have to go?'

'You? No.'

'But the mines, his attack on Winthrop – surely that must all come out?'

'Nobody knows anything about that,' said Poppy. 'He was taken by the flood. That's enough, isn't it? For everyone?'

'I see,' said Alice. The same system which had protected Tore when he was alive would conceal the facts about his death. Fear of scandal, fear of losing face: all these would conspire to present him as the tragic son of a famous man. The irony of this made her smile, faintly.

'Are his parents very ... ?'

'His mother is. Poor Tara. It was one of the worst days of my life, seeing her. But Gore? I really couldn't say.'

'But they were so close. All those holidays Johnny spent with him ... '

Poppy shook her head.

Alice said, wondering, 'Do you mean he lied? That it was all made up? But he is his son, isn't he?'

'Oh, yes,' said Poppy. 'He's never had any problem fathering children. He just isn't interested in them. That's why I never told him about you.'

'Me?' said Alice, in vague surprise. 'Why on earth should you?'

Poppy said, 'Haven't you guessed? He's your father.'

'But how could he be? Mama never . . . she couldn't have . . . '

'She wasn't your mother,' said Poppy. 'I am.'

'I hate her! I hate her! How could she have done that to me? I hate her!' said Alice, sobbing in Ruth's arms. 'I don't want her to be my mother! I don't even like her as a sister. She isn't my mother. I loved Mama, and now she says Mama only took me in to spite her.'

Ruth made a fierce face at Grub, who was hovering anxiously outside the door.

'Did Poppy really say that?'

Alice hiccuped, and muttered, 'Not exactly.'

'What did she tell you, exactly?'

'She said . . . she said that when I was born, I was going to be taken into care, because of her being an addict, and Mama found out and adopted me because she thought she'd make a better job of it.'

'That doesn't sound like spite to me.'

'But they hated each other!'

'Oh, Alice! Love and hate are so closely intertwined, particularly between parents and children. It's the saddest thing. But I refuse to believe that your grandmother adopted you out of some sort of petty revenge.'

'You didn't know her.'

'No, but I do know what it's like to raise a child or three,' said Ruth dryly. 'Listen, every single person who is alive today isn't there because they just happened to pop up like bean sprouts. Babies need a lot of care to survive. You can't imagine how much, until you have one. It's the greatest single endeavour of anyone's life to make a brand-new person. Most parents screw up, but not so badly as their children like to think. You had that from someone. Perhaps it was Poppy, perhaps it was your grandmother, but somehow you got it.'

'But I didn't get love,' said Alice. 'Nobody loved me. Not Poppy, not Mama, not Winthrop. I'm just utterly rejected, everywhere. I think there's no point in going on living.

'Rats!' said Ruth. 'Don't be a wet blanket. Let me tell you something. It is absolutely impossible for anyone to give love if they haven't received it as a child. I can tell you that, as a professional. You must have had bucketfuls of affection from someone if you were able to love this pain in the ass you're in mourning for so passionately. Someone has loved you, and more people will in the future. Chew on that, and stop feeling so sorry for yourself.'

'Wouldn't you be, if you were me?' said Alice, gulping.

'No,' said Ruth. 'I would not. You're young, healthy, smart, you're not having a baby at sixteen, and my sons think you're gorgeous. That sounds like a lot of good reasons not to commit suicide to me.'

'I brought you these from St John's Wood, they're Belgian chocolates and the best, but if you don't like them I'll take them away,' said Fay, perched on the end of Alice's bed. 'You do still like chocolate, don't you?'

Alice nodded, reluctantly, and opened the white and gold box. 'They look too beautiful to eat.'

'Oh, come on,' said Fay. 'That's what they're made for.'

'You're in love with him too, aren't you?'

'Was. If you mean Super Rabbit.' Fay's self-assurance hardly grated on Alice now. Instead, she found herself rather envying her resilience. 'No longer. It was', said the Infant Prodigy, 'merely a passing phase. Actually, I rather fancy Grub more, now he's got contact lenses. He's awfully handsome, don't you think?'

'Is he? I hadn't noticed.'

'It's nice, living so close by. London's really just a lot of little villages, you know. You'll soon adapt.'

'I don't think I'll ever get over it,' said Alice, staring at the wall. 'Like Poppy and Gore.'

'Oh, she told you about that, did she? I guessed ages ago.'

'You would, wouldn't you?'

'I must say, Alice, you are a bit of a nit, really. Anybody could have seen he was just using you. Boys are like that. They'll walk all over you if you get soppy. You've got to treat them like dogs, you know, with no exceptions. Then you keep the upper hand.'

'Why should it always descend to that? Why can't people just love each other and be happy?'

Fay made a vomiting noise. 'Yuk! Ugh! Pass the sickbag! Because love is about power, you twerp, not wallowing in a warm bath. There are winners and losers, and you have to make sure you aren't the loser. You need to be more streetwise, less of a romantic.'

'Romantic? Me?' said Alice, outraged. 'But I'm a classicist.'

'Of course you are. All that dripping about in black and going for long solitary walks. Look, I'm sorry I was such a bitch to you on Parents' Day, because you were the only person at Knotshead who remotely stood up for me, but you do sort of ask to be trampled on. It's all those Highland mists and things on top of the liberal ideology.'

'Oh, bog off, you little brat!' said Alice. She caught Fay's eye, and suddenly began to laugh as the truth of what she had just heard, however partial, sank in. 'Have another chocolate first, though. Where are you going next?'

'Well,' said Fay, 'not to another boarding school. I failed my Grade Eight, and my parents don't believe in them any more.'

Where the former Knotes would continue to be educated was a subject for much debate in many households. Those who had taken their GCSEs and A levels had less to worry about, but neither Grub nor Alice fell into this category.

'Hew thinks I could go straight to the Royal College, if he pulled some strings,' Grub said, stroking Leo, who stretched, yawned and subsided back on to the kitchen table.

'Lucky you.'

'I'm not sure that I'm ready to go. Or even if it would be the right thing to do any more. I can't play the piano any more. It reminds me too much of . . . '

Grub swallowed.

'Oh. I thought you got a Distinction?'

'Yes, but . . . '

They were silent, thinking of Jono. Grub had been to see Mrs Tore, at her invitation, and had sat there watching her chip the varnish from her silver-painted nails, crying. She had given him Jono's crossbow, sent to her by Delus. Gore didn't want it, and she said there was no place for things like that in her mews house in Notting Hill. It had shocked him, that house, for from floor to ceiling it was covered in pictures of Gore. Gore singing, Gore dancing, Gore photographed by David Bailey and Snow-don and God knows who else. The whole house was a flipping shrine to an ex-husband and absent father. No wonder Jono had wanted to keep normal people away; the miracle was how he had been able to cope with the outside world at all.

More and more, Grub wondered whether the only reason Tore had liked him at all was that they both longed for their absent, feckless fathers. He himself was starting to come to terms with Sam, as his brothers had done, but Jono, he thought, had been doomed. He remembered that awful night in Block 3, the night which had cemented their friendship. He had found Jono choking at the feet of the boy, the one everyone thought had committed suicide, who was hanging there, dead, with his pyjamas down. There had been a rope round Jono's neck, too, and a purple weal. Grub had never really understood what it had been about, except that it had something to do with sex, or sadism, or just despair. He had never really been able to accept that once someone crosses over a certain line, they are unlikely to be capable of returning to normality; for he, too, had believed too much in the school ethos that evil was made by en-vironment rather than choice.

'At least there's something you can do. All I'm good at is declining Latin verbs,' said Alice. 'Not much prospect of employment there.'

'What's happening to Poppy and Simon?'

'Oh, they seem to be all right. They aren't breaking up, or down, or whatever. Simon's getting out of teaching, which is probably a good idea. He wants to go into marketing in Bristol.'

'Yuk.'

'Well, someone's got to do it, and it's always been what he's been best at. Not education. I think they'll be all right once they move out of that awful mushroom house.'

'Toadstool,' said Grub.

Alice looked up and smiled suddenly. Oh, Grub thought with longing, how beautiful she is, how alive, her face is so gentle. I'd die for her, and she doesn't even notice I'm here. He remem-bered how he and Tore had called her ugly, and blushed.

'That was a good joke, really, wasn't it? The gnomes, I mean.'

'No,' said Grub honestly. 'The timing was wrong.'

'What d'you think will happen to the Arabs?'

'I expect they'll go off to crammers and things.' He looked at her long brown hand on the fabric of her dress. She was up, now, and wearing something she had bought in the summer sales with his mother. It was a plain, pale-blue cotton, and showed her collar bone and, sometimes, when she moved, the shape of her breasts and legs. 'Are you going to go back to living with the Harts?'

'I don't know. Possibly. Poppy says she can break the trust before my eighteenth birthday, so I can go somewhere else if I want. She's very fair like that. I wanted to split the money Mama left, but she says not, that her mother wanted me to have it. I think she does feel something, sometimes, you know, though she'll never be as she is with the twins. So I could go back to Edinburgh, or anything. I could even have had Winthrop's baby. It would have been nice to have had someone to love, although that would have been pretty disastrous, really.'

'Do you still mind a lot?'

'Yes. Even if I made a mistake, it doesn't just go away. It hurts like a leg that's been cut off, sometimes – you know, you can feel it itch although it isn't there. The Librarian said that women should put off falling in love for as long as possible, because it's so bad for their intellects. I think he's right. He's staying on, you know. He wrote. Mr Kenward, I mean.' She smiled slightly.

The postcard had been one from the Wallace Collection: a Claude called 'Ariadne on Naxos'. The Librarian had written: 'Cui deus "en, adsum tibi cura fidelior" inquit', and under it, 'Advise reading Ovid's Ars Amatoria.'

Alice had puzzled over this, then recalled how Ariadne had been rescued. But she did not like her Dionysus.

'He says the Slythes are planning to set up a smaller, more ideologically pure version of the school somewhere else, and he can't bear to leave all those books. I'm glad someone like him will still be there, in case someone like me comes along by mistake. But he's sending me the names of other teachers in London, and says that if I wanted I could learn Greek, too. Then I could read classics at university. I think I'd like that.'

'You could stay here, if you wanted,' said Grub eagerly. 'It's far too big for Mum on her own.'

Alice looked at him and shook her head.

'Think about it.'

'It would be too much of an imposition. I've been dumped on people all my life.'

'But we'd all like you to stay. I'd like it. Honestly.'

He touched her hand for an instant. She looked at it, expressionlessly, and he snatched it away, blushing, then remembered what she had said about it clashing with his hair, and blushed again. Such ugly hands, for a pianist. If that was what he was going to be. When he had opened the letter from Hew and learnt that he had been marked 140 out of 150 in his Grade Eight, he had looked at them in amazement.

'Honestly, I'm not teasing.'

'All right. I'll think about it. Thanks.'

She was not going to stay, he could see that. Too much had happened for her to trust him. She still thought of him as a trickster, a joke, her persecutor. Perhaps women just found it easier to be nice. He wished everything had been different. Oh, school, school. Half of him still thought it the best thing that would ever happen to him, but the other half knew it had been a disaster. It had distorted everything, fitting people's perceptions of each other on to a frame and either chopping bits off or adding bits on. He and Alice could never even become friends, because of it. She had never got to know the other sides of him, the places that weren't Tore or Knotshead or Grub, but the private Daniel-self.

He went into the drawing room, where the grand piano reared up, monochrome and solid in the familiar chaos of home. The Liszt Sonata was on top of a pile of dog-eared sheets. Ruth, he supposed, trying to cheer him up.

There was still that, of course. He didn't believe in the consolations of art. It was something you couldn't have faith in, not if you were inside it, sweating away to make it go. Music was just bloody hard work. It didn't exalt your spirits, it didn't reveal your inner soul, it simply blotted you out for a while, like any other system. You could go down to the deepest depths of yourself and pull out a wonder of the world, and people would still get it all wrong, through malice or carelessness or just stupidity.

Alice stirred in the kitchen. He lifted the lid and began to play.

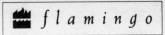
flamingo

Flamingo is a quality imprint publishing both fiction and non-fiction. Below are some recent titles.

Fiction
☐ News From a Foreign Country Came *Alberto Manguel* £4.99
☐ The Kitchen God's Wife *Amy Tan* £4.99
☐ Moon Over Minneapolis *Fay Weldon* £5.99
☐ Isaac and His Devils *Fernanda Eberstadt* £5.99
☐ The Crown of Columbus *Michael Dorris & Louise Erdrich* £5.99
☐ A Thousand Acres *Jane Smiley* £5.99
☐ Dirty Weekend *Helen Zahavi* £4.50
☐ Mary Swann *Carol Shields* £4.99
☐ Cowboys and Indians *Joseph O'Connor* £5.99
☐ The Waiting Years *Fumiko Enchi* £5.99

Non-fiction
☐ The Proving Grounds *Benedict Allen* £5.99
☐ The Quantum Self *Danah Zohar* £4.99
☐ Ford Madox Ford *Alan Judd* £6.99
☐ C. S. Lewis *A. N. Wilson* £5.99
☐ Into the Badlands *John Williams* £5.99
☐ Dame Edna Everage *John Lahr* £5.99
☐ Handel and His World *H. C. Robbins Landon* £5.99
☐ Taking It Like a Woman *Ann Oakley* £5.99

You can buy Flamingo paperbacks at your local bookshop or newsagent. Or you can order them from Fontana Paperbacks, Cash Sales Department, Box 29, Douglas, Isle of Man. Please send a cheque, postal or money order (not currency) worth the purchase price plus 24p per book (maximum postage required is £3.00 for orders within the UK).

NAME (Block letters)_____

ADDRESS_____

_____

_____